UNRAVEL

BOOK 2 OF THE LOCKWOOD TRILOGY

MELISSA CASSERA

Book Cover by Damonza
Editing: Dawn Ius, Jessica McKelden

2023 Edition
Print ISBN: 979-8-9873878-2-5

Published in the United States of America

AUTHOR'S NOTE

Unravel is the second installment in the Lockwood Trilogy, a dark, upper YA paranormal romance series. This book is not a standalone and is meant to be read after *Control*.

Unravel is told from the POV of both Natalie and Wes. Because Wes was raised as a precog assassin, his inner thoughts are significantly more twisted than the other characters. Reader discretion is advised.

This is not a typical love triangle romance, though if you find yourself pining for Wes at any point, we certainly do not judge.

For those who are "Team Henry," don't worry. You will be rewarded.

Enjoy the ride.

PLAYLIST

"Cry Me a River" - Tommee Profitt, Nicole Serrano
"Saints" - Echoes
"Honour" - Black Hydra
"Lacrymosa" - Evanescence
"Animal" - J2, Keeley Bumford
"Horns" - Bryce Fox
"You Put a Spell On Me" - Austin Giorgio
"You Are So Beautiful" - Tommee Profitt, Brooke
"Knights of the Night" - Pieces of Eden,
Amadea Music Productions

CHAPTER ONE

NATALIE

I HATE HOW he consumes me.

Who am I kidding? I don't hate it at all. I crave this distraction. A soft moan escapes my lips as I sink deeper into the mattress, feeling the weight of Wes's strong body on top of mine. My brain is so crammed full of confusion that I'm desperate for any sort of reprieve, a way to keep Henry alive in my mind since he took off without reason and hasn't reentered my life since.

And Wes is proving to be the perfect distraction.

Wes's tongue pries my mouth open and heat floods my body as he deepens our kiss. I keep my eyes clamped shut, picturing Henry on top of me, as Wes grazes his lips down my neck.

Henry Thorne. Contempt and desire whirl around my body, weaving through my insides, stirring around my heart. What did I ever do to him—besides protect his secret and do everything in my power to save him?

And here I am, in my bed, making out with Wes, while playing out my fantasy with Henry.

Is this toxic? Yes.

Does Wes have 146 different red flags? Yes.

Is this self-destructive? Yes.

Am I going to allow myself this distraction while I search for answers about literally everything in my life?

For now... also yes.

It's been thirty-three days since, well, since everything changed. Thirty-three days since I figured out I may have some kind of special powers. Thirty-three days since I learned my mother didn't die in a random accident, but likely at the hands of a group of people who can see the future known as the precog authority. Thirty-three days since it was hinted that I'm not human—that something is to happen to me before I turn nineteen. Thirty-three days since I killed someone.

It's also been thirty-three days since I last saw Henry.

Wes traces his palm along my side, grazing over my chest, dusting his fingers around my neck without applying pressure. He doesn't need to. For some inexplicable reason, when I kiss a precog, I lose consciousness. It happened with Henry too.

Heat spreads through my body when I think about Henry, and no matter what I try, I can't shake it. That single kiss is seared into my memory like an obsessive tick. It feels pathetic, and at the same time, necessary. If a precog can literally suck away all my oxygen with a simple kiss, that's a way they can destroy me.

And I can't let that happen.

So I've been practicing with Wes for thirty-three days, and I can make it almost an entire hour now before I reach the brink of blacking out. I look at it like training for a boxing match. If—or more likely, *when*—I need to fight for my life again, I can at least survive kiss-related warfare.

I used to tease my friend Ciel about her back-and-forth dynamic with her boyfriend, Adip, and here I am being a total hypocrite. But according to Ciel, fucking up is a teenage rite of passage, as is occasionally indulging in a guy who's totally wrong for me.

And make no mistake—Wes is very, very wrong. He's manipulative. And a liar.

He's also very, very good at kissing.

Ciel said he looks like a young Keanu Reeves mixed with a more evil version of Adam Driver, and now I can't unsee it.

"You're getting better at this," Wes says. More like, growls. His words wrap around my body, making every part of me clench. My lungs beg for air and he notices, moving his lips to my hairline, lightly brushing up to my ear.

Wes is the only precog I know besides Henry. And certainly the only precog who'll give me access to information about them, information that can lead me closer to the truth about my mom. About me.

About Henry.

Henry hasn't been back to school since the incident at that precog prison, or whatever the hell that place was. He also hasn't tried to get in touch. Sure, we don't have cell phones here at Lockwood, but we do have a school email address. Or he could take five minutes to send a letter. Maybe he thinks it's too risky or maybe he hates me. And if so, why? Things were good between us before he was taken away by the authority. Maybe they've shifted his perspective on life. *On me.*

What reason does he have to be angry? Why did he run off? And why do I care so much?

Ever since the last day I saw him, it's like something animalistic, feral even, has unlocked inside me—as if an electric current is always coiling around my limbs. Hate and longing and anxiety and pleasure skittering over my flesh. I don't understand what I'm feeling, or why I'm feeling this way.

Wes is back to kissing me again, tightening his grip on my skin. Every time we do this—lie here in my bed making out—I start rationalizing my decision to keep him around.

The information I need. The distraction, the numbing out is temporary. I'll be done with him soon.

Another part of me wonders why I need to rationalize it—to myself or anyone else. I was nearly murdered, twice. I suspect I have some weird hidden powers and learned I may not even be human, if I take Oliver's word for it. My father has a whole new family he never told me about. And on top of that, Henry broke my heart.

Don't I deserve this one distraction from everything? Anyone who wants to judge me for keeping Wes around can fuck right off.

Anger radiates through my body at the same time Wes deepens his kiss. The truth is that no one is judging me, at least not outwardly.

I'm over here judging myself.

My lungs start to seize and my mind begins to darken. "Stop," I say, nearly breathless.

Wes immediately backs off. "Sorry, did I take it too far?"

"No." I push myself up onto my hands, sitting up in bed.

Wes pulls me back down, curling me into his arms, twisting his fingers gently into my hair, stroking my scalp, and planting a kiss on top of my head. Goosebumps ripple over my skin. Another reason I like keeping him around: he gives me endless scalp massages—my favorite.

We're having one of those calm moments, where the world grows quiet, and just for a bit, I can tune out the pain coasting through my emotions.

"I love you, Natalie," Wes says.

My heart ricochets into my throat. *Love?* No, no, no. He can't love me. This is all a game. He lies to me. I lie to him. He's wearing an eye patch, after all, faking an injury, thinking I'm some idiot who will swoon and feel bad for him. I'm only sticking around for the distraction and the hope that I can use him to unlock some answers.

Speechless, I inch away from Wes's body.

Disappointment paints his face. "You don't have to say it back. It's only been a month, but I couldn't hold it in anymore."

I paste on a grin, acting flattered. He takes that as a cue, leaning into me, hovering his lips over mine.

"I need a break," I say, climbing out of my bed. "Do you want some tea or something?"

Wes shoots me a look. "Covington, when do I ever drink tea?"

"Right, sorry." I cross over to the kettle, feeling Wes's gaze boring into me from behind.

"Remember we have dinner with my father tonight." A lump forms in my throat. My father is the last person I want to see, now that I know he's unceremoniously dumped me and moved on with a new family. But I need answers. And so far, my hunt for the truth about things hasn't been going so well.

"How could I forget? I get to meet your dad. That's a big step." Wes heads over, curling his strong arms around my body. "I look forward to meeting the man who created the smart, beautiful, amazing Natalie Covington."

Before I can shrug off meeting my dad as any sort of meaningful step in our situation-ship, a siren wails in the distance. It's deafening, piercing my brain.

"What the hell is that?" I peer out the window as Wes cranes his head over my shoulder. Dozens of Lockwood students rush out of the buildings into the courtyard down below.

"Fire alarm?" Wes says.

But I know it's not that. We had several annoying fire drills the first day at Lockwood and it did not sound like that.

The ominous wail continues, and I get the feeling that something is very, very wrong.

CHAPTER TWO

NATALIE

My boots slosh over the muddy ground as Wes holds a large black umbrella over us both. It's November, and the sky is gray and thick and rain falls without a break. This is the reason most people hate living in the Pacific Northwest, but I like it. There's something about the moody atmosphere that feels right, even when everything else feels wrong. Besides, the sun is kind of bullshit.

My friend Ciel tiptoes over to us, careful not to splash mud on her new boots. "Why is that alarm so loud?"

I used to think our friendship was fickle and fleeting, like most friendships at private schools I've attended in the past, but we've grown close over the past couple months. I haven't told her about precogs, or powers, or anything that went down. Not because I don't trust her, but because I want to protect her. Ciel is a good person and friend, she doesn't deserve to get wrapped up in this mess.

I shrug about the alarm, looking up at Wes and noticing his gaze cutting to the far end of the property. I follow his eyes, spotting a much larger group of guards than we had earlier this semester. What the hell? Are these guys multiplying?

I turn to Ciel. "Why are there more of them?" I motion to the creepy guards that make me feel anything but protected, unable to forget that Wes's uncle was one of them—that he would have ended my life if it wasn't for Henry. Or Wes, if I'm to believe he convinced Henry to save me.

"Adip overheard that the school needed to heighten security," Ciel says.

Since we arrived at Lockwood back in September, Adip has basically become Lockwood's version of Gossip Girl. A really hot Gossip Girl, as Ciel would say, since they're in a very casual, very sexy open relationship. Adip knows everything about everyone and isn't afraid to spill. Well, he knows *almost* everything. He certainly doesn't know the extent of what I've been through since arriving at Lockwood, but not for lack of trying.

"Maybe we're getting a new student from, like, a very important family. Someone with a target on their back," Ciel says.

I stifle the urge to laugh. No one has a bigger target on their back than me, and arguably, Wes. Jury's still out on him. I've been hiding at Lockwood in plain sight, searching for clues about precogs, my mom, and what the hell happened back at that prison where they held Henry captive—and how I was able to kill Oliver.

Terror spikes through my chest at the memory. *I killed someone.* I know it was self-defense, that Henry's foster dad was trying to murder me, but it still doesn't make what I did any better. It's possible all of that was some bizarre surge of adrenaline. I've read about other humans having unimaginable bouts of strength when faced with impossible circumstances.

But something in my gut tells me that's not what's going on with me. A voice in my brain whispers that there's a bigger reason, along with Oliver's words about what's to happen to me when I turn nineteen.

And secretly? I'm hoping to draw one of these precog authority assholes out of hiding and have them come after me. At least then I can get some answers, even if my life's at risk.

The guards circle around everyone gathered in the courtyard. Their presence is intimidating as always. There's way more of us than them, but they have weapons. Wes also has a weapon—a dagger concealed in a leather sheath, tucked under his uniform jacket. He carries it everywhere, and while I don't doubt his abilities as a trained assassin, the guards have rifles.

Plus, Wes can't be trusted anyway.

Wes clasps my hand, his fingers tightening around mine. His gesture is pointed, and painful, as he clenches my palm, draining the blood from my fingers.

"Ouch," I say.

He doesn't seem to hear me.

"What's wrong?"

Still no answer.

His face draws away from mine as nerves singe through my veins. It's rare to see Wes rattled. This can't be good.

The alarm cuts off and a thick blanket of silence looms over Lockwood, making this entire scene feel even more eerie.

A woman I don't recognize works her way through the crowd and the guards part to let her through, nearly bowing as she passes. She looks to be in her early forties and is shockingly beautiful. Chestnut brown hair with glittery gold highlights that gleam even though there's no sun. Even at a distance, I notice her deep green eyes, the kind that bore through your soul.

My ex-boyfriend Jack walks next to her, holding an umbrella over her head, getting himself wet in the process. I study his ass-kissy expression, realizing he's doing whatever it takes to impress whoever this woman is. Classic Jack, zeroing in on the person he needs to impress most and clinging to them for dear life. Although our relationship is over, I can still read him like a book.

Every student twists their gaze to this mystery woman, as if they're all hypnotized. Impossibly transfixed. Except me. Does everyone know who this woman is but me?

Wes squeezes my hand even tighter and I wonder if he knows her too. I notice his jaw clench, his dead giveaway that something's wrong. I get the distinct feeling he's hiding something from me, yet again. *No surprise there.* I could fill a book with his lies.

The eye patch—which he's still wearing right now and does not need. He lied about being Canadian. I found that out when I went searching through his bags one night and found his US passport. I assume telling people he's Canadian is his way of coming off as more endearing. Who knows?

He also lied about his knowledge of the precog authority. That night, when he looked at the photo of my mom and recognized her with someone from the authority—that happened after he *explicitly* told me he didn't know anyone involved with them. My mind was so jumbled at the time that I didn't catch him in the lie. Now it's stuck in my mental notebook, crammed full of his deception. That little slip makes it even more important to keep him around, because there are things he knows, things he's purposely not telling me.

The charismatic woman holds court easily in the center of the common area, commanding attention without even trying. "Hello, Lockwood students," she says in a perfectly pitched voice. If she wasn't mysteriously showing up at private schools, she could have a great career as a voiceover artist. "Headmaster Rochester is unfortunately no longer with us."

Excuse me, what?

Headmaster Rochester has apparently been at this school for thirty years—a staple of Lockwood culture. Why would he suddenly disappear without fanfare? Lockwood goes all-out for the most basic things, like student elections. Why is there no retirement party for a man who dedicated thirty years of his life to this place?

"My name is Amelia Collins and I'll be taking over as temporary headmaster. I apologize for announcing this all so suddenly. I'd hoped that we could have a more distinguished first meeting."

Amelia scans the crowd and her fierce green eyes meet mine, locking there for a second too long. Anxiety winds through my middle and I swallow the thick knot in my throat. Maybe I'm just imagining things. Or not.

"I called this emergency meeting today because Lockwood is under threat of an attack. No one is to leave campus until we provide further instructions."

Attack? My stomach floods with tension. Have the precogs finally come for me?

Or is there another enemy lurking out there?

CHAPTER THREE

WES

AMELIA COLLINS.

I felt her arrive before she even showed her face. When you live your entire life trained to kill, you get damn good at sensing danger before it arrives.

And Amelia Collins is definitely dangerous.

But the question is, who the hell is she?

She continues her speech, her voice slipping over the entranced crowd. "Lockwood has received several anonymous threats over the last month, and those threats have only increased as the weeks passed. Our administration has decided to take swift and informed action. That's going to mean some changes happening here on campus," Amelia says, her voice smooth like whiskey. "The cameras situated around campus have been turned back on for your safety. We've ordered additional security guards. And no one is to leave unless there's a medical emergency."

How convenient that we're being watched and can't leave. I scan the terrified faces of the other Lockwood students, suppressing a chuckle. The worst threat these kids have probably ever received is

Daddy refusing to give them access to their trust fund. They sure didn't grow up like me.

I saw my first dead body at age five, after my uncle brutally murdered someone out in the woods when I thought the two of us were just out on a fun summer fishing trip.

Five was the age he'd decided to expose me to my destiny—to serve the precog authority as a trained killer. Can't imagine any of these other Lockwood fucks taking that news as well as I did.

My mind fills with images of death, of all the people I watched die while I was in training.

If Amelia Collins is here for me, good luck to her. Killing a trained assassin? More power to you, lady.

My brother was supposed to follow the same legacy, but he was the absolute worst. No skill. No talent. Like teaching a fish to play basketball. God rest his incompetent soul.

It makes sense, as he's not my real brother. As far as I'm aware, no precogs have family that's related by blood. We're all just placed together in some fucked-up foster care system. We were placed with Warren, who didn't want the dad label, so uncle it was.

Despite not being related by blood, it was clear early on that I was the talented one in the family, primed to carry on our sworn duty. At least until I killed my uncle, slicing away his expectations and effectively putting a target on my own back.

Natalie wriggles her hand from my grip and I realize I'm squeezing her too tight. I always feel protective over her, though I'm not an idiot—I know she doesn't really need my protection. She clearly handled her own with Henry's foster dad. Hell, she was the one who pulled Henry away from me when he flew into that rage. Though I can't blame him—I did leave him in that place.

She tugs her green hat down until it settles over her ears. It's emerald, the color her eyes shift to when she gets pissed. A primal urge stirs within me, a longing to remove her hat and every last piece of her clothing.

I blink some wetness into my eyes. Wearing this bullshit eye patch really messes with my vision and I wonder how long I should keep up this charade of the wounded boyfriend who was beaten by the guy my girlfriend loves.

I'm no idiot. After Natalie falls asleep, I take my time going through her room, searching for clues. Another side effect of being raised as an assassin—you learn to live on very little sleep. After digging through her things and coming up short, I found a secret trap door at the bottom of her closet. Lo and behold, she hid a box of research in there—about supernatural beings, about her mom, and about Henry.

But nothing about me.

I'm not sure if that means she trusts me, doesn't trust me, or if she doesn't care enough to even figure out if she trusts me. All options make me boil with anger and disappointment, so much that I nearly forget this Amelia woman is still droning on and on.

"I look forward to getting to know you all better and we'll keep you apprised of what's happening. Just know that your safety is our top priority." Amelia walks off with Natalie's pathetic ex-boyfriend, Jack, scurrying behind her with an umbrella.

"What the hell is going on? This can't be good." Natalie says, her eyes flooded with fear.

I tilt my gaze down to her and fake a smile. "It'll be okay." I wrap my hand around the back of her head, pulling her to me, planting a comforting kiss on her head. She relaxes into my arms, or at least it feels like she's relaxing. I can never really tell what's going on with her, and maybe that mystery is what makes me so excited…what makes me latch on to her and never want to let go.

᪣

I shove open the door to my dorm room. Well, technically, it was Henry's room, but he's gone, so now…all mine. After the whole incident at that precog prison, Natalie came up with an ingenious plan to convince Lockwood to let me in as a student.

Of course, she didn't tell them who I really am. She fabricated a backstory, claiming we were childhood friends, and that after her attack on school grounds, she'd feel much safer with an old friend here. Headmaster Rochester didn't go for it at first until she threatened to alert the media about her attack, and that Lockwood did everything to cover it up.

Immediately, they accepted me as a student.

Natalie's almost as good of a liar as I am. *Almost.*

Living life in the shadows, lying is second nature for me. Sometimes I lie because it's necessary and sometimes it's just out of habit. Sometimes I don't need to lie, but do it anyway. A default, if you will.

After our little emergency assembly this morning, Natalie rambled a bunch of excuses about why she needed some alone time. *Lies.* She had to study for chemistry (bullshit, she can ace a science exam in her sleep). She was tired (also bullshit, because I watched her sleep for nine hours last night). She made lunch plans with Ciel. That one might be true and I'm okay with it. It was easy to win Ciel's favor, and now she always talks me up to Natalie, gushing about how I'm the perfect "hot and mysterious" boyfriend and how lucky Natalie is to have me. All I need to do is toss a compliment at Ciel here and there and she eats it up.

At least I'll see Natalie tonight, when I finally get to meet her father. My first time ever meeting a parent. Fitting, as Natalie is the first girlfriend I've had—or cared to have, anyway. I've messed around with plenty of girls in the past, never telling them my real name, never planning to see them again. It was easy to pull this off because my family moved around a lot, always chasing a new mark.

There was nothing technically wrong with any of those girls, they just couldn't captivate my attention for more than a night.

Only Natalie holds that honor.

I light up the end of my joint and take a deep puff, the smoke filling my lungs and cleansing my mind of any stress. *Amelia Collins, huh?* Let's see who you are and what the hell you want.

Yanking the eye patch from my face, I blink in rapid succession, hoping to restore my vision as quickly as possible, but it doesn't work. I grab my laptop, searching for Amelia Collins with one stupid, blurry eye. Time to fake a doctor's appointment and tell Natalie I'm finally cleared to remove the patch. Maybe I can pretend that something else is wrong with me, spiking her guilt so she doesn't get any ideas about ending our relationship.

Resting my joint on a makeshift ashtray, I scroll through the search results on Amelia Collins. Tons of photos of her handing off checks at charity events, grinning alongside politicians and prominent businesspeople, likely every single one with a secret to hide. Most of all, her.

I'll give her credit—fabricating some kind of school security breach is an effective way to maintain control. After watching so many people on the brink of death, I can say for sure that when your life is threatened, when the blade of a dagger is scratching at the surface of your skin, you'll agree to anything.

My hand twitches at the thought of this woman creating an army…for what? Is it to close me and Natalie inside the Lockwood gates, turn the entire student body against us, and hang us in the courtyard while everyone cheers?

Amelia Collins. I bet she thinks she's so smart coming here, puppeting as a school headmaster with our best interests at heart.

All she's done is serve herself up to me on a silver platter. She thinks she can come here and kill me?

Not if I kill her first.

CHAPTER FOUR

NATALIE

MY FATHER SCANS the dining hall, barely able to contain his repulsion. His annoyance tripled when I told him he had to come here to campus because none of us are allowed to leave. He's not being waited on hand and foot at some award-winning establishment... *what an extreme inconvenience for him.*

It took thirty-three days to convince my father to have dinner with me. He still doesn't know what I know—that he's got a secret family, a new baby and everything. He was out of the country, hard to pin down. It feels like he's ignoring me, and he probably is. I'm eighteen, legally an adult in the United States. I'm sure he's more than ready to move on and forget I ever existed.

Now I'm sitting here next to Wes, my father across the table, looking like he'd rather be anywhere else but here. I know his secrets and lies. I know why he sent me away after Mom died—to boarding schools, wellness retreats, humanitarian missions, and now Lockwood. He wanted me out of the house and out of his life.

The dining hall is unusually quiet. Only two tables are occupied; one by a single student, headphones on, studying, and the other by a group of girls chatting loudly—their attention absorbed in their own worlds. Perfect. They can mind their own business so I can focus on mine.

"So, how are things, Dad?"

Wes holds my hand and my nails dig into his palm, not because I need him, but because I'm overflowing with frustration and his hand seems like a great place to take that out on. He gives me a reassuring squeeze. That was nice, I guess.

"Busy as usual," my father says, taking a sip of whiskey, screwing up his face. "One hundred thousand dollars in tuition and you can't get a decent drink on this campus."

Aggravation snakes through my insides. The only reason I'm here with him is because he's my last hope to get some information about me, my mom, my powers. What's to happen to me when I turn nineteen, like Oliver said.

I went back to visit Ray, Mom's friend in Vancouver who manages the Nine O'Clock Gun, the guy who gave me the note from Mom. But when I knocked on the door to his house, a woman answered. Said she bought the place and didn't know where the owner moved. I tried finding Ray at the historical society, but they said he'd retired and left no forwarding address. I searched his name online, but couldn't find any information about him anywhere. He just vanished.

I also convinced Wes to come with me, back to that precog prison, which was even weirder. We expected a pile of rubble from the fire that broke out, but instead, we found only flat land with lush, green grass that appeared untouched. I wondered if we accidentally went to the wrong place, but the spot where I killed Oliver was unmistakable. It's as if the precog prison *also vanished.*

Night after night, I stayed awake, obsessively researching Henry, Oliver, everything I could think of online. But there was nothing at all. Even the old research I had on Henry, the article about his charity work in Istanbul, was *gone.*

And then there's the question of my own powers. I considered so many possibilities. Do I have special powers, like Henry and Wes? Who am I? *What* am I? I'd scoured every possible supernatural explanation—angels, fairies, vampires, witches. I even wondered if I was a precog, maybe a different type who doesn't have visions. My research resulted in dead ends all around.

My father has to have some answers. He must know, or at least have suspected, something.

"What really happened to Mom?" I ask, heat prickling down my spine.

My father snaps his gaze up from his whiskey glass. Worry passes through his eyes. There's definitely something he's not telling me.

He paints on his best exasperated tone. "What are you talking about, Natalie?"

"You know what I'm talking about."

We lock eyes, and I hope my icy gaze challenges him enough to start giving me the truth.

Instead, he turns to Wes. "I apologize for my daughter. She's known to act a bit crazy from time to time."

I barely resist the urge to smack my father across his clean-shaven face. Of course he'd try to brand me as crazy. To discredit anything I'm about to ask.

"Oh, I love your daughter's crazy, but that's not what's happening here. You owe her some answers." Wes fondles a steak knife with his free hand.

I whip my gaze to Wes, surprised by his bravado, and at the same time, not surprised at all. That cocky overconfidence is Wes to the core, and I can't deny it feels good when it's aimed at my father—someone who actually deserves it.

The air grows thick and my father's eyes stay locked on Wes. I'm wondering if he wants to kill him right now, and also imagining what would happen if he dared try to kill a trained assassin.

"What do you want to know?" my father says, oddly compliant, and goosebumps sprout on my arms. Did Wes just hypnotize him or something?

"I know it wasn't an accident. Mom was killed, wasn't she?" I ask.

My father swallows, finally breaking his gaze from Wes and lowering his eyes. He looks… sad. Certainly not an emotion I've ever seen him express before, even at Mom's funeral.

"How do you know?" he asks so quietly that the words barely register in the room.

His question burns through my heart. *So he does know.*

"That doesn't matter. What matters is why didn't you tell me. Why aren't we doing something about it? Why haven't you tried to find out who killed her?"

My father smacks his palm against the table, causing the dishes and silverware to clatter. "Natalie, that's enough," he says.

Wes stands, looming over him, threatening. His stance seems to throw my father off balance. "Don't ever speak to her that way."

Blood rushes to my cheeks as I watch my father, the man who doesn't usually take any shit, completely back down to Wes. "Sorry," he mumbles.

Wes slides back into his seat. I peer around the dining hall to see if anyone else noticed the commotion. The group of girls have already left, leaving the lone student with his nose still in a book, headphones on, paying us no attention.

"Your mother was a complicated woman. We had a complicated relationship."

My patience shrinks. "What the hell does that mean?"

He sighs, taking a dramatic pause and finishing off his whiskey before saying another word. "We had a marriage of convenience. I got myself into some hot water, money-wise. Your mother needed a green card. She was presented to me as a way out of the hole I dug myself in. Marry her and my debts would be cleared. She was obviously beautiful, intelligent, it didn't seem that hard of an ask. At least, not at first."

My nose crinkles in confusion. "Green card? So Mom wasn't American?"

My father shakes his head. "She was from Turkey. At least, that's where she was born. I don't know a whole lot about how or where she grew up."

My mind combs through memories. Mom never mentioned being born anywhere else in the world or having relatives in Turkey. She certainly spoke perfect English with no trace of an accent. I try to recall any photos from her childhood, but now I realize… I never saw any.

"Your mother was in danger as well. Apparently, she got into some trouble doing a story overseas. The marriage was a way out for both of us."

"Who made that deal with you both?" I ask, my stomach churning at his revelations.

"I don't know who was in charge. Didn't ask questions. That was a part of it—to keep quiet and not question things. It was presented to me by a third party."

My mind knots with sheer confusion. This all sounds so bizarre, and yet, there are supernatural beings among us, so I guess anything is possible.

"Your mother and I had separate lives," he says. "I cared for her, I really did. But we did our own thing. It wasn't a romantic partnership."

Not romantic? "So how did I come into the picture?"

He sighs. "I really shouldn't say. Your mother made me promise…"

"Just say it," I snap.

But he doesn't speak. Wes locks eyes with him again, and my father slips into that bizarre, trance-like state. He finally opens his mouth and the truth drips out. "You're not my child. When I was connected to your mother, she was eight weeks pregnant with you and completely terrified."

My heart stops and Wes must feel it because he wraps his arm all the way around me, lightly pressing his palm to my chest.

"I'm sorry. She made me swear not to tell you." *He's sorry?*

"I don't get it. If you're not my dad, why did you want me to date Jack? Why were you forcing me into Harvard? Why did you bother coming all the way here earlier in the semester to make sure I was keeping Jack happy?"

He sighs. My father… the stranger. "I'm not proud of how I acted. I felt trapped, controlled by the whole situation. Jack's family is very influential and I saw a way I could benefit from this circumstance we're in. If you went to Harvard with Jack, maybe even married him, that could be advantageous to me."

My stomach churns. I'm nothing but a circumstance to him. *An advantageous circumstance.*

"Your mother had a lot of secrets. I didn't ask questions. That was part of the deal."

No. No. No. No.

None of this makes sense.

"You said you cared about Mom. Then why didn't you do anything when she was killed?"

He winces and his eyes begin to water. "Again, Natalie, I wasn't supposed to ask questions. Even if, or when, she disappeared. Your mother knew how to make enemies, her work made it impossible not to. But I made good on my promise to her."

I eye him with disgust. "And what was that?"

"To take care of you until you turned eighteen."

I stand, shoving back my chair, causing a loud scrape on the floor. This gets the other student's attention and his eyes turn to us, along with the waiter filling his water.

"Well, I'm eighteen now, so you're off the hook."

"Natalie," he says, a trace of pleading in his voice.

"I know you have a new wife, a new child."

"I'm sorry. I was dating Adelina when your mother was still alive. She knew about her. They were friendly. Again, it was just a business arrangement—to benefit us both. And I figured that you'd expect me to move on. I just didn't know how to tell you."

Bile rises in my throat. *Adelina. An arrangement. Marriage of convenience.*

This is all too much for me. I throw down my napkin and storm out of the room, needing to be anywhere but here.

CHAPTER FIVE

WES

WELL, **THAT WAS** fun.

Not so much for Natalie, but certainly for me. Especially her father bending so easily to one of my tricks.

Magic is something I began practicing several years ago, when I found an old book that belonged to my uncle. Well, it didn't actually belong to him. The owner of the book was this guy, Burak, the man who trained my uncle to be an assassin, who in turn trained me.

Wielding magic is forbidden for precogs, punishable by death. Burak wanted my uncle to familiarize himself with magic so he could better spot if someone was attempting to use it out in the field. One night, while my uncle was out on a job, I stole the dusty book from his bedside drawer, taking mental notes. This continued, night after night, until I got caught. My body still flinches, recalling that punishment.

Luckily, my uncle wasn't able to beat all the memories out of my brain, and I remember quite a bit of the magic from that book, trying various things over the years. One of those things is the ability to coax truth from people, lulling them into a hypnotic state. I've tried this on numerous occasions and it doesn't always work. Some people have an invisible shield that I'm unable to mentally penetrate. Or my magic could use some practice.

Either way, I'm glad Patrick Covington was easy. That weak-willed simp cracked within moments, spilling everything Natalie—and I—wanted to know.

Natalie's off, probably in the dining hall restroom, or maybe she raced back to her dorm. I'll give her a few moments and look for her. In the meantime, I'm enjoying this scene far too much. Sitting across from her fake father, a pathetic little man, as he drowns his pathetic little life in another glass of whiskey.

I knew they couldn't be related by blood. Natalie, so ethereally gorgeous, with her wild curly hair, her deep brown eyes that glitter with green depending on her mood, and her throat that begs for my hand to wrap around it while I kiss her.

Meanwhile, her father is devastatingly mediocre. He's average height, average frame, his hair thinning at the crown, combed over in some feeble attempt to cover his pasty head. His eyes are a muddy grayish brown—remarkably unremarkable, just like the rest of him.

My hand squeezes around the dagger inside my jacket, wondering what it would feel like to slice it into her father's chest, watching his miserable life drain away. How delightful it would be as he stares up at me, having spent all his life cowering to someone he owes money to, when I'm the one he really should have watched out for.

"Please don't kill me," he says.

My blood chills. Did he just read my mind? Or is he assuming that's the only logical next step in this situation?

"What makes you say that?"

"You're one of…" He trails off, his fingers drumming alongside the empty glass.

"One of what?" I say, snapping back. If this fool knows something, it's likely I'll need to kill him. I wonder how Natalie will repay me when I spill the blood of her own father, the man she hates most. The idea makes ending his life all the more tempting.

"I was married to Madeline for a long time. I suspect she wasn't exactly human. And neither is Natalie. That's one reason I was always so distant with her. I was terrified of who she was. What she might become."

Leaning forward, I study his trembling face. "What do you think she is? That I am?" I toy with him, assuming he's just trying to get me to confirm his suspicions, as if I'm some idiot. *Like him.*

"I… I don't know. I was hoping you could tell me," he says.

A laugh erupts from my throat as I toss my napkin on the table. "We're done with your conspiracy theories. If you really believe there are people who are not human living among us, there are pills and psych wards for that. I trust you'll stay away from Natalie, or you can kiss your new wife and child goodbye."

As I walk out of the dining hall, I can practically feel the terror dripping off him. *Job well done.*

I track Natalie down inside the ladies' restroom right by the dining hall, the first place I checked. Slipping inside, I lock the door behind me.

"What are you doing? This is the ladies' bathroom."

"It's where you are, so I'm here."

Natalie huffs in frustration. I wonder if she knows how it drives me crazy when she does that. How every roll of an eye or frustrated breath makes me want to clamp my hand in the back of her hair, holding her head perfectly still so I can explore her lips, her mouth, her neck…

She plants her hands on the counter, staring into the mirror. I come around behind her, resting my hands on top of hers, meeting her gaze in the reflection.

"Did you do something to my father?"

Heat races up my arms. Did she want me to kill him? Maybe I've disappointed her.

Nuzzling into her neck, I whisper, "I let him go, but it's just as easy to track him down. How do you want him to die?"

She shoves me back, a coldness slicing between our bodies. Spinning to face me, she rolls the tension out of her shoulders. "That's not what I meant! Can't you get death out of your mind for one second?"

"No," I answer, honestly. What does she expect? Death is what I know. Death has been my whole life.

"Okay, whatever, I meant did you use some kind of powers on him? He was like a totally different person."

My lips twist at the corners, an innate reaction I don't intend. She picks up on it right away.

"So you did. What did you do? Do you have powers I don't know about?"

"Of course," I say honestly.

Her eyes widen in some mix of horror and betrayal and excitement. Which, of course, thrills me to the core.

"Why didn't you tell me before?" She smacks her palms against my chest.

I grab her hands with mine, holding them in place as she attempts to tug them away. "You didn't ask."

"You're ridiculous. You know I've been looking for information."

"Yeah, about yourself. Your mom. And of course, about *Henry*." My voice drips with disdain. "It's been thirty-three days and you haven't bothered to investigate the person standing right in front of you. The person in your bed every night."

She attempts to tug her hands away, but I don't let her.

"Let me go."

"No." I squeeze harder, moving my body into hers. "Ask me. What do you want to know?"

"Fine. What power did you use on my father?"

I take another step closer, still clenching her hands to my chest. "It's magic that hypnotizes people into telling the truth. It doesn't work all the time. But it did on him."

Her perfect lips form into an "o" and her pretty eyes widen with shock. "Have you ever used that on me?"

"No." *But not for lack of trying.*

"Bullshit," she says.

"Okay, fine. I tried it on you but it didn't work. Maybe you're immune to it."

Her eyes trace along my face and I can tell she doesn't quite believe me. "What other powers or magic or whatever do you have? That you decided to keep from me."

My mind struggles to focus on anything but turning this little interrogation into a game. She asks a question and I answer, as long as she does something for me. This night has already been pretty thrilling. Nothing wrong with kicking it up a notch.

"Wes, this isn't a game. What *else*?!" Natalie snaps at me.

Oh, but it is a game. I release her hands and watch as they clasp the sink behind her, her body shifting backwards, putting distance between us, which only makes the game more thrilling.

"I can resurrect things."

I hadn't considered telling Natalie this before, telling anyone, really. Resurrection was listed last in the book of magic, accompanied by four pages of warnings and disclaimers, much like one of those pharmaceutical ads in a magazine. I have to admit the risk of it all drew me in deeper.

Natalie glares at me in absolute horror. "You can't be serious."

I take a step closer to her, sliding my hand over her cheek. She bats it away, but I'm back on her, swiping my finger across her lips, smearing her pink gloss as she twists her face away.

"I'll tell you, but you should do something for me."

"I said this isn't a game. Why are you messing with me? There's absolutely no way you can bring people back to life."

"I'll tell you more about it if we can *practice* tonight in a different way." I trace my finger down the front of her skirt, hooking it under the hem and gliding it up her thigh.

She gasps, squeezing her thighs together and blocking my hand with hers. "You're being such an asshole right now. More than usual."

I have no time to protest when a shrill voice comes through the door, followed by a bang. "Hey! Is someone in there? I've got to pee!"

Natalie takes advantage of the interruption and pushes me away, straightening her skirt.

"I'm not lying to you. We'll continue this later," I say.

She scrunches up her face at me, clearly annoyed, the very expression that drives me absolutely crazy.

I'm already imagining a perfect evening ahead.

CHAPTER SIX

NATALIE

BACK IN MY dorm room, I can't stop my mind from rolling over the information that tumbled out of my dad's mouth. *Patrick.* Guess I should stop calling him Dad, since all of that was just a bitter twist of lies.

Why wouldn't Mom tell me? I loved and respected her for many reasons, one of them being her steadfast commitment to the truth. And now to find out she was lying to me all these years? It had to be for a good reason. Right?

"Why are you so far away from me?" Wes asks, leaning back against my headboard.

He's here with me now, of course. He's always here. I'm firmly planted across the room, far away from him and his bullshit. I'm grateful that he used his hypnotic magic on my father to extract the truth, but resurrecting people? He must really think I'm naïve to believe he's that powerful. But my body betrays me, dread pooling in my chest—a small part of me worrying that he's telling the truth.

I take a few steps back on instinct, practically cowering in my closet, getting farther from him. "Because I need to focus."

"So I distract you, eh?"

His little blip of Canadian speech nags at me. I haven't heard him say "eh" in a while, and it's interesting that he's chosen to bring that lie back now. Like he forgot he was supposed to be Canadian and something tugged at him in this moment to make sure I still think that.

Joke's on him.

Scowling, I turn and pretend to busy myself in the closet. "This isn't the time to play around. I just found out my father isn't even my real dad. I have some things to process. Including the fact that you apparently have some secret magical powers."

"It's magic that layers on top of my powers. But fair enough. I'll enjoy the view from over here."

Normally, his incessant need for attention would get a rise out of me, but right now, I can't stop thinking about Mom and why she wouldn't tell me any of this directly. Sure, she left that note in the framed photo, which led me to the Nine O'Clock Gun, then to the box she left at my apparently-not-dad's house that helped me find Henry. But how does it all connect?

None of it makes any sense.

The only thing I know for sure at this point is that my dad isn't my dad at all. That's good news and bad. Good because he was an awful father anyway, and I guess that tracks. It was a marriage of convenience, like he said. And I was clearly an inconvenience to him.

My hand traces the frayed stitches of my mom's leather jacket hanging in my closet. If Patrick isn't my father, who is? Mom left behind clues—wouldn't that be one of them?

Before I stormed out of dinner tonight, I really should have asked him who my real father is. A stupid move on my part. That's assuming he even knows. I could call him, but of course, phones are forbidden at Lockwood, and family phone time isn't until next Wednesday.

My memory snaps into place. *Ciel has a phone.* She snuck it into

Lockwood right around the time of the masquerade ball, the night Henry warned me to run. That moment is seared into my brain, along with so many moments with him, replaying over and over on a tortuous loop.

"I'll be right back," I say to Wes. Before he can argue, I'm out the door and down the hall—knocking on Ciel's door.

"One second!" she yells from inside, and I can hear some rumbling and an echo of laughter. Clearly, she's not alone.

She yanks open the door wearing a short, ivory, very see-through robe. Adip shrugs on a shirt in the background. A small bit of envy pings at my heart, but I quickly shove it away. A part of me wishes I could be a carefree eighteen-year-old, having sex on a random weeknight with my hot boyfriend instead of fighting for my life.

"Sorry to interrupt, guys."

Ciel seems unbothered. "No worries, we just finished," she says, winking at me. "What's up?"

"Can I borrow your phone?"

Ciel grins, like I've just made the best ask of all time. "*Obviously.* But I want to know every detail about who you're calling. Is it a new guy? You know I like Wes, but I'm always team Natty, so if you're eyeing up someone else…"

I shake my head, which causes Ciel to pout in disappointment. "It's nothing like that. I just need to call my dad about something."

Ciel scrunches her face in confusion. "Didn't you just have dinner with him?"

"Yeah, I forgot to tell him something important."

Ciel shrugs, fishing the phone out of her drawer. "Here." She hands it to me and I squeeze her hand in gratitude.

"I'll bring it right back."

As I approach my dorm room, Wes is waiting for me in the doorway, hands draped on the top ledge, a cocky smile on his face. "What are you up to, Covington?"

"Calling my dad. Move." I duck under his arm, dialing Dad's number. It goes straight to voicemail. I leave a message, hoping he'll pick up on the urgency and not write me off for good before I can get more answers.

Wes follows me back inside the room. "Why do you want to speak to him? What use is he to you?"

I whirl around to face him, irritation flickering in my gut. "He said he wasn't my dad, but I didn't ask him who is. That's something I should know."

"You really think he's gonna have that information? He said the deal was *not* to ask questions."

My lungs tighten—squeezing out the oxygen. Wes is probably right, which irritates me to the core. But it's worth trying to ask him anyway.

Another idea springs to mind. "Maybe I should take one of those DNA tests. You know, the ones that tell you who your ancestors are."

Wes crinkles his brow. "You could try, but it's only going to tell you names if those people are registered and gave consent to share their information. It's a medical privacy law thing. And if your family is *that* secretive, I doubt they're over there chilling and posting their information publicly on some corporate-owned DNA site."

He makes a good point. "How do you know all that?"

"I used to bore easily and would research random shit online. Until I met you. Now I'm never bored." He grins, his gaze smoldering into mine. That egotistical, enraging gaze that I hate—and sometimes enjoy, depending on how desperately I need a distraction.

Shame blooms in my chest, knowing tonight will be yet another night that I'll shut off my brain, mute my problems, and get lost in Wes.

Shaking off my impending weakness, another idea wedges into my brain. "What about Adelina, or whatever his new wife's name is?"

Wes takes a few steps closer to me. "What about her?"

"He said she was friends with my mom. Maybe she has information."

Wes shoots me a skeptical glare. "Natalie, I love you, but what would make you think your mom would confide in some random woman? She didn't even tell *you* anything, and you're her daughter."

His words bleed out and all I can hear are those three damn words. *I love you.* I swallow, pretending I didn't hear it, shaking it away. Luckily, he keeps talking.

"Besides, we need to focus on something more urgent. Amelia Collins. I've got a bad feeling about her and I'm pretty damn good at reading people."

Amelia Collins, huh? Luckily, we have a mutual in common.

"I have an idea."

CHAPTER SEVEN

NATALIE

AFTER SPENDING WHAT felt like an eternity convincing Wes to go back to his room, I raise my fist, banging on Jack's door. I want to handle some of this on my own, involving Wes as little as possible. Things are growing more complicated, and the less mixed up we are, the better.

Annoyed, Jack whips open the door wearing a towel, his hair dripping. Realizing it's me, he looks slightly less annoyed. "Nat, what's up?"

"Can I come in?" I say, but by that time, I'm already shoving past him, entering his room. That's when I walk right in on a half-naked Josephine. She quickly covers her body with a sheet.

"I'm so sorry," I say, lowering my eyes. And I am.

There was a time when I hated Jack for sneaking around behind my back. But let's face it, I wasn't in love with him, and clearly, he felt the same about me. Sometimes people are meant to be in your life for a spell and then you move on. They're a better match than we ever were.

Besides, I couldn't care less about their romance. I'm here for answers.

"I can give you two some privacy," Josephine says. She climbs out of bed, the sheet wrapped around her body.

"No, it's cool. Stay. I really didn't mean to interrupt anything. I just wanted to talk about what happened earlier today."

Jack eyes me, acting confused. "What do you mean?"

How could he be confused? We were told our entire school is under attack and given no other information. Obviously, he doesn't know what's been happening in my life, but he's got to at least be worried for his own safety.

I rattle off my concerns. "What happened to Headmaster Rochester? What threats did Lockwood receive? What's the deal with this Amelia chick? You're like her shadow already and she just got here."

Jack watches me with a concerned expression, like I'm insane for even asking. "Headmaster Rochester decided to step down once the threats started coming in. And Amelia—Headmaster Collins—was pretty clear about everything today. I'm our class president, so of course we've become close. What don't you understand?"

Ugh. Just when I think Wes might be the most annoying guy on the planet, here's Jack to remind me he's actually the worst.

I look over at Josephine, who gives me an apologetic glance. The familiar beep of a text alert fills the silence.

"Was that a text message?" I ask.

My question is answered when Jack grabs a cell phone from his desk.

"How did you get a phone?"

He doesn't answer right away, his eyes glued to whatever message just came through. "This phone is for administrative purposes. Presidential perk."

Jack quickly dresses as I turn around to give him privacy.

"Where are you going?" Josephine says, her words laced with disappointment.

"Headmaster Collins needs to see me." Jack finishes getting dressed, ignoring her feelings. Nothing new for Jack.

"And you're just going to rush off at her beck and call?"

Poor Josephine. She clearly doesn't know how selfish Jack can be. Whatever Jack wants, Jack does.

"Sorry, babe." He plants a quick kiss on her cheek before rushing out the door, leaving his ex-girlfriend and new girlfriend behind.

Josephine looks over at me, her cheeks flush with embarrassment. "I'm sorry about that."

"You don't need to apologize. That's just how Jack is."

Her eyes still twist with concern. "I thought what happened earlier was weird too. In fact, all of this is weird," she reveals.

Intrigue stirs in my brain and I take an uninvited seat on the chair next to Jack's bed. "Weird how?"

Josephine shakes her head, cobbling together her thoughts. "Two nights ago, Jack got a call in the middle of the night. He snuck out of the bedroom, but it woke me up. I followed him."

Damn, Josephine! Maybe I was wrong about her. I'm already beginning to think she's way too good for Jack.

"What happened?" I ask, treading carefully. I can tell by the way she's clenching the sheet around her body that she feels embarrassed and exposed in more ways than one.

"I think something happened to Headmaster Rochester," she says, her voice so quiet I barely hear her.

My mind burns with anxiety. "Like what?"

"I only heard Jack's side of the conversation, but it definitely sounded like he's gone missing. No one knows where he is. I've tried asking Jack about it, but he won't say a word. And ever since he met Amelia, he's been acting so strange. Like he's under her spell or something."

Under a spell. A shiver coasts up my spine. Could this Amelia woman be a precog? Is she wielding magic like Wes?

Josephine's crystal-blue eyes fill with tears. "What goes around comes around, right? I wanted him when he was with you, and now look what's happening." A single tear spills down her cheek.

"Look, there's no karmic revenge happening here," I say, trying to comfort her, or at least thank her for spilling some information. "Everything between us is cool, water under the bridge. Jack and I were basically arranged anyway, set up by our dads."

I swallow and my breath scratches against my throat, thinking of my fake father trying to get something out his messed-up arrangement at my expense.

Josephine wipes away a tear. "Jack's dad hates me."

I can't help but giggle, not in an offensive way, but to commiserate with her pain. "Who cares what his dad thinks? If Jack makes you happy, that's all that matters. And if he doesn't, you'll find someone better."

"Thanks, Natalie. And I'm really sorry. For everything."

I can tell she's sincere. Everything that happened between me and Jack feels like a lifetime ago. When it comes to Josephine, all is forgiven.

She's the least of my worries.

Back in my dorm, I'm relieved that Wes followed my orders and went back to his room. My stomach tightens with anticipation as I search through news articles, trying to find any shred of information about Headmaster Rochester and his disappearance.

But there's nothing. No missing person's report. No headlines about him. How is it possible this man could just vanish into thin air?

Then my mind clicks to something Amelia said this morning—the campus security cameras have been turned back on. But when? Did they do it at the first sign of a threat? Or more recently? If something happened to Headmaster Rochester, the cameras may have picked it up. Maybe the footage has already been turned over to police.

Unless they have something to hide.

Wes's concerns about Amelia dance through my mind, along with Josephine's words, that Amelia seems to have put Jack *under a spell.*

If only I could get a peek at the surveillance footage, which is not an easy task, considering I have no idea exactly where the security monitors are on campus.

But I bet I know someone who does. Someone who has studied every single inch of this campus.

Someone who had to be careful…because he came here to kill me.

CHAPTER EIGHT

WES

It doesn't take long before Natalie is inside my dorm room, right where she belongs. I made a plan while she was gone, the next steps to keep her—*us*—safe.

I'm prepared when she arrives, my hair pulled back in a knot, the patch I don't need tucked neatly back over my eye. Before I got to Lockwood, I didn't pay much attention to my appearance. I was living in the shadows, usually under a hooded jacket where I didn't have to worry about grooming my hair or shaving the stubble off my face.

Blending in at Lockwood is a little different. Wandering around in a hooded jacket looking feral won't fly here. I'd stick out like a sore thumb. I studied the kids, noticing that most guys wore glasses and shoved that sticky pomade shit in their hair to make it look spiky on purpose. I suppose that's the current trend for overprivileged prep douchebags.

One day, when I was sitting in the dining hall, eavesdropping on Natalie, her friend Ciel was playing some game of hot or not, ranking celebrities. She brought up some guy named Jason Momoa, and Natalie noted that he was hot. My research showed that he often wears his hair pulled back and doesn't have glasses, so I gave that look a try to see if it would impress Natalie.

Given our last month together, the nights I've spent exploring her mouth, her body, I'd say the look is working pretty well for me so far.

"Jack was useless," Natalie says. "But Josephine said he's been acting weird, like Amelia hypnotized him. Do you think she's a precog? That she's using the same magic as you?"

My head tilts and I paste on my best look of concern. "I don't know."

I want to tell her my plan to take care of things, but I'm not sure how she'll react if she learns I'm plotting to kill Amelia. It might be better to keep Natalie feeling in control, taking the lead. I know she likes that, even if it is a false sense of security.

Natalie shakes her head. "But it's definitely weird that Headmaster Rochester is just gone and there's no one looking for him, at least that we know."

I nod in agreement, grabbing my half-finished joint from earlier and lighting it up, the end crackling as I inhale.

"Do you think something bad happened to him? Did this Amelia woman do something to him? Is she here for me, for us?"

I make an attempt to keep her calm. "I'm sure they gave Rochester a very attractive retirement package. Or some shady fuck forced him out with a threat. Who knows? We'll figure out what her deal is." I take another drag off my joint, smoke billowing between us. What I don't tell her is that by the time we figure out Amelia's deal, she'll be dead—by my hand.

Natalie studies me and I know that look. She doesn't like where this conversation is going. I quickly stub out my joint, hoping to smooth things over.

"Why are you being so cavalier all of a sudden? You were just saying you had a bad feeling about her."

She's right, of course. I was attempting to direct her attention to something new so she wouldn't stress and obsess over her dimwit of a fake father. That was a mistake on my part, alerting her to Amelia being trouble.

But she doesn't have to worry, because I'll smash anyone's face in and leave their bodies blooded and broken before they get anywhere near her.

Just the delightful thought of that sends adrenaline pumping through my veins, causing my skin to sizzle. I haven't killed anyone since my uncle, which I certainly chalk up to being one of my best moments—watching the life drain from his eyes after all the years of torture and torment he put me through.

There's not much better than staring down your prey, watching things click in their mind. That moment they realize they're about to die and can't do a thing about it. It's exhilarating.

My uncle had to have known I'd someday put my training to use on him. If he didn't see it coming, he's even more deserving of his fate.

And Amelia Collins is next.

I grab Natalie's hand, pulling her to me, gently tracing my thumb along her wrist. Her expression is full of frustration, but her body tells a different story. I trace my eyes over her throat, then her chest, watching the rise and fall quicken. Having studied every inch of her, I can tell when she craves a distraction from everything.

When she craves me.

My free hand brushes a wild strand of her curly hair behind her ear. "I'm just trying not to panic because it won't do us any good." I lean into her ear, nuzzling into her neck. "We have to stay calm and focused. There's no use freaking out. We'll get to the truth."

Pulling back slightly, I notice the confused expression on her face. I can tell she doesn't agree with me, but we can work on that later. My eyes study the curves of her lips, wanting to consume every inch of her.

Her hands press against my chest and she crosses her arms, closing herself off from me, bruising my heart. I don't like it when she coldly pushes me away, stripping us apart.

"Do you know where the security cameras are?" she asks.

A surge of something hot spears through my chest—a feeling of distrust. Is there something she's not telling me? That familiar bad feeling claws up my stomach, the feeling I get when something bad is about to happen.

"No, I'm not sure where the cameras are," I say. *I lie.* Of course I know where the cameras are. But if she wants that information, she's going to have to tell me why she's asking.

I can feel her stretching farther away from me, walling up her emotions. "That's interesting because you *must* know where they are."

A grin slides onto my lips as I try to turn this conversation playful. "What would make you say that, Covington?"

"Because you came here to kill me. It would be pretty stupid of you not to have clocked where the security cameras are. And I know you're not stupid, Wes."

Damn, she just called me out. So much for playful.

"Why do you want to know? Is there something on those tapes?"

Natalie cocks her head, appearing to grow more aggravated. "If the school has been getting threats, there's got to be something. What about Headmaster Rochester? Maybe we can see when he left campus, learn what happened to him."

I lean back against my desk, gripping the edges. The desk that used to be Henry's. For a split second, my mind skips to their time together. Natalie was in this room with *him* not that long ago. Did she sit at this desk? And where was he? On the bed? Was she on the bed with him? Did he kiss her, like me? Touch her, like me?

Suddenly, I'm consumed by a twisted kind of jealousy, unable to fathom Henry's hands ever being on what's mine.

"Where are the security monitors? You have to know." Natalie interrupts my vicious thoughts. I can't risk her finding any disturbing footage, growing more worried than she already is, potentially putting us both in more danger.

Or worse, taking off to look for Henry.

I'll just take care of Amelia myself and anyone else who threatens to tear us apart.

"Covington, I agree with you. I'm with you on this. But there's no surveillance room, at least not one that I know of. I looked everywhere when I got here. Besides, they said the cameras were off before, right? I wouldn't lie to you."

Her lips work into a pout and she unfolds her arms, stepping closer to me, appearing to warm up. She wraps her arms around my waist, lifting her eyes to meet mine, bouncing her gaze between my eyes and lips.

A smile stretches across my face as I twist my fingers into her curls, planting a gentle kiss on her lips. "It's going to be okay. I'll protect you."

My reassurance must work because, within seconds, she shoves me back onto my bed. She climbs on top of me, straddling my hips, the skirt of her uniform bunching around her waist. My entire body tenses with anticipation. I know it's not possible for us to do it, *do this*, but hovering on the edge, getting so damn close, sends me spiraling. She leans down, her lips centimeters from mine, her sweet breath dusting over my mouth.

Before another heated thought can arouse my brain, she rips off my eye patch in one swift movement.

My body seizes in panic and I quickly shut my eyes. "What are you doing? I need that."

"Open your eyes," she whispers.

I'm not sure what's happening here. Is this some kind of kinky eye-based foreplay? I blink my eyes open, ready to continue my wounded rouse. But I immediately notice her icy stare.

"I know you don't need this thing, so let's stop playing this game, okay? You *would* lie to me. You *do* lie to me, all the time. And now you're going to take me to the room with the security footage."

CHAPTER NINE

NATALIE

THE SILENCE IN the security room is absolute.

I can feel Wes's eyes, both of them without that stupid fake eye patch, claw into the back of my head. We tuck ourselves into the room where the campus surveillance footage is held, in a hidden wing of the McNulty Building. It's a makeshift space, certainly not high-tech, with low ceilings, unpainted cinder block walls, cement floors, and no windows.

Wes hasn't breathed a word to me since I called him out on his lie. I was saving that for an occasion when I needed leverage. He led me here, helping us duck the now-working cameras, head hung low in what looked like shame, but he's probably just pissed that he got caught.

I pulse my finger on the keyboard, clicking through security footage from a week ago, the last time I remember seeing Headmaster Rochester. Wes leans against the door. His task is to keep watch while I go through the tape. Although this building is so dirty and decrepit, I'm not sure anyone comes back here often. Or at all.

On the monitor, I spot the footage of Headmaster Rochester leaving the administration building.

"There. He's going right, maybe to his house." Headmasters have their own house on the Lockwood campus, not unlike deans at universities.

Wes still doesn't say a word to me. I gaze back at him. His head is lowered, messing with the cuffs of his coat. I've never seen him so quiet. It's unnerving, if I'm being honest. Shaking off the bad feeling, I get back to the task at hand.

I switch over to the feed outside of Headmaster Rochester's campus house. On the tape, he walks through the oversized foliage, heading inside. A single light shines over the porch. I fast-forward through the footage, but everything seems calm and annoyingly untouched. I press play, watching the tree branches billow in the wind, the same frustrating light illuminating the front yard.

This footage is a whole lot of nothing.

"Does the camera only point to the front of the house?" I ask.

Wes doesn't bother answering.

I snap my eyes to him. "Are you just going to stand there or are you going to answer me?"

He lifts his gaze, meeting mine, and I swear I can see the ghost of a grin on his lips. Smug asshole.

"Oh, *now* you need my help?"

My insides tighten with frustration. I could say the same to him. Shouldn't he be apologizing and begging for my forgiveness? It's a good thing this relationship is fake, because as a boyfriend, he really sucks.

"You lied to me," I say.

"And *you* lied to me," he retorts.

I freeze, feeling caught, even though I'm not exactly sure what he's referring to. Playing it cool, I fold my arms over my chest as anger balloons in my brain. "Don't deflect your shit onto me."

Wes pushes away from the door, closing the distance between us. He thrusts his hands into his pockets, beaming his confident and cocky eyes right at me. "You don't think I know what you're doing, Covington?"

I stand my ground. What the hell does he know?

"You're in love with him." I can see the anger stir in his eyes. Whatever affection he was harboring towards me now seems to have disappeared. "Henry. You love him, right?"

I swallow back the dry, musty air. I don't love Henry. How could I love someone who completely ditched me without enough respect to explain why? I risked my life to save him, and he just took off and disappeared. What kind of stupid girl would I be to allow someone like that to consume my heart? He broke it. He's not getting it back.

So no, I don't love him. And I'll keep telling myself that until it becomes true.

Playing it off, I sneer at Wes. "I don't love him. Stop saying that."

He steps closer, leering over me, and I can see he doesn't believe a word I breathe. "I may have sold you some lie for sympathy, told you I was injured, but that was the only way to get you to see," he says.

Exasperation leeches through my bones. "See what?"

"That the person you need is standing right here in front of you. I'm the one who saved your life. Not him. I'm the reason you're still here. I didn't leave, he did."

My chest squeezes at his words. Technically, he's right. But I don't buy that Henry would defy his entire kind and put his life in danger just because some random precog told him to do it.

There's got to be more to his reasoning. And one day, I'll find out the truth.

Something catches the corner my eye on the security monitor, and I cut my gaze to the footage. "Wait, what was that?"

Wes sighs in frustration. I know he wants to talk things out, but I can't deal with his drama right now.

I pause and rewind the footage, then hit the play button. On the monitor, a silhouetted figure emerges from behind Headmaster Rochester's house, appearing to flee the scene. Who was that? And have they turned this footage over to the police already?

"Rewind that," Wes says, leaning in, just as curious as I am.

I swallow the thick knot in my throat as I roll back the footage and press the play button again, this time, watching in slow motion.

On the monitor, we watch the shadowy figure circle around the front of the house. They're wearing all black and the single light from the porch is the only way this person doesn't completely disappear into darkness. In slow motion, the mystery person twists their head for a split second, and I notice a strange flash of white.

Ice leeches through my veins. "What the hell was that?"

I rewind the footage once more, pausing on the moment the whiteness appears on screen. Using the dilapidated mouse next to the keyboard, I zoom in.

My hand begins to tremble as I notice what's appeared before me. A surge of nerves rises up through my body as I see the clearer picture of the mystery person, wearing a bizarre white mask.

The mask conceals everything, like a *Phantom of the Opera* mask constructed to fit the entire face. The nose is prominent and the lips are contorted into a menacing grin. The hollowed-out slats for the eyes are so small, I wonder how this person can see. If they're even a person. *Or even human.*

"I've seen that mask before," Wes says, the words stuttering from his lips, as if he didn't intend to speak them out loud at all.

My eyes snap to him. "Where did you see it?"

"Come with me. I'll show you."

CHAPTER TEN

WES

MY MIND SHATTERS into a million pieces as I lead Natalie down the long hallway to my room. Twisting the key in the lock, I shove open the door, Natalie following closely behind.

"Lock the door behind you."

She hesitates for a moment, but then does as I say. I wonder how long this will go on for, how long everything I ask of her will be laced with ten layers of distrust. I guess I should blame myself. I miscalculated, thinking I could guilt her into a relationship, but it turns out she knew all along. That must mean the only reason she's sticking around is because she thinks she can get something from me.

Probably to get closer to Henry.

Pain splinters my mind. The thought that she's using me to get to him makes bile rise up in the back of my throat. What the fuck is so great about Henry Thorne? Maybe I should have just killed him back in that prison, plunged my dagger right into his stomach.

"What are we doing in here?" Natalie says, crossing her arms with impatience.

I ignore her little temper tantrum and rip open the desk drawer, pulling out a small leather book, the one possession I carry with me everywhere. My thumb brushes over the inscription on the cover. *The Decalogue.*

The Decalogue comes from the Greek name for the Ten Commandments. Precogs steal quite a bit from Greek culture, all the way down to the branding on our forearm of the psi symbol. Psi is the twenty-third letter of the Greek alphabet and is associated with a numeric value of 700. My uncle told me this is significant because, centuries ago, there was a war amongst precogs. 700 of them split off into a fringe group, attacking the rest of us. Twenty-three brave soldiers on the "good" side lost their lives in that battle. From that moment forward, we were all to be branded with the psi symbol so that we can never forget their sacrifice. It's a decent story that I always suspected was a crock of shit.

I carefully peel open the worn pages of *The Decalogue*, this version being the precog ten commandments specifically for people like my family, the assassins, ordered to right the wrongs of precogs who dare to defy the authority, to kill off those who present a problem to our kind.

Natalie peeks over my shoulder as I rifle through the pages, finding a black-and-white photo of an army of precogs, all wearing the same mask we just saw on that security footage.

My stomach wrenches at the photo. "I fucking knew it."

"Who are they?" Natalie asks, her voice dripping with anxiety.

"The Armory. From what I was told, they were a fringe group of precogs devoted to a more militant world order."

"More militant than what you already do? Your job is to execute people."

"I'm not entirely sure of their criteria for 'militant.' My uncle said the Armory hasn't been seen in public for years. He thought they disbanded, went their separate ways."

"Then why are they in your book?"

Memories of my uncle's words seep into my brain. "This book exists to warn us about any potential threat that might get in our way to execute a hit."

Natalie blows out a frustrated breath. "So if they're working against the authority, what are they doing here at Lockwood?"

My heart begins to pound, picking up speed. And that's when a vision begins. The first I've had all year.

The back of a woman standing on a balcony overlooking the Lockwood campus. Her hair is brown, glossy, and she's wearing a black blazer and skirt with high heels. Is she a student here? A teacher?

The woman slowly turns, mouth crinkling into a smile that appears both warm and sinister. Amelia Collins. *She's greeting someone on that balcony.* But who? And where on campus is this balcony?

Amelia extends a manicured hand, as if she's luring a child to the candy jar. A girl steps into my view, only visible to me from behind. She's wearing a Lockwood uniform, but it's styled differently. A student.

The girl turns to the side, facing Amelia, allowing me to see who it is. It's Natalie's friend, Ciel.

Amelia reaches out, tracing her finger along Ciel's necklace, hooking her finger underneath the dainty gold ringlets. Ciel isn't pushing her away. In fact, she seems to be enjoying it.

Amelia steps closer as Ciel flutters her eyes shut, like she's preparing for a kiss. Do these two have something going on?

Amelia tugs at Ciel's necklace, pulling her closer, hovering her lips dangerously close. Ciel's eyes flutter. I can practically feel the anticipation in my bones. Is this the first time they've messed around together? Or has this little affair been going on for some time?

Amelia pulls back as Ciel pouts at the rejection. Ciel moves her lips, about to mouth something in protest.

And then...Amelia shoves her off the balcony.

"Wes. Wes. Wes!"

Natalie's muffled voice cuts off my vision in one vicious slice. I try to get my bearings. It's been awhile since I've had a vision, and never one that went on for this long before.

It's hard to focus. Hard to think. Hard to breathe.

My senses must be returning, as I can feel Natalie's grip on my shoulders, shaking me.

"Wes!"

I squint, blinking quickly, trying to restore my eyesight and slow the speed of my heartbeat. My head pounds as I reach my hand up and touch my tender scalp.

"Wes, can you hear me?"

I manage to nod through the pain in my head, noticing the alarm in Natalie's voice.

"You started shaking and you fell and hit your head," she says.

Fuck. Being a precog really is a curse.

"You might have a concussion. We should get you to a doctor."

My hand smacks down on Natalie's wrist, squeezing harder than I intended. I look up into her eyes, seeing the old Natalie, the one with concern for me. Care for me. The one I thought—I hoped— might one day fall for me.

Maybe all is not lost between us, but there's no time to focus on that. Not with a member of the Armory sneaking around campus and Amelia Collins tossing students off buildings like a gum wrapper.

"I had a vision," I say, causing Natalie's arm to tremble under my grip.

My heart splits as I realize the last time someone must have said that to her. *Henry.* I hate the parallels between him and I, that Natalie had these experiences with him before me. Maybe I should have gotten involved sooner, changed his vision myself instead of letting him take the risk. A bad move on my part.

"The vision wasn't about you," I tell Natalie.

I watch the rise and fall of her chest, exhaling with relief. But it won't be for long.

"But unless you and I do something about what I just saw, our new headmaster is going to kill your best friend."

CHAPTER ELEVEN

NATALIE

CONFUSION PEPPERS MY mind as I try to process what Wes just said to me. Our new headmaster is going to kill Ciel? Is this some kind of joke?

Determination bubbles in my gut. I can't let this happen to her, but how am I supposed to keep her safe without exposing everything that's going on, potentially putting her in more danger?

It occurs to me that I'm now in the same position Henry once was. He made the decision to warn me about his vision without revealing the whole truth, and we all know how well that went.

Wes is hunched over on the ground and it's clear he's still struggling from that vision. A bead of sweat trickles down his face. I grab a Lockwood-branded sweatshirt from his drawer and kneel down in front of him, wiping the moisture away.

"You good?"

He nods, but I can see in his face that he's anything but good. Sure, our situation is complicated, but it's hard to watch someone struggle. My heart lodges in my throat at the dilemma of caring for someone you know is bad for you.

Before any more positive feelings for Wes have the chance to sneak into my brain, I shake them off, focusing back on his vision. "We have to tell Ciel."

Wes meets my gaze, a coldness passing through his eyes. "No, we don't."

Is he serious?

"I'm not going to sit around while my friend dies."

"She won't," Wes snaps, cutting me off.

"Bullshit. You had a vision. It's going to happen. You can't lie to me about this."

Wes pushes to stand, suddenly more focused and pulled together. "Visions are real. Very real. But Amelia won't get the chance to kill your friend." He pulls aside his coat, showing off his dagger encased in the leather sheath. The gestures smacks against my bones, sending a sharp chill down my limbs.

"So your plan is to march across campus and stab our new headmaster? Are you insane?"

"The longer we wait, the greater the chance that your little friend is a goner."

I wince at his callous way of talking about Ciel's impending death. I suppose as a trained assassin, one would think or speak differently about dying. But that doesn't mean the best decision here is for Wes to openly murder someone on campus, especially not one with a ton of guards around her.

Fear weaves around my body, pinching at my skin, as I attempt to rationalize with a trained killer. "Wait a second. This doesn't all make sense. Why would Amelia want to kill Ciel?"

Wes groans, and I can tell he's getting frustrated. "I don't know, Natalie. My vision didn't include Amelia explaining her reasoning. Sorry."

I brush off his shitty attitude. "When is it going to happen?"

Wes seems to get even more annoyed. "My vision also didn't include a clock or calendar."

Something inside me bursts open and I snap, yelling into his smug face. "I'm trying to figure out how to handle this mess, okay? I don't want Ciel to die and I don't want anything bad to happen to you." The words fly out of my throat before I've had time to think things through.

Wes tilts his head, eyes narrowing in curiosity. "I thought you'd be thrilled if I was out of your life, Covington."

My chest twists with confusion. He's right, there are times when I wish I'd never met him. But if I'm being honest, there are other times when I can't imagine not having him around. *Serves me right.* An entire month of indulging, letting myself get distracted with him, widened the path for a few stray emotions to worm their way into my mind. Maybe even my heart.

"You're a liar, about more things than the stupid eye patch. But that doesn't mean I want you gone for good."

Before I can utter another word, Wes scoops me into his arms. His lips crash into mine, as if he's kissing me for the last time.

I push at his chest, shoving him off. "What are you doing?"

Wes doesn't let go of me. He breathes into my ear. "Taking advantage of the moment."

Ugh. I wish I could say that the last fuck I have to give for him flies out the window, but that's not true. Despite my complicated feelings, we need to focus on getting Ciel out of this situation without killing someone else in the process. Even if our new headmaster is some undercover murderer, we don't need that blood on our hands. At least, I don't need any more blood on mine.

"We need to focus right now, not do this."

"Or we can do both." Wes swoops in again, curling his arm around my waist, but I bat him away.

"Enough! I'm serious. Let's think through this. Why would

Amelia want to kill Ciel? What would be her motivation?" I lower my gaze, combing my brain. It really doesn't make any sense.

"Maybe to get to you," Wes says.

I lift my eyes to meet his blunt, matter-of-fact expression, chewing on the inside of my cheek. "So you think Amelia is here to kill me?"

"Or me," Wes says.

"Your vision shows otherwise, so why would you think that?"

"When you're trained to be a killer, you get pretty good at sensing when other people want to kill you… and the people you love."

My body quietly shudders at his words. I'm not sure which is worse, being reminded that he's a killer, or the reminder that he loves me.

"Okay, so how do we stop Amelia from getting to us without making Ciel a casualty?"

Wes slides his dagger out of his coat, rolling it in his hand, volleying his eyes between mine and the weapon. "I was planning to kill her now, but you're still talking."

I blow out a frustrated breath. He's cocky and impossible and I really shouldn't care what happens to him, but this feels like a terrible mistake. There's got to be another way to handle this without shedding more blood.

"Give me your medieval knife and stop being dramatic."

I grab the dagger, attempting to wrench it from his hand. He overpowers me easily but then there's a strange crackle, kind of like an electric shock shooting up my arm, breathing life into my limbs. It doesn't cause me any pain.

"Ouch, fuck." Wes yanks his hand away and the dagger falls to the ground in a perfect upright position, the blade piercing the floor. Odd that he felt pain when I didn't.

"What the hell was that?" Wes asks. I notice a flicker of fear in his eyes.

"I don't know." *But I want to find out.*

I bend down to pick up his dagger, but the sensation is gone. I twist it around in my hands. No electric current, just the heaviness of the metal blade. I extend my hand, holding the dagger out to Wes. "Touch it again."

Wes hesitates a beat and I get a glimmer of satisfaction, knowing he's momentarily freaked out. Maybe he'll finally calm down and stop trying to murder people. Maybe we can find some rational solution to this mess.

Wes reaches out his fingers, touching the blade. Nothing. Maybe it was nothing all along. But I know we both felt it.

"I'll be holding onto this so you don't do anything stupid."

Wes leans back against the dresser, folding his arms over his chest, looking me up and down. "I've got to admit. This whole thing is working for me. You annoyed with me, holding my dagger. You sure we can't get into bed now?"

Now I understand the urge to want to stab someone. I roll my eyes at him, cutting him off mentally. This isn't the time to flirt or kill. I need to protect Ciel and get to the bottom of why Amelia is really here.

"Tell me exactly what happened in your vision. Word for word. I want every detail."

"And what do I get in return?"

Wes is playing a dirty game because he knows he can. He has information that I need about my friend, and possibly about me. I hate this cat-and-mouse bullshit, but at the same time, I have to admit the frustration of it all feels a bit thrilling.

Dammit, Natalie.

I slowly cross over to Wes, realizing that the room is much darker than when we first entered. I was so carried away with everything, I didn't even notice night fall. Wes's face is illuminated by the building lights outside the window. Shadows flicker on the wall as I watch for his reaction. His eyes are hooded, darkening as I move closer. His gaze sweeps over my face and down my entire body. I know exactly what he's thinking.

I get closer, nuzzling my face into his neck as Wes sucks in a sharp breath. I move my face closer to his, and he stares at me with a fevered look. I hover my lips over his and I swear I can hear him almost growl.

Just as our lips are about to touch, I press the dagger to his neck, grazing the tip along his skin.

Wes chuckles and a smile blooms on his lips. I thought he'd be angry or perhaps even a tiny bit scared, but he's acting like this scenario amuses him.

"You're going to tell me everything about your vision. Got it?" I say in the most threatening tone I can muster.

Wes raises his hand, fingering one of my stray curls and tucking it behind my ear. "Like I said, I'll tell you everything if you do something for me."

"You're in no position to bargain. I'm holding the dagger."

"*My dagger*," he says.

"I took it from you once. I can do it again."

Wes heaves out a sigh, appearing to resolve to this fate. "Fine."

A smirk crosses my face as I lower the dagger. In a split second, Wes curls his hand around the back of my head, fisting my hair. He yanks me into him, our faces so close, they nearly melt into each other. A slice of fear darts up my spine and I remind myself that I'm holding the weapon, my knuckles tightening around the handle.

"You should remember that I'm not some preppy schoolboy, Covington. I'm a trained assassin. Remember who you're messing with."

Using all my strength, I shove him back. He stumbles against the dresser.

"I'm not scared of you. Now quit stalling. Tell me about your vision."

CHAPTER TWELVE

WES

My head splinters with an awful fucking headache. It's been so long since I've had a vision that I forgot about the aftermath. It's like your head isolates from your body, goes on a death-defying rollercoaster, and winds up back on your neck again.

At least, I think it's like being on a rollercoaster. I've never been on one myself. Instead of amusement parks, my childhood was spent hunting down rogue precogs with my uncle, watching them bleed out on the ground.

After filling Natalie in on my vision, we made a decent plan. She will warn Ciel to stay away from our new headmaster without revealing that there are people in the world like me with special powers and other people who want to kill them. Which means I need to work on figuring out who Amelia Collins is. It would be so much easier to just kill her, but Natalie brought up a good point. If she's here for me, or us, there will be others waiting in the wings. There will be more Amelias, who, one by one, will try and take us down.

I won't let that happen.

The more strategic play is to try and get information from Amelia.

Pose as a student—which I'm already doing—and pretend that I've got an issue only the headmaster can solve. Then do my best to get her to crack, or at least distract her so I can dig through her personal things.

This whole plan feels very anticlimactic, but it'll do for now. Driving my dagger into Amelia would be far more fun, though. What a thrill it would be to watch Amelia take her last breath, knowing I did it purely to save the girl I love.

A crunching sound interrupts my fantasy and I duck behind a mossy tree, disappearing into the thick, forested night. I was supposed to wait until tomorrow and go to Amelia's office in the administration building, make an appointment like a normal student. That's what I promised Natalie, at least.

Instead, I'm crouching outside of the headmaster's house where she's staying, watching and waiting. My heart quickens with the elicit feel of tracking someone. Watching their every move. Straining to hear their secrets. The excitement of nailing down their routine, making it easy to hunt them and strike at the perfect moment.

It's been a while since I've hunted someone like this. The last person was Natalie, who still remains my favorite target. My lips split into a grin as I remember the first time I saw her. It was in her dorm room, and I was hiding in her closet. Sweet, sweet memories.

My uncle had given me vague instructions about a new target, Ms. Natalie Covington. All I had was her name, room number, and class schedule. It was surprisingly easy to get into her dorm when Ciel, head buried in a phone she wasn't supposed to have, held the door open for me. I hadn't even stolen a Lockwood uniform yet, but she didn't seem to clock some plain-clothed guy waltzing into the building. I easily slipped by her and crept up to Natalie's dorm room.

Natalie's room looked like an average eighteen-year-old girl's. Nothing surprising or special. I remember feeling disappointed at what a bland target they'd given me. Surely, she'd be easy to kill. Why was I wasting my time on this girl?

But then the doorknob twisted and the door creaked open. In walked Natalie when she was supposed to be in class. Luckily, I was able to duck into the closet before she saw me, but her arrival caused a thrill to shoot through my veins. Nearly getting caught by the beautiful girl I was tracking? A girl who skips class, perhaps breaks more rules, like me?

Now this… this was interesting.

Not even a moment later, some idiot entered her room. I later learned this was Jack, her boyfriend at the time, now ex. They got into a long, drawn-out argument that killed my buzz until, right at the tail end of their fight, Natalie started talking about missing her mother. A strange feeling simmered in my gut as I thought about my own brother, Timothy, who, at that time, had disappeared after changing one of his visions.

Timothy's not my real brother, biologically speaking. He's older, so he got to pick his title for us and chose to call us brothers. Despite being a useless assassin with no other marketable skills, he was a pretty decent guy, and when I learned he was gone, there was an unfamiliar shred of hollowness in my heart. I'm not accustomed to caring about people, so when I saw his dead body, a strange feeling crept into my brain.

That day, hiding in Natalie's closet, watching her cry over the loss of her mother, made me strangely…sad. If there were an Olympics for bottling emotions, I'd be the fucking gold medalist. And the silver and the bronze. But watching Natalie break down weirdly awakened something in my heart, a place where I'm not used to not feeling anything.

And just as quickly as she began crying, she stopped herself, breathing in and out as if psyching herself up for a fight. I was mesmerized by her control and intensity. I recognized that same thing in myself.

After she kicked her boyfriend out, I watched as she unbuttoned her school uniform jacket, throwing it on the bed, followed by her uniform blouse and skirt. It was as if she was shedding a heavy weight, the clothes restricting her. The anticipation of her catching me was almost too much to bear, thrumming through my veins and other parts of me I probably shouldn't admit. In that moment, I wanted to get caught, to see what she would do when finding a stranger in her closet who was watching her every half-naked move.

A door creaks open in the distance and I'm rocketed back to the present, so lost in this memory of Natalie that I almost forgot my mission here tonight.

Two guards greet Amelia at the front door to the headmaster's house, and my eyes stray from the ground, fixing on her. They hand her a binder of some sort. She sets it down inside the house and leaves with the guards, following them down the path to the right. Anticipation simmers in my gut. Not quite as good as the feeling I got when I first saw Natalie, but decent, nonetheless.

I'm torn between following Amelia and finding out what's inside that binder. After a moment of deliberation, I pick the binder, carefully crossing the property to avoid the working security cameras.

I circle around to the backyard and twist a pin from my pocket into the lock. It's not as easy to pick as many other locks on campus, but after a few moments of trying, it pops open.

I've never been inside the headmaster's house before. It's musty and ancient, old furniture lining the room that doesn't even seem to match. The room is both cold and clammy, which doesn't make a lot of sense. Surprising that they'd give such a dump to the headmaster of a one hundred thousand dollar-per-year private school, but who am I to judge?

I move through the house, scoping for any hidden security cameras. This place doesn't even seem equipped for Wi-Fi, much less high-tech surveillance. In the entryway, a lone antique lamp glows on a rustic wooden table where the binder lies.

I rush over, ripping open the binder. The entire thing seems to be in some kind of bizarre code. Not another language necessarily, more like symbols or glyphs. I don't recall seeing anything like this before and I wonder if this is some secret language. And if so, what the hell is it?

I flip through the pages, glancing at the annoying symbols that don't reveal any helpful information. Maybe I should have followed Amelia instead.

I'm about to give up when I turn to the final page, feeling something smooth and slick on my fingers. It's a few Polaroid photographs, taped down to the page, of about a dozen members of the Armory, a group I thought had disbanded but now seems very much together…very much alive.

My eyes comb over the members, all wearing those weird *Phantom of the Opera* masks and all-black service uniforms. Maybe this binder is about them? Is this a secret language they use to communicate? And is Amelia one of them, or in charge of them?

Slamming the binder shut, I decide to take it with me. I pick it up, tucking it into my coat, when a small, thick manila envelope drops to the floor. It must have been underneath the binder the whole time.

Unraveling the thread to the envelope, I pull out the contents, finding a series of photographs of guys who appear to be around my age, each labeled with a number. They're wearing the Armory uniform, holding their mask in their hand, revealing their face.

I rifle through, one by one, until I land on a photo of a person I recognize.

The photo is of Henry *fucking* Thorne. In an Armory uniform, mask in hand.

My stomach churns as I take a better look, chest pulling tight as my fingers twist around the photo, nearly disintegrating it in disgust.

It's been a month, and I was secretly hoping he'd tucked his tail between his legs and hidden away for good. Either that, or I hoped he was dead. Didn't matter to me either way.

But here he is, not only alive but a member of this insane fringe group. There's no questioning things now. He must have been the one on that security footage the day Headmaster Rochester disappeared from campus. His plan is obviously to come here, sneak onto campus, and kill me. Maybe Amelia is here to lord over the job, make sure it's done properly. He must be hiding somewhere on campus right now, watching us, waiting to strike.

I collect the photos in the binder and make my way out of the house. There are only two things on my agenda:

1) Killing Henry Thorne.

2) Doing it before Natalie finds out he's here.

CHAPTER THIRTEEN

NATALIE

I KEEP AN eye on Ciel all night and the rest of the next day. Things are normal: deciding how she is going to style her uniform, styling mine, making out with Adip in the hall, class, studying, more class. It isn't until around seven o'clock the next night that I lose track of her entirely. Shockwaves float through my body when I realize she managed to slip past me.

I search everywhere on campus for her until I finally track her down at an intimate on-campus dinner party—hosted by Amelia. Fortunately, she's not wearing the outfit Wes described in his vision, so at least I don't have to worry about attempted murder tonight. Though, this brings me zero relief.

My hands clench around the ornate wood trim wrapping around the door to a private dining hall. Luckily, Adip tipped me off that our new headmaster invited Jack to some special dinner tonight, and he couldn't track down Ciel either, so I put two and two together. Amelia invited Ciel to this party, carefully making sure I wasn't aware of it. She must have known I was attached to Ciel all day and waited for the right time to strike.

About a dozen people circle around a table, none of them I recognize except for Ciel and Amelia. Jack isn't even here. Ciel sits right next to Amelia, looking absolutely stunning as always. And Amelia seems to notice. Her finger brushes back a strand of Ciel's hair and I can almost hear her pay her a compliment. The headmaster is openly flirting with a student and no one in this crowd seems to bat an eye. That would be odd for a normal school, but at Lockwood, not so much. No one seems to care or pay attention here, another odd fact about this school.

A familiar voice echoes behind me, and I startle.

"Nat, what are you doing?" Jack speaks to me in a rage whisper, yanking my arm to lead me away from the room. "You're not supposed to be in here. This is a private party."

"Sorry," I say, my voice dripping with sarcasm as I remove my arm from Jack's grip. "There was no sign barring me from entering. Besides, I'm looking for Ciel. Why is she in there with that creepy new headmaster?"

Jack recoils in shock. "Creepy? Headmaster Collins is amazing. Do you know what she's accomplished?"

I cut him off before he rattles off facts I don't care about. "She's getting a little too close to Ciel in there. Don't you think that's gross?"

I point to Amelia and Ciel, but Jack makes a confused face and shakes his head. "It's dinner. There's nothing inappropriate happening." An unsurprising answer from Jack, who always has his head up his ass.

I continue my interrogation. "Why are you and Ciel the only students attending? Who are those other people at the table?"

"They're important connections. Amelia—excuse me, Headmaster Collins—gave the opportunity to two promising students to meet some of her former colleagues. She selected me and Ciel." Jack studies me for a second. "Oh, I get it. You're jealous that she didn't invite you."

I try not to be offended by his statement. He has no idea what's really going on. It's just Jack being Jack.

"No, I'm not jealous. But I do need to talk to Ciel."

"Now?" Jack eyes me, exasperated.

"Yes, it's an emergency."

"Why? What's going on?"

I make up a quick excuse. "It's girl stuff."

Jack seems to buy that, lucky for me. He straightens his suit jacket, making his way into the dining room. I watch as he leans over to Ciel, convincing her to come talk to me. My gaze cuts to Amelia, noticing the way she seems engaged with the crowd, smiling brightly, while keeping an ear open to Ciel's conversation.

Ciel slips out of the room as Amelia clocks her every move. My spine bristles as Amelia looks over my way. I duck out of view, hopefully before she noticed me.

Ciel greets me in the hall, lips pursed together with panic. "Natty, are you okay? Jack said you had some girl emergency."

I rest my hand on Ciel's arm, attempting to calm her down and pry for information. "I'm fine. How's the dinner going?"

Ciel brightens. "It's great. Our new headmaster is so cool. Amelia. She told me to call her that."

My words bubble up without thinking. "I bet she did."

Ciel's lips turn down. "What's that supposed to mean?"

"Don't you think it's odd that she showed up out of nowhere? Then suddenly invited *only* you and Jack to a private dinner and was *clearly* flirting with you in there?"

Instead of concern, Ciel looks almost flattered. "I never thought about it that way. You think she's interested in me?"

Frustration spikes through my chest. "Ciel."

"Oh come on, Natty. It's not the first fling I've had with a teacher. I told you about that."

She's right. One night after too much wine, Ciel filled me in on this sexy yet illegal fling she had as a sophomore with her English teacher. I don't judge her, of course. That's a fantasy lots of people have, even if it's not mine. Her last teacher-student affair may have been dangerous in a legal sense, but it's nothing compared to what might happen if she pursues things with Amelia.

"I don't think it's a good idea for you to spend time with her," I blurt out, realizing how unprepared I am for this conversation. I don't really have a good excuse to get Ciel away from Amelia. And I didn't expect that Amelia would have moved in on her target so soon. That I'd find them together already. My thoughts float back to Henry, trying to warn me about his vision. I wish he was here now to help me deal with this.

I wish he was here, period.

"I'll be fine. I know how to be discreet," Ciel rationalizes.

"That's not what I mean." I make up a fast lie. "I've heard things about Amelia."

Ciel's eyes widen in shock. "Wait, you know her?"

I continue my fabricated story, hoping she buys it. "Not personally, but I have a friend who went to the last private school where she worked. Apparently, she does this shady thing where she tries to entrap the students, get them to act inappropriately, and then suspends them from school. Like revenge porn. Basically destroys their future."

If Wes's vision is correct, what Amelia is about to do is far worse than that, but hopefully Ciel buys this fabricated explanation.

Ciel gasps. "That's so messed up. Why would she do that?"

Good question, Ciel. I'm already mired in my own lies, too late to back out now. Wes would be better at this. I'm pretty sure he gets off on deceiving people.

I continue, weaving more lies into this story. "I think it's one of those revenge missions. You know, the woman who was scorned in high school and decides to make it miserable for girls who remind her of the people who never accepted her." *Whew, where did I pull that from?*

Ciel nods in understanding, and I feel immediate relief.

"Why don't you excuse yourself from dinner and just come back to my dorm and hang with me?"

Ciel makes a face. "I can't just leave. That would be rude, right?"

Suddenly, a buttery voice slices through our conversation. "Is everything okay out here, girls?"

I twist my head, noticing Amelia behind us in the distance. Blood chills in my veins as she takes a few steps towards us.

Amelia fixes her gaze on me. "I don't think we've had the pleasure of meeting yet."

I paste on a smile, playing nice. "Headmaster Collins. Welcome to Lockwood. I'm Natalie Covington."

I notice a glimmer of recognition pass in her eyes, but it's gone in a split second. Long enough for me to realize she definitely knows me. She extends her hand for a shake. "It's nice to meet you, Natalie."

I clasp her hand, my finger grazing her plum-colored silky blouse. A dainty gold bracelet loops around her wrist and her manicured hands are so smooth, it seems unreal.

Everything about her is perfection, which makes it easy for my eyes to latch on to the one thing that's out of place. A black spot on her wrist, peeking out from her blouse. A tattoo? Or a branding?

Amelia removes her hand from mine.

"Your bracelet is so beautiful," I say, clumsily grabbing her wrist and twisting it to get a better look. "I've been wanting one just like this."

Using my finger, pretending to look at the bracelet, I bunch up the fabric of her blouse, discovering exactly what I suspected.

The psi symbol. The same thing branded on Wes and Henry. It's confirmed: Amelia is definitely a precog.

Amelia quickly yanks her arm away and I can't tell if she knows

I saw the marking or if she's just uncomfortable at my bold move to assault her wrist.

"Well, I'll be getting back inside now. Ciel, are you coming?"

I glance over at Ciel, who shrugs, joining Amelia. "I'll come over to your dorm as soon as we're done here, okay, Natty?"

I nod, my heart sinking, realizing I'll need to stay here and hide out to protect her. "Sounds good. Have fun."

Amelia leads Ciel back into the dining room as my gut clenches.

CHAPTER FOURTEEN

WES

ANGER SPLINTERS MY insides as I sit in my dorm room, staring down at the photo of Henry.

This fucking guy.

What I wouldn't give to drive the blade of my dagger into his stomach—to make him my second kill. How satisfying it would be to watch the life drain from his eyes, knowing that Natalie can finally forget about him and be with the person she's meant to be with—*me*.

Is this what love is? I suppose so. I'm not familiar with that emotion, or many at all. A crucial part of my training as a boy was learning to turn them off. I vividly remember a lesson my uncle taught me.

As a kid, I was fascinated with birds—the freedom they had, the power to fly. My uncle didn't believe in connection to any living thing, so my fascination aggravated him. One day, a bird flew into our window, and I used some magic I got from my uncle's book to try and resurrect it. A small slice in the side of my wrist, very small, let the blood trickle slowly into the mouth of the dead being, count backwards from ten.

It worked.

As the bird fluttered to life, I felt elated. But I didn't realize my uncle was spying on me the entire time. He marched over, smashing the bird back to its death with a hammer, its blood splattering across my face.

From that day on, my uncle devoted himself to bashing the emotions out of me. Night after night, as a sick bedtime routine, he shoved me to the ground, pain lancing through my body, daring me not to feel anything. Over time, it morphed into a game—one I desperately wanted to win. So I excelled at my training, successfully removing all of my feelings. That is, until my brother wound up dead.

And to a greater extent, emotions flooded in when I met Natalie. There's something so intriguing about her that I still can't put my finger on. And maybe that's what keeps my interest—that she's the key that finally unlocked my feelings.

Sure, she's beautiful. Intelligent. Witty. Sexy. But lots of girls have those qualities or can fake them really well. My uncle would frequent a club with hot women ready and willing to do whatever he asked of them. I used to watch, half-enthralled, half-bored. What's the fun if there's no challenge? No connection?

I was propositioned by girls many times, even taking a few up on it. There was no emotion, and physically, it was mediocre. Even though I could take things farther with other girls than I can with Natalie—because for some reason, when we kiss, it literally sucks the life from her—those experiences were unfulfilling.

But with Natalie, our connection is special, something I'll never be able to replace. And I'll never have to—because I refuse to let her go.

And I won't need to, as long as I can get rid of Henry Thorne. The only thing standing in our way, keeping her from fully becoming mine.

I take a long drag of a joint, my hand twitching around the photo of Henry, trying to soothe my hammering chest. Excitement thrums in my veins, picturing Henry cowering in front of me, falling to his knees, begging for his life. Then I'll head back to Natalie, his blood smeared on my hands, marking her with it. Showing her what I've done for her. How much I love her.

That must be love, right?

The door to my room creaks open and I quickly shove the photo of Henry in a drawer, burying my fantasy. Natalie storms in, looking distraught, as usual. If only she would just calm down and let me take her pain away.

"Ciel was with Amelia," she says, flustered. "She's already moving in on her."

Natalie paces around my room, unable to relax. I wish she would just let me handle this. Amelia would be dead. And I'll take care of Henry, as well as anyone else who tries to tear us apart.

"What did you find out? Anything?" She spits her questions at me fast and furious, and I nearly forgot my mission for the evening. At least, the one I told her.

"Not much, but I made an appointment with the admin to meet with Amelia tomorrow," I lie.

I can't risk her seeing the photo of Henry. The binder is already hidden in a secure place in my ceiling, where a loose tile allows me to tuck away secrets. Henry's photo needs to go up there, too, and soon—before Natalie finds it.

Her eyes flare and I can tell she's annoyed that I just sat here all night, doing nothing, while she tried to help her friend. That's not what I did, of course, but it's better to have her think that rather than discover the truth.

I quickly act interested in her friend. "Where is Ciel now?" Truth be told, I don't really care. It's not that I don't like Ciel, but I also wouldn't think of her again if she ceased to exist.

"I waited there until the dinner was over and walked her back to the dorm. I think I freaked her out enough to stay put. And I convinced Adip to keep her company, which wasn't hard."

Natalie blows out a breath and all I want to do is yank her into bed and get lost in each other. Sadly, I don't have powers or know how to wield magic to make her fully mine right now.

"I should go back to my dorm," she says, effectively shutting down my evening fantasy.

She turns to leave, but I clamp my hand around her wrist, stopping her. She yanks it away and excitement erupts in my gut. The more she resists me, the more I want her, a twisted little game we play that makes everything I've endured in my shitty life totally worth it.

"You just said Ciel is fine. Adip is watching over her."

Our eyes lock, and I can tell she's searching for an excuse to leave. But I don't feel like letting her. Her hands press against my chest, pushing me away, and a surge of adrenaline pulses through my core. I grab her shoulders, spinning her around, and pin her arms up against the wall. Her breath quickens and her chest grazes mine as it rises and falls. I'm certain that she's loving this as much as I do until she digs her nails into my wrists.

"Ouch, fuck." I pull my hands away, inspecting the damage.

"Good, I'm glad that hurt," she says, shoving past me, leaving me empty and alone. "I have your dagger, remember?" She pats the bag slung around her shoulder, resting on her hip. "I'm not afraid to use it."

I smirk, tracing my eyes along her. "Come on, stop messing around. Get over here."

I swear I catch the ghost of a smile playing on her lips as she twists the knob to my door.

"You can leave all you want, but nothing is stopping me from coming to your room tonight," I say.

Natalie rolls her eyes as she leaves, shutting the door behind her. Her spurn feels like an invitation, one I'd like to take her up on. But maybe, just for tonight, I'll let things breathe. Allow that sensation of desire, of wanting someone so fucking badly, to consume my every thought. Just for tonight.

⚶

Allowing that pent-up aggression to build all night was a decent idea. Fixating on Henry's photo like a vile effigy, indulging in dark fantasies of erasing him from this world entirely. It's intoxicating. I even prowled around campus, searching for him, but unfortunately, came up short. He must've found a great hiding place. But he can't hide forever.

My adrenaline is now at an all-time high as I sit in this sterile, boner-killing administration building, waiting for my appointment with Amelia. A cappuccino in an expensive white teacup sits on the table in front of me. I watch the steam drift away as the liquid grows colder and colder, eerily similar to watching someone die. Something I've done many, many times, even though it wasn't always by my own hand.

A young, plucky secretary peeks her head into the waiting room. "I'm sorry, but Headmaster Collins won't be available today after all. I can reschedule your appointment."

Well, that was a waste of time. A waste of a morning. And worse, a waste of an evening without Natalie.

"Sure," I say, acting agreeable.

As I make my way to the secretary's desk, I gain a clear view inside Amelia's office. She's on the phone in some heated conversation. Maybe it's about the missing binder. I can't help but smile, imagining her freaking out that she lost her little precog burn book.

"Does Wednesday at ten work?"

I lift my gaze, meeting the secretary's smile. "Perfect."

I smile back and wink, making the secretary whose name I've forgotten already blush and her breath hitch. She appears to be in her twenties. Probably attractive to most guys, but not to me. Her response feels so basic, expected.

As I turn to leave, my eyes latch on to a figure outside the window, someone clad in all black, the stark white gleam of their mask unmistakable. A member of the Armory, standing between a dense assembly of trees, watching me.

Henry.

I race outside to get a better look, but if it's him, he's already gone. My eyes scan the campus. When you spend your life watching and tracking other people, you always know when someone is watching you. So where the hell did they go?

I need to find Natalie. And fast.

CHAPTER FIFTEEN

NATALIE

My electric kettle whirs and pops as fresh steam floats out. I pour two cups of my favorite mint tea as Ciel sits on my bed, acting like she's a prisoner.

"Natty, you can't keep me in here all day. I'll go crazy!"

I hand Ciel a mug of hot tea, hoping it will calm her down. "I just don't trust Amelia. Like I told you—"

Ciel cuts me off, setting down her tea without a sip. "I know, I know. She's like entrapping students or whatever. But listen, I already went to, like, the most evil private school before this one. It was as if someone mashed the original *Gossip Girl* with *Euphoria* and added in season five of *Game of Thrones*."

I shudder, unsure if Ciel is kidding or not. Instead of asking questions, I remind myself what's at stake—Ciel's life. If she wants to spill details about her old school, at least that can kill some time without her getting killed.

Ciel adjusts herself, lying down on her stomach, propping herself onto her elbows. "If you're going to hold me hostage, you at least have to give me some juicy details about Wes."

Oh God. I may have just made a grave mistake not allowing Ciel to gossip about her previous school's drama using television metaphors.

"Come on, Natty. Spill. I see the way you two look at each other. Tell me everything. Is it the hottest sex you've ever had? He seems kind of dominant."

I certainly can't tell Ciel the truth, that if I even tried having sex with Wes, it would literally kill me. And if I tell her we haven't done anything other than kiss, she'll grow bored and want to leave. Maybe I should just lie.

A knock on my door saves me from this predicament.

"You're not getting out of this," Ciel calls after me as I head to the door.

I don't say another word, twisting it open to find Wes standing there with a worried expression. My nerves flare. He never looks worried.

"I need to talk to you," he says in a hushed, urgent tone.

Ciel stands, says in a singsong voice, "I'll just leave you two alone."

I step in front of her, blocking her way. "You're not going anywhere."

Ciel huffs in frustration. "Oh my god, Natty, you're being the worst!"

"Just wait here a minute. I need to talk to Wes in the hall."

"Whatever you have to say, you can say in front of me. Unless it's some weird sex stuff, in which case, you should *definitely* say it in front of me."

Without indulging her any further, I shove Wes into the hallway, closing the door behind me. "What's up? What happened?" I ask, my heart hammering against my ribs.

His worry seems to have dissolved as his lips curl into a smirk. "You told Ciel we had sex? Does that mean you think about that?"

I slap his chest. He's insufferable. And hot. And rage-inducing. Ciel's got it wrong—Wes is the worst. Not me.

"I can't exactly tell her the truth about us."

He circles his muscular arm around my waist, pulling me so our bodies are flush. My body betrays me again as excitement ripples over my skin. *No, no, no.* Not this. Not now. Not ever again.

"It *will* happen, don't worry. If we keep practicing," he says while I writhe out of his grip.

Batting him away, I focus back on what's important. "Did you just come here to torture me or do you have news about Amelia? How did your meeting go?"

"Meeting was canceled."

"Why?"

Wes shrugs. "If you would just give me back my dagger, I can take care of her. Then you wouldn't need to keep your friend a prisoner, and you and I could have a much more interesting afternoon."

Aggravation leeches through my veins. Amelia is here to kill Ciel, and likely intending to come after us. Why does he treat this like a joke?

I suck in a breath, trying to calm my nerves. It's easy to forget that Wes grew up much differently than I did. He doesn't have parents and was raised alongside his brother by his uncle, an assassin. When I was ten, I was sneaking through my neighbor's house with Jack, giggling as we hunted for innocuous buried secrets. When Wes was that age, he stalked people so his uncle could murder them. He told me that his brother tried to shield him from seeing his first dead body, hoping Wes could hold on to his innocence just a bit longer. But his uncle found out, later beating Wes within an inch of his life while his brother watched as punishment.

Faced with death, Wes comes to life. Me on the other hand...

I soften a bit. As maddening as Wes can be, I do have compassion for him. How could I not when he was raised like that?

"We're not killing Amelia. We both agreed that there will be others besides her coming for us. We just need to make sure that Ciel stays safe until the time that your vision takes place."

"And then we kill her?" Wes asks.

"No. I'll stop it from happening," I say.

Wes looks at me like I have five heads. "Natalie, you're not killing anyone. I'm the one trained who is for this."

"I'm not going to kill Amelia. I already told you that."

"Then how exactly do you think we're going to get out of this mess?"

"Look, we know that when I'm faced with severe danger that something happens to me. When I shoved Henry away from you, he went flying. I think I can fight her off."

Wes's jaw ticks and I can tell he's getting frustrated with me. "You told me that was just adrenaline. You even pulled all these articles and scientific studies about people getting unimaginable strength when faced with certain circumstances."

I don't broach the topic of my powers with Wes very often, mostly because I don't trust him. But right now, I need him to trust me. "What about last night, when we both touched your dagger? There was that weird electricity."

Wes shakes his head. "It could have just been an electrical shock. When you touched it again, nothing happened."

"Then how do we explain us? When you kiss me, you know what happens. And you told me that didn't happen with the other girls. There's got to be a reason that precogs can be intimate with other people, but with me, I nearly die. It's like a defense mechanism built into your blood or something. Maybe you're designed to weaken me because deep down, you know my strength."

Wes is surprisingly quiet, his snarky demeanor seems to have melted into something more sinister. "When a precog kisses you, huh? You mean like me and *Henry*?"

Wes's gaze is cold, and I know I've offended him. He's aware of our past, yet every mention of Henry's name seems to unfurl some kind of rage-filled jealousy.

"This has nothing to do with him. It's that a precog and a human can be intimate, but a precog and I can't. Why is that?"

Wes snorts, shaking his head. "I don't know, Natalie. I'm sure you'd like to figure it out by the time you see Henry again."

Wes turns, stalking down the hall in the opposite direction. I was only trying to get across to him that I'm a threat to precogs, that I've unlocked powers before, that I can handle Amelia without bloodshed, but it seems that any hint of Henry Thorne will permanently sour a conversation.

A tug in my stomach tells me to go after him, as if it's my responsibility to smooth things over. But that's the old me—the one who used to try and please others, like Jack or my stand-in father.

My palms grow clammy and my conversation with Wes nags at my heart, wavering my confidence.

What if Wes is right? What if the only solution is to kill Amelia?

What if all we can do is sit by as precog after precog comes after us, in a vicious cycle that never ends?

CHAPTER SIXTEEN

WES

ANGER FLOODS THROUGH my body. Both at the fact that Natalie will take off with Henry the minute he crawls his ass back to Lockwood, and the fact that even if I kill him—*and I will*—it still won't make her forget him. Make her love me.

This I didn't plan for. As far back as I can remember, I was taught to carefully plot and plan everything. Every detail was to be meticulously thought out. The last thing you want as an assassin is a surprise.

And Natalie Covington is a surprise.

I realize, as I head back to my dorm, that I never told Natalie that a member of the Armory is on campus. Of course I won't let on that it's Henry, just that she needs to be careful.

It's as if every moment that passes with Natalie, the core of who I am becomes more and more out of control. More *unraveled.*

And I'm really beginning to hate it.

I attempt to invite logic back into my brain and take stock of the situation. Amelia is here, clearly on some mission to get Natalie or me. Or both. My vision shows that she's going to kill Ciel. Henry has joined the Armory, who seem to be working for Amelia. And now he's trailing me around campus, lurking in forests like a fucking creep.

My brain twists in a way that almost feels painful and then another vision slams into me.

Amelia and Ciel on that balcony. I've seen this already, but now the vision is zoomed out—revealing some twisted branches and an open field underneath. There's something bronzed and glistening on the ground, peeking through the darkness. What is that?

Amelia pulls Ciel closer. But this time, I can't make out the details of what they're doing. Not like I care—I know how this ends. I wish my vision would do me a solid and let me see what's on the ground so I'd have some idea of where they are.

My vision suddenly twists away from Amelia and Ciel, giving me a clear view of the ground. Almost as if I commanded it.

A bronzed statue of some old guy holding a rifle. Ah, yes. I know where this is. It's in the old Lockwood Commons, an area tucked way in the back of campus. No one really ventures there because, why would you? All you'll find is overgrown grass and a statue of a dude no one cares about.

Ciel's body slams into the ground, right next to the statue, the earth rumbling with her fall.

I blink as my vision snaps to a close. Where the fuck am I? Something dark and wet seeps through my clothing, the coldness stinging my back. Trying desperately to smooth out my eyesight, I realize I'm outside, lying on the ground.

I quickly push up on my hands, shoving to my feet, staring right at the statue I saw in my vision. *Fuck.* How did I get here?

Oxygen squeezes from my lungs as I dart into an alcove, wondering if anyone saw me. How long was I passed out? Did anyone see me? Was *he* watching me?

Fear kicks into my chest. I can't afford to show any weakness, and lying here on the ground unconscious for who knows how long is not the vibe I need right now.

A sharp pain sears through my head. These new visions are the worst. I never had side effects this intense before. What the hell is going on?

I volley my gaze around the Lockwood Commons. Everything's dead silent. Not a soul in sight. I hate this. I'm used to being in control, everything and everyone bending to my whim. Except Natalie, of course.

And now? I feel something I'm not used to. *Unsettled.*

Focus. Focus. Focus.

I pull myself together and make my way down the overgrown trail to a more lively part of campus. I need to get back to Natalie. Now that I know exactly where Ciel is going to die, it will make it easier to save her.

The problem is, we still don't know *when* Amelia is going to fling her off that balcony, crashing Ciel into a bag of bones next to that corny statue.

I take a few steps before my head twitches again with pain. Dammit. My stomach rolls and I try to remember the last time I ate. I had some weed and then…

Bile rises in my throat and pours out of me onto the ground. *Fuck me.*

In the distance, I hear a door to one of the campus buildings creak open and slam shut. My instinct is to hide, but my stomach empties yet again, all over the ground.

"You good, man?"

I look up to find Adip standing in front of me, his face filled with concern.

I make a half-ass attempt to act normal, even though this guy most certainly saw me dump my guts all over this lawn. Adip is nice enough, but I'm not up for small talk right now.

"Hungover?" he asks.

He gives me a good excuse. "Yeah. Damn whiskey got me again."

"I feel you, bro. I can go find Natalie if you want," he says.

I shake my head. "Really, I'm cool."

Adip grins. "I get it, man. You don't want her to see you like this. You really care about her, don't you?"

Do we really need to have a heart-to-heart right now? Yes, I care about Natalie. I fucking love her. She loves somebody else. The bile threatens to rise in my throat again.

"It's nice to see her so happy," Adip says.

Happy? I wouldn't exactly describe her that way with me. Exasperated, maybe. Turned on, yes. Although she won't admit it. I'm pretty sure Natalie just loves to hate me. But happy? Only in my dreams.

"What makes you say that?" I ask, even though this is the last thing I should be doing right now, probing for information about Natalie's happiness. But I'm curious what Adip knows. Plus, the searing pain is gone and I'm no longer vomiting. Maybe this distraction is exactly what I need.

"You know, she was with Jack for so long. And they were basically an arranged marriage without making it to the altar. But you? She chose you. And I can see how she acts around you. How she looks at you. Nat's had a rough couple years, especially after her mom died. Thanks for giving her a reason to smile again."

My heart twinges and my head floods with possibilities. Did I misunderstand things? Does Natalie actually love me? Adip didn't mention anything about her feelings about Henry. If Adip, her good friend, didn't even notice that moody fuck, maybe Henry wasn't that special to her after all.

But a nagging feeling beats against my logical mind. Adip knows a slice of Natalie. I know the real Natalie. And the real Natalie is in love with a guy who is not me, as much as I attempt to push that truth away.

"Thanks for saying that, man. I think you cured me." I give Adip a good-natured slap on the shoulder. Which, I think, is what you're supposed to do when you have guy friends. I wouldn't know. I've never had them. Or any friends at all.

A figure darts by in the distance and my head snaps up. What the fuck was that?

Adip follows my gaze. "Everything okay?"

That's when I see it again. A figure wearing all black, a slice of their white mask peeking out behind the branches. It's got to be him. *Henry.*

Instinctively, I reach into my coat, realizing that Natalie still has my dagger.

"What are you looking at?" Adip asks, craning his neck around, surveying the area.

I'm staring right at this fucker as he watches me from behind a tree. "You don't see that over there?"

Adip follows my eyeline, shaking his head. "You mean the trees? I guess they are kinda dead this time of year. Maybe interesting to look at? I dunno."

My chest tightens. How does Adip not see the masked creep standing right there? Or is there some weird shit happening that only I can see?

I jerk my eyes to Adip, pointing over at the man I'm one hundred percent sure is Henry. "Right there."

But when I look back over, no one is there.

CHAPTER SEVENTEEN

NATALIE

My heart flutters with anxiety as I clutch onto Ciel's arm, leading her through campus. The air is surprisingly dry today for Washington state in November. My throat burns and it almost hurts to breathe.

"Natty, can you let go of your death grip on my arm?" Ciel begs.

Her plea makes me realize I'm white-knuckling her poor arm so hard, I've likely cut off her circulation. I release my grip, choosing to sling my arm gently through hers. Can't take any chances of her running off.

She wriggles away from me, stopping us both in our tracks. "Okay, you are being way too clingy. I've gone along with your whole Amelia is evil thing so far. But it's obvious what's going on!"

My heart bangs against my ribcage. "What do you mean, obvious?"

Ciel folds her arms over her chest, rolling her eyes at me. "Come on, Natty. It's clear you're in some existential crisis!"

What is she talking about? Does she know something? Maybe

she went snooping through my room or my laptop. No, I barely had her out of my sight. Except for that brief argument with Wes.

"I guess I need to spell it out for you," she says.

Anxiety flares up my spine as I swallow a gulp of dry, cold air. Whatever Ciel thinks she knows, I'll just deny it. The most important thing is to keep her safe, which means making sure she doesn't die at the hands of Amelia, and ensuring she doesn't find out any information that could put her in more danger.

"You and Wes are having relationship problems, aren't you? It's the sex, isn't it? Dominant guys can be so challenging."

I exhale deeply, and suddenly, my throat feels a tiny bit better. She thinks my crisis is boyfriend issues. She's sort of right, but not in the way she thinks. I go along with her theory, just to keep her distracted.

"You're right. Why don't we get you one of those honey pistachio matcha lattes you love so much and then head back to my dorm to talk about it?"

Ciel huffs. "No, Natty, you will not swoon me with flavored lattes. And look, I love giving boyfriend advice, but you've had me cooped up in your room all day. I know I seem like an extrovert, but I'm really an introverted queen and need my alone time. Why don't you give me a little time to recharge and study, and we'll have some wine later in my room? You can tell me everything about you and Wes then."

I shake my head, but Ciel is already moving at a clip, racing away from me.

"Ciel, wait!" I call after her, but she disappears into a throng of students exiting the courtyard building.

Chasing after her and trying not to make a scene, I crash into someone, toppling to the hard concrete. I look up to see what happened, but no one seems to be anywhere near me. Chilled wind curls around my body, sending shivers through my veins. What the hell just happened?

Heels clack across the pavement and a manicured hand reaches down to mine.

My gaze traces up her arm, staring right into the face of Amelia Collins.

"Need some help?" She grins at me, sincerity glistening in her eyes. But I see through her bullshit. At least by having her in my presence, I know she's not trying to kill Ciel.

Amelia helps me stand and there's a strange gentleness to her touch. I study her face and it seems impossible for her to be capable of killing someone. Guess that's all part of her charm.

"Natalie, right? We met last night."

I nod, pasting on a grin, deciding to comb her for information. Two can play at this game. "I'd love to set a meeting up with you, Headmaster Collins. Ciel told me how wonderful that dinner was. I'm always looking for opportunities to network on campus."

Amelia eyes me, acting impressed. *Acting* being the key word here. "What do you want to major in when you get to college?" she asks.

"I want to be an eye doctor." That might be the first true thing I've said to her since we met.

"Interesting and impressive to be that specific about what you want at such a young age. I can see why you might be so intrigued by the eyes."

I stare at her in confusion. "Why do you say that?"

"The eyes tell a story. They never lie."

I stiffen, not sure what to say. Is she just a precog? Or can she read minds too? Maybe she's wielding magic like Wes.

"And your eyes are such a beautiful shade of green," she says.

My heart cracks open as the words slip from her mouth. *A shade of green.* My eyes are brown. My mom's were, too, until they changed to green when she turned eighteen. Henry told me that my eyes looked green in certain moments. Maybe they're changing. Maybe I'm changing too.

Without thinking, my hand glides into my purse, clasping the handle of Wes's dagger. A surge of electricity jolts up my arm—the same feeling as before, but this time, it doesn't go away. As if it's tempting me to stab the blade right into Amelia's fake façade and slice away her lies.

"Make an appointment with my office," she says, before sauntering away.

I choke out a breath as my fingers go limp and the dagger flattens in my purse. *Get a grip, Natalie.* I'm not a killer.

Except, that's not the truth. I killed Henry's foster dad, a mark that weighs heavy on my soul, but also brings me a sick sense of pride. I didn't have a choice—he would have ended my life if I didn't do something. Though I'm still not sure exactly what I did, how I mustered that strength, to deliver the final blow.

A surge of adrenaline smashes into my chest and my entire body begins to tremble. The clock is ticking and Ciel's life is at stake. A bead of sweat trickles down my spine despite the frosty air.

Amelia just knocked me off balance in more ways than one.

I take the stairs to Wes's dorm room two at a time. It's still daylight and his vision happened at night. That means Ciel is safe, at least for now.

I bang on his door and wait a moment for him to answer. It's eerily quiet up here, sending shards of fear through my bones. This would be the perfect place to get rid of someone and no one would hear. I whip my head around, making sure no one is watching me.

Where is Wes? I knock again, recalling our earlier argument.

He's pissed because he thinks I still carry a torch for Henry. And he's not wrong. But Henry left Lockwood, left me. His actions have made it more than clear how he feels. I know I need to let it go, let him go.

But I can't, at least not yet. Feelings that strong don't just disappear. At least for me, they don't.

Wes was pissed—*is* pissed—at me. That means he likely came back to his room, smoked a joint, and is lying in bed with his headphones on.

I try knocking once more, but still no answer. I've got a feeling deep in my bones that he's in there and either can't hear me or he's purposely tuning me out because his feelings got wounded.

I fish the key to his dorm out of my pocket and twist open the knob. He gave me a key almost immediately—a sign of trust between us, he said. I've never trusted him, but I'll take what I can get. Keep your enemies closer and all that, right?

As I shove open the door, I realize he's not here. The room is quiet and undisturbed, bed made, everything tidy. I've never met such a clean guy before in my life, unless they had a maid picking up after them 24/7. In Wes's case, he's just meticulous.

Doesn't research show that most serial killers are?

I shiver at the thought. My boyfriend—or pretend boyfriend—is a real assassin. Even worse, despite the fact that he's tracked hundreds or maybe thousands of people, our body count is even. *One for one.*

Shifting that sick fact from my mind, I turn to leave, but a part of me hums to stay. I've never been in Wes's room alone. Not even when Henry stayed here.

It's a smaller room than my dorm, but more charming in a way. Certainly more private. Suddenly, this space looks decidedly better than mine. Maybe I can convince Wes to switch rooms with me. He'd probably take that as an invite to move in with him.

I wander around his room, eyeing a few items on his desk,

remembering that weird manual or whatever it was that he had. I poke around, looking for it on top of his desk, but it's not there. Pausing a moment, my hand lingers on his desk drawer. Technically, this is considered snooping if I go through his things. *It is snooping.* But I'm more than certain he's snuck through my room, so I justify it to myself.

Sliding open the old drawer, I find a mess of papers inside. Apparently, Wes really isn't that clean, he just swipes his clutter into a drawer. Got it.

I close up the drawer, scanning the room until my eyes catch on to something odd on the ceiling—a tile slightly parted from the rest.

Climbing onto Wes's bed, I reach upward, my fingers latching on to what appears to be a binder tucked into the ceiling. With a tug, it comes loose, a photograph floating onto the bedspread.

Is this some kind of photo album? I've never seen Wes with a photo. I didn't even know he had any pictures since his life is so shrouded in secrecy. Heat pricks the back of my neck as I take a closer look.

The photo is of Henry, wearing a black uniform, a white mask dangling from his hand.

My body quakes with anger as I process what's in front of me. So Henry has joined that precog fringe group and Wes knew about it? How long has he known?

Resentment billows from my chest. Why wouldn't Wes tell me about this? Why would Henry join this group?

My stomach cramps with realization. Wes said this group is dangerous, looking to maintain an archaic type of order, destroy anything that doesn't fit their beliefs.

Does that mean Henry joined this group because he wants to destroy me?

CHAPTER EIGHTEEN

WES

I FLING OPEN the door to my room to find Natalie standing there.

Not just standing there—she's holding the photo of Henry. *Well, fuck.*

I'm the idiot who stashed it in the ceiling. The possibility of her snooping through my room had occurred to me, but I dismissed it, allowing myself to get sidetracked. Another core tenant of precog assassins—don't get distracted. If my uncle was alive, he'd have beaten me senseless for this mistake. I'm not someone who makes mistakes. Not usually someone who gets distracted. But Natalie… she knocks me off balance.

She turns to me, her eyes welling with tears. I can't tell if she's sad, hurt, angry, or just wants to kill me. She has my dagger, so this is a real possibility.

"I can explain."

But really, I can't. The only explanation is the truth—that I didn't want her to know Henry was around, possibly close to campus or even here watching us. I want her to stop thinking about him, to strike him from her memory so all that's left is thoughts of me.

But I know that's not our reality. And I'm sure revealing the truth will send her running away from me for good, although that might happen anyway.

"How long have you known about this?" she asks.

Part of me wants to tell her the entire truth and beg forgiveness. I've never begged anyone for anything, but for Natalie, I'd do it.

But a darker part of me wants to take control, to tear that photograph from her hand and shred it into tiny pieces. Press her down on the bed, forcing her to look up at the ceiling she went through without my permission, and make *her* beg *me* for forgiveness. Excitement boils inside me as I think of taming her, wrapping my lips over hers until the last breath is almost gone from her body and she's pleading for her life. The only way I'd cave is if she promised to strike Henry Thorne from her mind and heart for good.

"Your silence speaks volumes," she says, snapping me back to reality and into this room with her.

My hand sweeps out, yanking the photo out of her grip.

"Give it back to me," she tries to demand.

I hold it high, out of her reach. I'm over six foot and she's barely five three, so there's no way she'll win. I crumple it in my hand, fisting it so she has even less of a chance of getting it back.

"You hid this from me, Wes. Why? What is going on?"

I turn my back on her, quickly grabbing the lighter I use for my weed, igniting a flame. The photograph slowly burns, melting away Henry Thorne —at least from this moment.

"No!" She grips at my arm, but it's too late. The photo collapses into dust right onto an ugly ceramic dish with the Lockwood emblem that I use as an ashtray.

"I can't believe you," she says, her voice laced with disgust.

I twist around to face her, deciding that matching her anger might be the best course of action. She yanks my dagger out from her purse, pointing it at me.

"What are you going to do, stab me? Go ahead!" I open my coat, motioning to my heart, testing her. Daring her.

The dagger trembles in her hand as she weighs her next move. An excruciatingly long moment passes before she drops the dagger to the floor. "It's all yours. Go ahead. Kill Amelia."

I eye her in shock. "What changed your mind?"

She shrugs. "Why would I tell you anything when all you do is lie to me? Just take care of it. Save Ciel. And stay the hell out of my life."

She storms out of my room and I don't stop her, even though every part of me wants to lunge forward and grab her into my arms and refuse to let her leave. I wish kidnapping was more acceptable.

Leaning down, I grab my dagger from the floor and a chill leeches through my body. My stomach rolls and heaves, bile thickening in my throat. All the excitement of the kill has shriveled up and turned into some cruel sickness.

I tuck the dagger into my pocket. Time to get this over with, get rid of Amelia, and then get to the real work—getting Natalie back.

Three hours. Three hours searching every inch of this campus for Amelia Collins. How the hell am I supposed to kill her when I can't even manage to perform a simple task like track her down?

If my uncle were here, he'd grip my jaw with his fingers, digging his dirty nails into the flesh of my chin, and thrash insults at me for letting a mark out of my sight. There were many times I'd thought about twisting my dagger into his mouth, ripping out his tongue, watching his blood drain down my arm, silencing him forever.

Thankfully, I was the one who watched him snatch his last breath.

I'm outside of the headmaster's house once again, but there's no Amelia in sight. Darkness looms over the Lockwood campus. If

Amelia gets to Ciel before I take care of things, Natalie will never forgive me. I've already fucked things up enough. I can't fail my most important mission yet.

Suddenly, I hear the crunch of leaves in the distance and my stomach swirls with anticipation. It must be Amelia arriving home. I'll let her go inside, get comfortable, let her guard down, and then sneak in—plunging my dagger into her perfect little world.

I curl my head around an evergreen tree, getting a better glimpse of the front door. Still no Amelia in sight.

A tree branch cracks behind me and I whip around just in time to see a figure darting right at me, wearing a white mask and black clothing. *Henry.*

Before I can reach into my coat to grab my dagger, he plows into me. My head smacks into the hard ground. A sharp pain slices through my skull, but there's no time to deal with that.

My fingers claw around his neck and I twist hard to the left, a move I've practiced over and over again, getting the upper hand and crashing his body against the ground in one violent swing. Blood rushes to my limbs and a deep feeling of satisfaction takes over. This is quite fun, destroying Henry Thorne. His white mask barely clings to his face and I rip it off in one movement, thrilled to watch as the life drains from his eyes.

But to my disappointment, it's not Henry.

It's some guy about my age. Buzz-cut blond hair and bright green eyes. He spits in my face and I drive my elbow into his stomach, reveling in the crack of his ribs. It's not Henry, but he will do in the meantime.

My hand fingers the dagger in my coat. The guy attempts to get an upper hand, but I plow my elbow down again, this time into his collarbone, getting way too much satisfaction at the sound of it snapping.

In a swift move, I slice the dagger from my coat, plowing it right down into his chest. The dagger lands with a thud, blood spurting up my hand.

And then, *he's gone.*

I'm staring down at grass and branches, but the fucker isn't here. Where'd he go?

And then I realize the blood on my hand isn't his. *It's mine.* When I drove down the blade with such force, my hand must have slipped down the handle, slicing into my palm.

Pain ricochets up my arm and explodes through my body. I'm here on campus, a few feet from the headmaster's home, bleeding out on the ground.

I push myself to stand just as the wound starts to close on its own. Fear slithers into my bones and I begin to wonder.

Was that real, a vision, or something else?

CHAPTER NINETEEN

NATALIE

THE CAMPUS IS a blur of students, giggling, gossiping, bitching, pretending to study, or arguing whose room the party should be in tonight.

At this point, it seems like everyone's caught on that Lockwood is nothing more than a cash grab, luring in our parents with promises of the highest level preparatory education. For most, it's a dream to get to spend the year before you head off to college chilling and partying on an island on the Washington coast where no one in the real world knows what you're up to. Lockwood looks great on college applications. That's all that matters.

The good news is that with everyone distracted or generally unbothered, things slip through the cracks. Like everything that's happened with me, Henry, and Wes. I was nearly killed right here on school grounds, and I'm not sure anyone would remember if you asked them.

The bad news is that no one seems to know or care where anyone else is. I've asked about fifty students if they've seen Ciel since she escaped from my clutches earlier, and every single one gave me the same shrug and blow off.

All I can hope at this point is that Wes took care of Amelia. But I can't seem to find him either.

In the distance, Adip flags me down. "Natty! Wait up!"

He jogs over to me and my body swirls with hope. Please let him know where Ciel is.

I interrupt him before he can say anything. "Have you seen Ciel?"

"Not recently."

My stomach turns over with disappointment and anxiety, the threat of Amelia lurking in the background.

"Is Wes okay?" Adip asks.

I recoil in surprise. Why is he asking me this? "I think so."

"I saw him earlier over at Lockwood Commons. He was vomiting up his guts and it seemed like he was hallucinating or something?"

Lockwood Commons? No one goes back there. It's what they call a dark part of the campus. There are several spots like that, roped off by metaphorical caution tape and treated almost like a crime scene. The school doesn't host any activities or classes or anything in that area of campus. Rumor is, it's a spot where wild animals creep out of the forest, and a few years ago, a student nearly got attacked by a bear. Apparently, there are a few cases of bears swimming out here in the San Juan Islands, going from island to island. They're supposed to be harmless, but maybe the school doesn't want to take any chances. They probably wouldn't want a parent to ask for a refund after their kid became a bear's lunch.

"I haven't seen him, but I'll go look," I say.

What was Wes doing at Lockwood Commons? Maybe he was just hiding out, blowing off steam before tracking down Amelia. Or perhaps Amelia was back there. But why was he sick? And what did Adip mean about hallucinations?

Unless he had another vision.

My mind splinters with the possibility that Wes might be with Amelia right now. What if things didn't go according to plan? What if his vision changed?

Suddenly, I remember a specific detail of Wes's original vision. Amelia was with Ciel on a balcony. There's an old, decrepit building at the Lockwood Commons with a third-floor balcony—his vision suddenly links to reality.

"Adip, I've gotta go."

I race away from him before he can say another word, making my way down the narrow path to the far-right corner of campus, hoping it's not too late.

❧

The overgrown evergreen trees finally part and my feet smack down on Lockwood Commons. A paint-peeled sign flanks the entrance. The lawn is empty and dark, but a single light shines from the third floor of the building.

My nerves spike as I race over to the entrance and yank on the door, but of course, it's locked. My throat balloons as if I'm kissing Wes and losing oxygen, except this time, it's driven from pure fear.

One of the windows off to the side has a giant hole smashed through it. I carefully push the broken glass with my fingers, shards falling to the floor. Gripping the windowsill, I hoist myself inside, tiny cuts tearing into my skin on the way, adrenaline masking the pain.

Voices echo through the vents and my blood crackles. It's Amelia and Ciel. I lean down to grab a shard of glass as a weapon and slowly inch my way up the winding staircase. The steps twist and crack and sink, and I'm not certain I'll ever make it without plunging to my death. But I've got to try.

My foot presses onto the landing for the third floor and I exhale the breath I was holding the entire ascent. Their voices are louder, clearer, as I tiptoe into the room.

Terror seeps through my veins as I watch Ciel and Amelia standing on the balcony, just like Wes said in his vision. Amelia is smiling, flirting, alive and well. Which means Wes wasn't able to do what he promised. What he so badly wanted to do. So where is he?

Tears bubble in my eyes and I choke back a sob. If Amelia is still here, that must mean Wes is not. Did she do something to him? Is he…gone?

My hand clutches tighter around the shard of glass, cutting deeper into my skin. Blood trickles down, leaving tiny dribbles on the floor.

Amelia is wearing a black blazer, a tight black skirt, and high heels, just like Wes said in his vision. Ciel has her uniform on, hair braided down her back, again, just like his vision.

I take another step into the room as they chat on the balcony. My hand curls around my back, hiding the shard of glass until the last minute. Until I need to use it. I know shards of glass aren't supposed to kill precogs, but at least I can do something as a distraction. I mentally kick myself for giving Wes back his dagger.

Amelia reaches out, tracing her finger along Ciel's necklace, hooking her finger underneath the dainty gold ringlets. Exactly like Wes said.

Amelia steps closer as Ciel flutters her eyes shut, like she's preparing for a kiss. Amelia tugs at Ciel's necklace, pulling her closer. Wes's vision is coming to life before my eyes. And I'm about to change it.

"Hey!"

My shout startles Ciel, but Amelia looks at me as if she expects my arrival. Her expression is disorienting.

"Natty, what are you doing here?" Ciel asks, a twinge of guilt in her voice.

I clutch the shard of glass behind my back and race over to them. "Get away from her, now!"

Amelia's lips turn into a sickening grin. My feet hit the balcony, and in one swift movement, Amelia shoves Ciel over the side. Ciel's screams echo through the night and cut off just as fast.

"No!" I lunge at Amelia with the shard of glass, but her hand grips my wrist, twisting it so hard I'm afraid it might snap. Agony spreads through my body, but I can't let her win.

"Natalie Covington. Right on time."

"What the hell are you talking about?"

"I was expecting you," she says.

My mind tries to process through the hurt and agony of my wrist, alongside what the hell she's saying. "Where is Wes?"

Amelia grins again, a sinister and sweet concoction that only makes me hate her more. "Nothing like a bit of magic."

Magic. I swallow my pain, wanting to make her pay. For Ciel. Even for Wes.

"What did you do to him?"

Amelia pops her eyes open, innocence teasing over her expression. "I didn't harm him, if that's what you mean. I have other plans for Wes. *You* are the one who really spikes my curiosity."

I swallow down my nerves, clenching on to my strength. "And why's that?"

She eyes me, unflinching, with the air of a guidance counselor giving you a serious talk about your future. Except I can tell that Amelia is ready to end mine.

I try to wrench my wrist free from her grip, but I can't seem to move even a centimeter, as if we're frozen in time.

"Let's see if it's true."

Before understanding what she means, Amelia crashes her mouth down on mine. I press my lips together, refusing to give her access, but suddenly, my neck locks into place, as if I'm trapped in some viselike grip of magic or powers or something otherworldly that I don't understand.

I might die tonight, right here, right now. But I'm not going out without a fight.

My mind parses through her plan. She's going to try and suck the life out of me. Which must mean she thinks this is the only way to kill me. Otherwise, she could stab me with this shard of glass or toss me over the balcony like Ciel.

But she doesn't know I've been practicing with Wes. That I'm able to buy time for my life now. Her plan is flawed and that gives me an advantage.

I open my lips seductively, giving her the access she wants. This small gesture seems to throw her off balance. Instead of resisting her kiss that could end my life, I'm welcoming it.

As Amelia pulls away from me, my limbs tingle, and suddenly, I can move again. Not well, but I can move.

"What are you doing? Do you *want* to die?" she says, and I detect a hint of fear in her voice.

"Maybe I do."

She glares at me in shock as I come unglued from her power.

"But not tonight," I say.

A jolt of electricity ignites my hand, just like it did when I held Wes's dagger. I rip away from Amelia's iron grip and jam the shard of glass into her chest. She stumbles back, clutching the glass, falling backwards over the balcony into the open, black air.

Shock rips through my core as I fist the edge of the balcony, expecting to see her body slam onto the ground below.

But there's nothing there, as if the night sky swallowed her whole.

CHAPTER TWENTY

WES

THERE ARE TWO things I know in this moment. One, Natalie's friend Ciel is lying dead in my arms. And two, I'm going to attempt to resurrect her.

If I do this, maybe Natalie will forgive me for my lies. The ones she knows about, and the ones she doesn't.

Twisting my body to the side, I maneuver Ciel's mangled body through the onslaught of branches, heading deeper into the thick, forested part of Lockwood. Her blood trickles down my forearms in a sticky syrup. One of her legs is warped from the fall in a way that doesn't quite make sense. But things rarely do when you're murdered, especially when your body is thrown off the third-story balcony of a building.

This wasn't my original plan. That was to kill Amelia, but I'm pretty sure she found some way to trick me and mess with my head.

My last vision showed Natalie taking care of Amelia. A shard of glass to the chest. Shoving her over a balcony. *That's my girl.* Unfortunately, it won't be enough to kill her and Amelia's body seemed to disappear into thin air. I'll have to deal with that later.

I always hoped I'd find someone with the same thirst for killing that I have. Even though the kill won't stick, Natalie's body count is technically higher than mine now, a fact that thrills me to the core.

The wind growls around me as I wind deeper into the forest, gently setting Ciel's body down on the ground. Physically, she looks broken, and at the same time, her expression seems almost at peace. An odd thing, really. It's something I got used to when watching my uncle carry out his kills. No matter how much he tortured his marks, no matter how much pain they were in, they always seemed at peace when the deed was done.

It almost makes me sorry that I need to bring Ciel back to life. *Almost.*

After my uncle cruelly disposed of that first bird I resurrected, I continued playing with magic, perfecting it over time in the shadows, behind his back. I've never tried to resurrect a human, though, just various animals who met untimely deaths, never by my hand.

I learned a few things through my experimentation. If you wait too long to resurrect, it doesn't work. You've got twenty minutes from the time of death, max. If you use too much of your own blood, it also doesn't work. Just a small trickle. If you cut from the wrong part of your wrist or anywhere else on your body, it fails. And you have to count all the way down from ten, never skipping a number or stopping too soon.

But when it works, when you use your own blood to breathe life into something, there's no greater power than that.

Guess I'm about to find out if it works on humans.

Kneeling down next to Ciel's body, I draw the dagger from inside my coat. Ciel's lips are closed into a glossy pout and I use my fingers to pry them open. I'll need to get my blood down her throat. It's the only way.

In a quick sweep, I gently slice my dagger along the side of my wrist. Just a small cut. Any pain is immediately replaced with a sort of exhilaration as I watch my blood drip into her mouth. I wait, counting down from ten, but when I get to one, nothing happens.

Disappointment whips through my brain as I realize that maybe this won't work on humans. Perhaps I'm not powerful enough.

Feelings of inadequacy snap into my brain, until Ciel finally sputters, her chest lurching forward like she's seizing. *It's working.*

Ciel's manicured, bloodied hands reach out, pulling my wrist closer to her lips. Her eyes blink open, staring up at me with a glimmer of adoration. Pride swells in my gut as she laps up more of my blood. That's right. *Drink up, good girl.* Then go tell Natalie what I did for you so she'll feel indebted to me for life.

Satisfaction rockets through my veins, until I feel a light gnaw of Ciel's teeth on my skin. She latches on tighter, bowing her head, viciously sucking the blood from my wrist. This definitely hasn't happened before. I yank away from her, which seems to cause an even bigger frenzy. She lunges at me, desperately grabbing at my arm.

I grip her wrists, pinning her down onto the ground, trying to reason with this girl I just brought back to life. "Ciel, stop. You're okay now."

But she's not listening, thrashing around like a wild animal.

"Ciel, enough!"

My command does nothing as she continues to writhe and thrash, kicking my limbs, her fingernails digging into my arms. I'm beginning to regret my choice. Maybe I should just kill her…again.

I make one last attempt to calm her down, moving my face an inch from hers, locking my gaze on her eyes. "It's me, Wes. Look at me. Just breathe."

She stills, her breath slowing. Her lips quiver, reaching up to brush against mine. I pull back an inch, not wanting her to get the wrong idea. I'm not sure if arousal is a side effect to having your life saved, but I'm not your guy. Nothing about Ciel turns me on. Although it takes every inch of my willpower not to imagine Natalie underneath me right now, thanking me for saving her friend.

"Wes?" Ciel's voice creaks and confusion contorts her face. "What happened? Am I dead?"

A chuckle escapes from my throat. "No, you're very much alive." I press myself up on my hands, pushing away from her.

Ciel looks down at her mangled leg and tries to move it. There's a loud, sickening snap and her leg flexes, appearing normal again.

I notice the terror flood into her eyes. "What's happening to me?"

"Just stay calm. Don't move for a few minutes, okay?"

Her breathing accelerates and her body shivers as she watches her wounds close up, one by one. I clamp down my hand over my wrist to stop the blood, then that wound magically heals too. Except for the bizarre vision I had earlier, that's never happened to me before. I wonder if resurrecting an actual human somehow unlocks other powers. *This could be promising.*

Natalie's voice booms across the woods. "Ciel?" Natalie races through a bank of trees, running over to Ciel and wrapping her in her arms. "I thought you were dead."

"So did I," Ciel says.

Excitement skates over my body as my gaze lands on Natalie, watching her little reunion with a resurrected Ciel, all thanks to me. Natalie glances my way, appearing grateful, causing a new thrill to ignite my entire body. There's no bigger turn-on than knowing Natalie owes me.

A small smile creeps onto my lips. This is a debt to me that Natalie will undoubtedly try to repay. And I'll enjoy every single moment.

CHAPTER TWENTY-ONE

NATALIE

Monday morning biology class.

There are so many things out of my control right now, it feels somewhat good to just sit here, staring at a textbook, the white noise of a teacher's lecture layering the background. A place to zone out and process what the hell is going on in my life.

Amelia disappeared into thin air last night, which means she's still out there, lurking. Waiting. Watching. Ready to strike.

Who knows what she, or any other precogs like her, have planned next. And if Henry's joined that group, working alongside or for her…

I think I might be sick.

On top of the danger constantly lurking, Wes brought Ciel back to life in some resurrection ceremony, and of course, she's asking a million questions. My only relief is that she was so exhausted last night that she finally passed out after I helped her shower and destroyed her bloody clothes. Dread sinks into my mind. How am I going to explain everything to her? And with Amelia still out there, she's still not safe.

My stomach wrenches as the bell rings with a deafening chime. Class was fifty minutes but felt more like fifty seconds. A sharp ache spreads across my chest, wishing there was some place to hide out, like home. But I don't have a home anymore. My fake dad hasn't even bothered to return my call from Ciel's phone or try to reach me at school.

Irritation stabs at my heart as I collect my books, accidentally dropping some papers to the floor. A pretty hand with a black, French-tipped manicure picks it up. I raise my eyes to meet Josephine.

"Thanks." I shove the papers into my backpack.

"Are you okay?" she asks.

I brush off her concern, making a desperate attempt to act normal. "Yeah, I'm fine."

"You look really pale. And you've got something on your forehead." Josephine reaches up to wipe whatever it is away. "I can't get it off. Wait, is that blood?"

Terrified, I cover up my forehead. "Um, I don't think so."

Josephine fishes out a compact from her purse. "Here, look."

I attempt to stay calm as I peek into her mirror, noticing she was right—it is a small patch of dried blood. How the hell did I miss that?

I ramble off a quick excuse. "It was a pimple. I was picking at it during class. I know I shouldn't do that, but oh well."

Josephine eyes me with concern and I'm not sure she buys my reasoning. "I have some acne cream in my room. It's really good stuff if you want some."

"Thanks, maybe I'll stop by later."

She smiles sweetly. "Okay. Oh, and by the way, did you hear about the new headmaster? They can't find her anywhere. Jack has been freaking out."

"Oh my god, really?" I hope my acting skills are better than my ability to clean up blood.

"Yeah, maybe she just couldn't hack the job, you know?" There's a small amount of glee in Josephine's eyes and I get the hint that she's thrilled that Jack is no longer up Amelia's ass. If only she knew the truth.

Wes appears in the doorway and sucks me into his gaze.

"I've gotta go." I go after Wes before Josephine can utter another word.

❧

Back in my dorm room, I inhale deeply, trying to minimize my frustration. Wes cups my face in his hands. I'm not sure what he thinks is going on right now, but I am certainly not in the mood for romance.

"I'm glad to hear that all that practicing we did came in handy with Amelia." He leans in for a kiss and I twist my head, refusing access. I back away from him in disbelief.

"Amelia's not dead. You said glass can't kill a precog, right? She's definitely going to come after us again. And now we need to tell Ciel the truth."

Wes takes a reassuring step towards me. "I'll handle it."

I shake my head. "Okay, did feeding your blood to my friend and bringing her back to life screw up your brain even more than it already is? Because you can't handle everything. Also, how did you even know how to do that?"

Wes steps forward, towering over me. "I told you before that I use magic. You brushed it off. And I know you're still mad at me for not showing you the photo of Henry. I'm sorry. And I'm even sorrier that you care so much about him."

My body explodes with anger. "Enough!"

A coldness passes through Wes's eyes and I get an eerie feeling that something's changed. He cocks his head, his eyes raking over me as if he's sizing me up. The tension swallows the room and my emotions bleed into each other.

"I saved your friend's life. I did that for *you*. And your words might push me away, but your body tells a different story. I can see it in your eyes, your lips, your—"

"Enough," I say again, turning away from him.

Wes surges forward, his hands gripping my waist, hoisting the front of my body against the wall. He breathes into my neck from behind, sending ripples of anger and twisted excitement through my body.

He's right. My body does tell a different story. Allowing him into my life, into my bed all those nights—I did that to myself.

"I will take care of you. Let me take care of you." His voice is nearly a growl, testing me as his teeth nip at my neck. My mind clouds and dizzies, unlocking that part of me that desperately wants, needs, a distraction right now.

My body trembles as he undoes the top button of my blouse, then another. My eyes flick to his wrist. He detailed for me exactly how he brought Ciel back to life. A slice in the side of his wrist, except there's no wound there. No scratch, no scar, nothing. The sight of it, the idea of it, sends a strange mix of shockwaves through my skin.

"You don't even have a cut on your wrist. How—"

"Shhh," he quiets me, grazing his fingers along my chest. He undoes another button and another button until a knock sounds at the door.

Sucking in a lungful of air, I wriggle free from him, quickly buttoning my shirt. I'm both relieved and annoyed at the interruption, which pretty much sums up my feelings about Wes entirely.

I twist open the knob to find an angry Ciel standing there, arms folded over her chest. She shoves past me into the room. "Oh good, you're both here. Now that I'm not drugged anymore!"

I flick my eyes to Wes, accusing. "Did you give her something last night?"

He shrugs, nonchalant. *Unbelievable.*

"She wouldn't calm down and she needed to rest. You didn't see how she looked when she was dead."

My eyes widen in shock at how casual he's talking about Ciel's murder, although it shouldn't surprise me.

"Okay, so your boyfriend basically roofied me," Ciel says, turning to Wes and shifting her tone. "But you did save my life, so thank you."

"You're welcome. See, Natalie? That's what gratitude looks like." Wes smirks at me, and I definitely want to punch him right now.

Ciel flops onto my bed and gives us both an expecting glance. "Okay, so one of you is going to tell me what the hell is going on. Which one is it gonna be?"

I exchange glances with Wes, kicking myself for not talking this through with him last night. After sneaking Ciel back into the dorm and cleaning both of us up, disposing of all evidence, I collapsed into a heap of exhaustion. I snuck out this morning for class before Wes woke up.

Ciel motions to Wes. "So what, you're some kinda vampire?"

Wes shoots her an offended glare. "Of course you would think that."

"You gave me your blood. What am I supposed to believe?" Ciel asks, making a decent point.

Wes grunts in frustration, and for a second, I wonder if he's about to bare fangs. At this point, nothing would surprise me.

"Vampires don't exist. But I, on the other hand, very much do," he says, his tone laced with threat.

"Okay, if you're not a vampire, what the hell are you?"

Do we tell Ciel about precogs? About Wes's ability to see the future and apparently save lives while being a trained assassin? About Henry and that prison and everything we went through?

And what is Ciel going to say when she learns that I killed—or at least attempted to kill—not one, but two people?

CHAPTER TWENTY-TWO

WES

KNEELING DOWN IN front of Ciel, I allow a smile to creep onto the corner of my lips. I'm aware of what my presence can do to girls, and I imagine it's all the more powerful when my blood has literally saved their life.

Ciel inches across the bed, getting closer to me, hoping to hear the truth about who, or what, I am. But I'm not stupid enough to reveal the truth to her. She seems the type to vomit secrets all over social media, hiding under some anonymous account. And sure, social media is forbidden here at Lockwood, but I already know Ciel snuck a phone onto campus. I'll just feed her a different version of events.

"How familiar are you with witchcraft?" I ask, toying with her.

"Like spells and stuff?" she asks, and I can see the goosebumps cover her bare arm.

"Exactly like spells," I answer, suppressing a laugh from bursting from my lungs. Nowadays, girls are into witches, tarot cards, crystals, angels, stuff that's leaked into the mainstream. So we'll go with that.

I let my eyes trail down Ciel's face, well aware of the effect I have on her. Dark magic and flirting, what a way to draw someone in and make them forget all their questions and reservations.

My eyes drive to Natalie, and I notice she's fidgeting with the fabric of her skirt, her fingers twisting around a stray thread. Is she worried that Ciel won't buy my explanation? A darkness flickers across her expression and I wonder if she's jealous. This is an angle I hadn't considered when I decided to save Ciel's life. I assumed Natalie would be indebted to me, whether she wanted to be or not. But a harmless flirtation with her friend might prick at her heart enough to realize I'm the one for her.

My hand knots at the bedsheet as I spill more lies to Ciel. "It's not something I can talk about too much—for your protection, of course." I emphasize the word *protection*, and I can see the bravado disappear from her body.

"I...I understand," she says in a breathy tone.

Good little puppet, performing exactly as I want.

My fingers glide across the bedsheet and Ciel follows them with her gaze in almost a trance-like state. I'll bet she's wondering what it might feel like if I was tracing my hand along her body. She'll never know, because the only girl I want to touch is sitting across the room, fuming at me. I have to admit, this whole situation has turned very fun, very quickly.

I continue with my fable, Ciel easily lapping up my words. "The women in my family were involved in witchcraft and I learned some things by watching as a kid. Unfortunately, they were found out and brutally killed. Witchcraft is extremely dangerous and even more risky to pull off. And if anyone were to find out, it would be over for all of us. But I know how much you mean to Natalie. Saving you was worth the risk."

Ciel exhales, a tiny moan of gratitude escaping her lips. Part of me would love to know how she'd thank me. Not because I'd ever act on it, but Ciel could give Natalie a few pointers on how to show gratitude.

"Well, thank you. I owe you," Ciel says, and I wish those words were coming out of Natalie's lips, preferably with her body pressed against mine.

I pull a joint from my pocket. My fingers tighten around the edge of the paper as I light it up, bringing the joint to my lips and taking a long drag. Ciel studies my every move, as does Natalie.

"Don't worry about it. There's no debt for *you* to pay." I shoot a glance to Natalie as I exhale, making it clear she knows that someone will pay for my generosity, and that someone is her.

She crosses her arms over her body and meets my eyes with an insolent glare. I rake my gaze over her pretty pink pout, imagining her whispering how thankful she is for me while I—

"So what do we do now? Where's Amelia? Is she going to come after me?" Ciel says, littering questions all over my perfect fantasy.

Time for her to go.

"Amelia is taken care of."

Ciel pops her eyes open, looking frightened. "You mean, she's dead? Did your witchery do that too?"

I reach out for Ciel's hand, pulling her up from the bed, keeping hold of her wrist. "The less you know about Amelia, about any of this, the better. It's for your own good. You're safe now, that's all that matters."

Ciel practically leaps into my arms, squeezing me into a hug. "Thank you. I promise I won't say a word to anyone."

Natalie glances over at us and lowers her gaze. Pleasure ripples through my stomach as I picture envy exploding through her body.

Ciel pulls away and heads to the door. "I'll leave you two alone now. And don't worry, my lips are sealed. Witches are, like, the ultimate feminists. I would never betray those badass bitches. It's so cool you were raised by them."

As Ciel leaves Natalie and I alone, that familiar friction returns, as if the flame from my lighter is grazing along my skin.

Natalie storms over to me, planting her hands on my chest and shoving me backwards, causing the joint to fall from my mouth. Luckily, I catch it in time and stub it out. Damn. This is about to get good.

"What do you think you're doing?" she asks.

"Jealous, are we?" I smirk, knowing that she hates it. That she *loves* to hate it.

"Ciel may have bought your bullshit witchcraft story, but if you think she's done asking questions, you're an idiot. And if you think she won't tell anyone, you're more of an idiot. So what are we going to do now? Amelia is clearly still out there. And what about Henry? Is he working for her?"

Her words stab at my gut. *Henry.* His name somehow sounds more vile every time it leaks from her pretty mouth. My fists clench at my sides and I exhale, trying to remove some of the tension.

"On top of everything, there are consequences for changing a vision," Natalie says. "You changed your vision. We know what happened to Henry when he—"

I cut her off. "No, I didn't."

"Excuse me?"

"I didn't change my vision. Amelia shoved Ciel off that balcony and she died. That was the vision. I didn't change any of that, only what happened after."

Natalie thinks that over, her expression growing even more confused at this precog loophole. "What about bringing someone back to life? Aren't there any consequences for that?"

"If you count my uncle's beatings when I resurrected a bird, sure. Otherwise, nope. Not that I'm aware of."

Natalie swallows, averting her gaze. I know it makes her feel uncomfortable when I talk about my uncle's treatment, which makes me want to do it more, play to her guilt.

And she's still not thanking me for saving her stupid friend.

I assumed she'd be thrilled, grateful, indebted. I pictured tears leaking from her eyes as she thanked me, over and over, in so many different ways.

Instead, she's here fidgeting, annoyed with me. It takes every ounce of my willpower not to curl my fingers around her throat and remind her how good she has it—make her beg for air and admit that I've been here for her all along.

I'm the real reason she's alive, not that other asshole.

I'm the reason Ciel is breathing once again.

It's time for her to start repaying my kindness.

Before she can utter another word, I walk past her, heading to the door. As I reach out for the knob, I expect she'll call out my name to try and stop me.

Sadly, she doesn't.

CHAPTER TWENTY-THREE

NATALIE

WHENEVER WES EXITS a room, it's as if all the oxygen flows back in again.

One moment, I loathe him. The next, I'm grateful that he brought Ciel back to life. And the next, I'm drawn to the thrill, the distraction he provides when he's not acting like a complete psychopath.

My gaze drifts to the window. Early season snow flurries leave a dusting across the fallen leaves. A few stray students hurry into nearby buildings to escape the weather.

Only one person is left, and they appear to be looking right up at me.

Shock spreads through my chest as I squint to get a better look. They're dressed in black with a white mask, watching from a bank of trees down below. The Armory uniform.

Could it be Henry?

I quickly duck down, nerves tightening as I peer over the windowsill. The person twists away, beginning to work their way through the trees.

My legs move at their own volition as I grab my coat, speeding out of my bedroom, down the winding staircase. I shove open the door to my dorm building and race across the lawn to where they were standing, noticing a trail of footsteps in the snow leading ahead.

Danger ricochets through my mind, but the idea that this person could be Henry keeps me forging on.

Branches smack against my arms as I move quickly across the damp ground. My stockings catch onto a sticker bush and rip along my thigh, a cold gust of wind stinging my bare skin.

The air is quiet and I can hear the faint sound of footsteps on the icy ground. They can't be too far away.

I quietly make my way through the maze of branches, trying desperately not to slip on the snow-dusted ground.

In the distance, I spot the person from behind—what appears to be a guy wearing a black, hooded coat and black pants. He's crouched over, head bent, mask in hand.

I crouch behind a tree, careful to quiet my breathing. His hood falls away, revealing a mass of brown, wavy hair.

Hair that looks exactly like Henry's.

I take a few steps closer to get a better look. A branch cracks under my shoe and I quickly duck behind a tree.

He turns around, and that's when my suspicions are confirmed. My heart leaps into my throat.

Henry Thorne is back. And he was watching me.

His chest rises and falls as he looks around. My knees shake as I study his hand, reaching into his pocket, removing a sharp dagger, not unlike Wes's. Do all precogs get one of those? Or just the ones who are ordered to kill someone?

He rolls the dagger between his fingers, studying it, frowning at it. My body ripples with anticipation of what he might do next.

His brow furrows as he fingers the blade. Then, in a split second, he grips the handle and drives it into a tree. The swift movement sends shockwaves through my core.

He doesn't move like the Henry I remember, the Henry that existed a little more than a month ago. He seems more visceral now. More frightening. More dangerous.

He rips the dagger from the tree and stares ahead, then yanks up his hood and storms off, still carrying his mask.

My head is screaming to run, but I'm glued to this spot. What's Henry's plan? Is he checking up on me? Baiting me?

I push through the thick branches, heading deep into the woods away from campus, giving Henry time to get ahead, feeling thankful for the dusting of snow so I can follow his footsteps. Eventually, his footsteps run out, leading inside a dilapidated, barn-like building that I've never seen before on campus. Probably because I've never dipped this far back into the woods before.

Swallowing my nerves, I wind around the building, peering through a broken piece of plywood. Henry paces inside, knotting his hair into his hand. Now that looks like the Henry I remember, the one whose frustration is palpable.

Another guy joins him, wearing the same clothing, with his mask on. "Did you see her?" the mysterious guy asks.

Her? Is he talking about me?

Henry still has his mask off, lowering his gaze, shaking his head no. If they're talking about me, then he just lied, or perhaps he didn't see me after all.

The mystery guy speaks again. "Get it done tonight."

"I need more time." Henry croaks out the words, his voice sounding pained, almost broken.

"We know what she's capable of." The man places his hand on Henry's arm, almost comforting. "It must be difficult, changing a vision to save someone, only for that person to betray you."

So he *is* talking about me. But how did I betray him?

Suddenly, the man wrenches Henry's arm, twisting it around in a sickening manner. It takes every ounce of my restraint not to run in and stop him as Henry howls in pain.

"We need her taken care of tonight. There's a school dance. Perfect distraction." The man tosses Henry to the ground as fear slithers through my mind. Henry Thorne was just ordered to kill me. *Tonight.* Apparently, at a school dance, which I didn't even realize was happening.

My stomach twists, adrenaline coursing through my insides as I process the reality of this situation. Do I tell Wes? Or do I handle this myself?

I quickly make my way back through the woods undetected, mind clouding with realizations. Henry left and joined a precog fringe group tasked with murdering people like me.

As I work through a dicier area of the woods, almost reaching the main part of campus, a rough grip latches onto my shoulder and terror slices through my chest. I spin around, only to find Wes standing behind me. How long has he been there? Did he follow me?

Wes wraps his arms around my shoulders, pressing my body up against a tree. "I saw you," he says, his eyes boring into mine.

"You were following me?"

"No, I *saw* you. In a vision."

My chest clenches as Wes cups his hands around my jaw, pulling my face closer. "You were with him. Henry. Right here against this tree."

Nerves erupt in my stomach as I process a very different reality for this moment.

Wes is shaking. "If I didn't have that vision and come straight here, do you know what would have happened to you? He would have caught up. Shoved your body against this tree. Told you everything you wanted to hear. Captured your trust."

Wes traces his fingers along the ripped part of my stockings.

"He touched you here. I saw it."

He runs his hand along my thigh, underneath my thick coat, tucking his fingers under the waistband of my uniform skirt.

Then he balls his hand into a fist, pressing hard against my abdomen, causing a gasp to erupt from my lips.

"And when you were distracted, he stabbed you right here."

His words smack into my mind, whipping through me like a tornado, realizing these past few minutes could have—*should have*—looked very different.

Unless Wes isn't telling the truth.

CHAPTER TWENTY-FOUR

WES

THIS.

This is what I live for—Natalie, pinned against a tree, attempting to figure me out. Am I lying? Or not?

Okay, sure, fine, I'm lying. Wouldn't be the first time. Won't be the last. Truthfully, it doesn't really matter what she believes as long as she's triggered enough to stay the hell away from Henry. At least until I can take care of him. Which clearly has to happen before tonight, since he got orders to kill Natalie from that other Armory fuck.

It's insane how those two can slither around this campus undetected. But at least I managed to find him, courtesy of Natalie, who unwittingly became my guide. The administration at this school clearly notice nothing, even with the cameras turned on. This school is truly the best catfish of all time—branded as a posh prep school but serves as more of a private island to dump your kids at so you don't have to deal with them until they're shipped off to university.

Unless there's some reason they purposely don't notice things. Which I've also considered.

"I know what I saw in my vision. It's up to you if you want to believe it or not," I tell Natalie, then push away from her because I know it's the last thing she expects. Normally, I'm the aggressor, doing what's necessary to get her to listen to me and come around. Gotta keep things interesting. I suppress the grin creeping onto my lips. Keeping up the charade, I start to walk off.

Natalie shouts after me. "Where are you going? You just said I was going to be slaughtered in the woods and now you're going to leave me out here?"

I spin to face her with a devious smirk. "You don't believe me, right? So I guess you've got this all handled."

As I study her face, I can see the confusion ripple through her eyes. Whenever I'm around her, it's as if everything else in the world is on mute. Even the fact that the Armory is here, that Henry was ordered to kill her.

Natalie claims she doesn't trust me, but I know a small part of her does, and that tiny nag in her heart is just enough to keep her on the hook. She's about to come around in three…two…

"Fine. Let's say you really did have that vision. Why would Henry do that here in broad daylight?"

"I think it's obvious that no one on this campus is paying much attention. And do you see any cameras out here?" I make a good point, if I say so myself.

Natalie exhales in frustration as irritation winds through my brain, but I shift it aside. I don't want that asshole occupying space in her head.

Footsteps crunch on the ground not far away. I try and shield Natalie from whoever is headed our way, but of course, she doesn't comply.

Warmth spikes through my chest. Maybe it's Henry, and if it is, I'll get to end his life right before Natalie's eyes. Come to think of it, that's a fairly delicious proposition. He attempts to kill her, and I save her.

She won't be able to deny my heroism in that scenario. Maybe she'll finally forget about him and start thanking me.

"Hey guys, what are you doing out here?" *Adip.*

He works his way over some branches, careful not to slip on the frosted ground. I nearly groan with disappointment at his arrival, while also wondering how the hell he knew we were out here.

"What's up, man?" I ask, scrunching my brow as I wait for clarification.

"I was just walking by and heard the two of you talking."

He was just casually walking by this uncleared spot, tucked away from the main part of campus? That seems like a load of bullshit to me.

Natalie seems thrilled by Adip's arrival, making her way over a few branches. The weight slips from her shoulders as she takes her place by his side, which is fine, because I know they're nothing more than friends. I'd still like to understand how Adip managed to find us out here. And why.

"What's up with this school dance tonight?" Adip asks. "Did you get the invite at your dorm? So much for giving us notice. I don't even know if I'm supposed to DJ. You know how long it takes to put together a set?"

Ah. Sweet, dumb, clueless Adip. Should have known his appearance out here was innocent.

"And it's another masquerade ball. How many of those things is the school gonna throw? It's like they've completely run out of ideas to entertain us. I may need to take over the planning committee because things are really starting to get stale here."

"Well, I'm looking forward to it," Natalie says, slinging her arm through Adip's.

My head tilts her way as anger ricochets through my bones. I know she's baiting me, trying to piss me off, by throwing herself willingly into Henry's arms.

The guy was ordered to kill her and yet she still would rather be with him than safe with me.

"Natalie," I say, the darkest parts of me coming through.

"Seems like you two are going through something. I've got class anyway." Adip tries excusing himself, but Natalie isn't ready to let him go. She doesn't want to be alone with me, that she's made clear.

But she'll risk her life to be alone with Henry.

"Natalie," I say once more, warning her to stay with me.

"What? You don't have to go tonight. I'm happy to fly solo," Natalie bites back, causing a burst of rage to explode through my bloodstream.

"It's mandatory attendance for all students," Adip says. "The dance is to welcome the new headmaster. Headmaster Collins."

CHAPTER TWENTY-FIVE

NATALIE

ANXIETY SURGES THROUGH my torso and up into my throat, practically choking me. Not only is Amelia still alive—which I already knew was possible, considering I didn't use a dagger to stab her—but she's back here. On campus. Throwing parties and ordering my death.

"Natty, are you okay? You look very pale." Adip shoots me a concerned look.

"I'm fine."

My eyes cut to Wes. He's glaring at me in a way that slices through my soul. I know he'll want us to skip the event, probably keep me under lock and key.

If I can just get to Henry, understand what's really going on, and figure out why he'd want to kill me. There's got to be some explanation.

"They even left masks with the invites. I guess that was pretty cool of them."

A choked laugh bursts from my throat. This school really loves their masquerade balls—always covering up for something. My attack. Amelia's bizarre arrival. Who knows what other secrets they're trying to keep buried.

And a masquerade ball is the perfect place for the Armory to hide.

Until I find them. Him. *Henry.*

∽

A thick knot forms in my stomach as I make my way inside the school dance with Wes. Of course, he refused to stay away, which is helpful at this moment as I use his arm to steady my balance on these ridiculous gold heels that Ciel lent me.

Wes and I made rules for tonight. Smile. Dance. Act as if everything is normal. Keep our eyes out for Amelia and every member of the Armory. Do not leave each other's side.

I plan to follow these rules. *All except the last one.*

I spent the afternoon pretending to come around, even thanking him for saving Ciel. Which I am grateful for, but not in the way he wants me to be.

We yank the Venetian masks over our faces and walk inside, energy crackling through the room as we take in the scene. Our classmates chat and giggle, a cluster of rich kids with not a care in the world. I can't believe I used to think I was one of them.

Ciel rushes over to us, ripping off her mask, clearly freaked out. "What the fuck, guys? This party is for Amelia? What, did she come back to finish the job on me?"

I attempt to quiet Ciel so no one overhears.

Wes looks down at her, meeting her gaze. "Don't worry, I'll keep you safe," he says, laying a reassuring hand on Ciel's arm.

"How many times can you bring me back to life? Does that witchy stuff you did on me work more than once?"

Wes nods, but he's full of shit.

With a deep breath, I squeeze Ciel's hand. "I promise you'll be fine."

She smiles at my reassurance, and I feel a heavy twinge of guilt that I, too, am full of shit.

"Just stay near me. Don't wander off alone," Wes orders.

Ciel nods, appearing eager to follow whatever he says.

Nerves flutter up my spine and I get a strange feeling that someone is watching me. My gaze bounces to a person standing in the hall wearing a black suit. The mask covers their entire face, but it's a different mask than the Armory uses. And they're staring right at me. They aren't tall enough to be Henry and they don't have his body. I should know, I've spent hours tracing over every inch of him in my mind.

The stranger disappears down the hallway, head twisting back to me once again, as if beckoning me to follow. My insides wring tight and I wish I was holding Wes's dagger, or any weapon, right about now.

I pinch Wes's arm. "Someone's watching me. In the hall."

Wes follows my gaze and immediately snaps into action, storming across the room, practically shoving our classmates out of the way. Several of them gasp and shoot him dirty looks. One girl eyes him as if his rude movement turned her on.

I chase after him, fear spasming in my chest. His hand slides into his jacket and I know he's gripping the handle of his dagger. He turns into the hallway, and I'm not far behind, struggling on my stupid high heels, trying to keep up.

The mystery person paces in the distance.

In a split second, Wes is in his face, shoving him against the wall, pointing the blade of his dagger against his throat. "Who are you?" Wes demands.

The guy deteriorates into sobs. "Please don't hurt me. I just wanted to talk to Natalie."

Wes tears off his mask, revealing a trembling Jack. Wes scowls, backing away, not lowering his dagger. "Never invite my girl to sneak off with you, understand?"

My glare cuts to Wes. "Stop. Leave him alone." I rush over to a shell-shocked Jack.

Jack nods, squeaking out a few sarcastic words. "Damn, Nat, you really know how to pick boyfriends."

Wes jabs the dagger at him. "Say one more thing."

"Wes, enough! Go back inside the dance."

His icy gaze cuts through me. "I'm not leaving you. We have a deal. Whatever he has to say, he can say it in front of me."

Not wanting to waste more energy fighting with him, I focus on Jack. "What's going on?"

Jack regains his breath. "I didn't know who else to talk to."

Wes lobs another jab. "Your girlfriend might be a start."

I twist back to face Wes, mouthing for him to shut up. He shoots me a vacant stare, an eerie thing I've never noticed him do before. Nerves balloon in my chest.

Jack starts to talk, keeping his eye on Wes's dagger. "Things have been a little weird between me and Josephine lately. I don't know, never mind. That's not what I wanted to say. It's about Amelia… Headmaster Collins."

My heart pounds as I pry for more information. "What about her?"

"I still don't know where she is. I planned out this entire event for her, and no one can find her."

Relief floods through my bones. So all of this was Jack's idea. Amelia may actually be gone. Jack innocently threw this soiree, probably to impress her.

"Okay, so what do you expect me to do about that?" I ask Jack. "I don't know where she is."

"Help me find her. I'm going to look like a complete idiot in front of the entire student body if she doesn't show up to a party that I threw for her."

I suppress the urge to roll my eyes. Jack is forever worried about his image, and the truth is that no one at Lockwood would care if Amelia showed up here or not. They're just happy to have an excuse to dress up and party.

"Why did you throw a masquerade ball?" I ask, genuinely curious.

"Her assistant told me they were her favorite."

My heart batters inside my chest. *Her assistant.* Did they suggest a masked ball so it would be easier for the Armory to move through this space? To get to me?

"So can you help me find her?" Jack asks. "It will be like old times, when we were kids, looking around for clues."

Right. When we were kids, I was always on some mission, roping him in to help me search for things. Now I realize how poor my investigative skills were, considering I missed so many major things happening right before my eyes.

My eyes swing over to Wes, who seems back to normal now. Deep green eyes glittering. No more vacant expression, just one of annoyance.

"Sure. We can look around for her," I say, not really meaning it. *I have someone else I want to find.*

Jack pushes away from me, straightening his suit jacket. He motions to Wes's dagger, still in his hand. "Never mind. I'd rather not bring a psycho along. And you're lucky I care about you, Nat, because I could have him expelled from this school in a heartbeat for having that weapon."

Jack storms off down the hall and Wes lets out a loud groan. "I can't believe you dated that guy. He's deeply annoying. I really should have just stabbed him."

I scoff. "What are you, just some cold-blooded killer now? You can't just go around stabbing anyone who looks at us sideways."

Wes raises his brow. "Sure I can."

The thought curdles my insides. He must notice my sickened expression because he slides the dagger back into his jacket and clasps my hand. "I'll kill anyone who is after the person I love. And I can count that on one finger."

His gaze transfixes on mine as he steps closer, wrapping me into his arms. Right. *Love*. In his fucked-up mind, he probably thinks this—*we*—are what love is.

I'd hate to know what else is rolling through his mind.

CHAPTER TWENTY-SIX

WES

IRRITATION SNAPS IN my veins. Yet another declaration of my love gone unanswered.

She'll never say it, feel it, as long as she's clinging to Henry as her lifeline.

Well, that will all be over tonight.

"We should get back in there," Natalie says. Her chest visibly rises and falls. *Hmmm.* Maybe it's nerves, or maybe a part of her wants to say it back to me.

Or maybe it makes her want to run away from me. Too bad, Natalie, because that's never going to happen.

I will never let you get away.

We walk hand-in-hand back into the main room, a glittering, revolting spectacle for a woman who isn't even here. How fun it would be to watch everyone in this room discover who Amelia really is. To watch the confidence drain from their souls as they realize they're not the only beings on this planet, and that they don't even have a millimeter of the power that precogs do.

A slow song comes on and I twirl Natalie around into my arms, tracing my finger along her spine, something I know turns her on, even if she doesn't want to admit it to herself. They've turned down the lights in the room, turning the space into shadows with a dusting of small bulbs illuminating certain corners of the space.

My eyes squint as I notice what appears to be a member of the Armory blending into the crowd across the room. They've swapped their black uniform for a black tuxedo, but it's undoubtedly the mask they wear.

The way this person is staring in our direction tells me it must be Henry. I don't even need a vision to know what this guy is thinking right now. I can practically feel his body twitching with envious rage, watching me with Natalie. Her back is turned to him, giving me the perfect chance to mess with his mind before I rip him to shreds. I run my hand over her hair, gently fisting her curls, bending down to kiss the top of her head—keeping one eye open to watch his reaction.

He reaches his hand up to rub his neck, averting his gaze as if to avoid watching us. Now *this* is delightful—relishing in his pain. How fortunate for me that he's served himself up on a silver platter that I'm about to shatter into a million pieces.

"I'll be right back," I say, excusing myself from Natalie.

She grips onto my arm. "Really? I thought you said we wouldn't leave each other's side tonight." Her eyes cut to mine, shooting me a skeptical glance.

"I have to use the boys' room. Unless you'd like to join me." I trace my finger over her bottom lip before curling my hand lightly around her throat, indicating what I'd really like to do.

She recoils from my touch. "Just go," she says, and I'm relieved she didn't agree, but only so I can take care of Henry.

I have other plans for us after he's dead and gone.

Patting my jacket to double-check that my dagger is safe and secure, I leave the room, hoping he'll follow. Watching from the corner of my eye, he slips into the hallway behind me. *Just as I planned.* Excitement erupts in my mind as I consider the possibilities. Should I end him swiftly or take my time?

Anticipation simmers in my gut as I duck into an empty room, baiting Henry to follow. I tuck around the open door, hiding, gripping my dagger. Maybe it's better to get this over with fast—don't want to risk Henry Thorne being alive a second longer than needed.

He enters the room, and in one swift movement, I have him on the ground, the blade of my dagger pointed at his neck.

He jerks his head back to put some distance between my weapon and his flesh. "Please, Wes, please don't hurt me!"

That voice…is most certainly not Henry. I rip off the mask to find Adip cowering underneath my grip.

A chill lurches through my body and I grip his face, wanting answers. "What the hell are you doing?"

Adip's eyes widen, his face trembling in my hand. "I…I just came to warn you."

Warn me? I'd always assumed Adip was just some bored rich kid with way too much time on his hands. Did I miscalculate things?

"Warn me about what?"

"There was someone watching you."

I release him from my grip, pushing away, and quickly tuck my dagger into my jacket pocket. His eyes follow my every move.

"Do you know who it was? What were they wearing?"

"I don't know, but I saw them come into the ball right after you and Natalie. And whoever it was, they were watching you dancing. I tried getting a better look. It was super weird, man. I didn't mean to freak you out. Also, why do you have a knife or whatever that is?"

So Adip wasn't watching us. He was watching someone else stalk us. Henry.

"Where did you get that mask?"

"The school gave it to me. They left masks for all of us."

Someone is fucking with us. They left an Armory mask for Adip because they knew it would be a distraction. Rage unfurls in my mind. I'm in here with Adip, which means Natalie must be out there alone…*with Henry.*

I tear off into the hallway, Adip shouting after me, obviously wanting answers. In the main room, the other students are waltzing in some horrid, choreographed number. I shove through them, hearing their yelps ring out behind me. A deep ache bleeds through my chest as I search and search for Natalie, but she's nowhere to be found.

Henry could have grabbed her by now, ended her life. How could I have been so stupid? How could I have fallen for this?

I spot Ciel across the room and yank her away from her dance partner. "Have you seen Natalie?" I shout over the god-awful music.

"No, why?"

Useless.

I shove past her and circle the room one more time before deciding Henry must have dragged her off somewhere. I'll tear apart every inch of this campus until I find her.

After ripping open every door inside the building and finding no trace of Natalie, my feet crunch against the hard ground outside, searching for footprints or any sign of the direction she could have gone.

I'm not sure what makes me more angry—that Henry has her, that she might be dead, or that he outsmarted me.

Let's go with all three.

My heart hammers inside my chest as I listen for any clues. There's nothing but the faint sound of music pouring from the masquerade party and the rustling of trees.

And while I see no one, *I can feel someone.*

I suck in a deep breath, taking a few steps forward, all my senses on alert. My foot catches onto something on the ground, buried underneath a pile of leaves.

I sink to my knees, shoving away the leaves, dirt, and debris, revealing a peek of gold.

The shoe Natalie wore tonight.

Ice runs through my veins as I picture Henry dragging Natalie away, knowing he'd bested me, leaving behind a single shoe like some fucked-up version of Cinderella.

I'll never be able to undo this.

My stomach clenches as a surge of grief rises inside me. Wetness appears in my eye sockets and a single tear trickles down my cheek. I don't cry. *I despise it.*

If only I was smarter and more capable, I could have prevented this. Maybe my uncle was right all along.

I was nothing. I *am* nothing.

And now I've lost the only thing that means something to me.

CHAPTER TWENTY-SEVEN

NATALIE

THE FIRST THING I register is a rocking motion, as if my body is being lulled to sleep.

A slosh of water awakens my other senses and I blink open my eyes. Wind bites at my skin and something underneath my back feels hard and damp. I squeeze my eyes open and shut a few times, trying desperately to focus my gaze on something, anything, but it's pitch black.

I shift my body, noticing that I'm lying down. Trying to push myself up is fruitless because I'm unable to move my hands. A sharp ache runs up my arms as I tug at my wrists, realizing they're bound. Awareness coils through my mind.

The dance.

Wes excusing himself. Finding that strange.

Going after him.

Someone grabbing me from behind, placing something over my mouth.

Everything going dark.

Panic floods through my body as I piece together the events. Where am I? How long have I been here? Who kidnapped me?

Then a familiar voice cuts through my muddled brain.

"You're awake."

My eyes snap open as someone crouches down in front of me. Their face comes into view, and I realize…it's him.

Henry Thorne.

I'm not sure whether to feel terrified or elated. This was my plan all night, to reunite with him, get answers. But now I'm here with him, drugged and tied up. My heart hammers as the memories flush back. The last time I saw Henry, he was ordered to kill me. A large part of me didn't want to believe it, figured I could reason with him, figure out the truth of what's going on.

Cold leeches around my skin and my body shakes as I make a sad attempt to inch away from him, shrugging off the blanket that had been casually thrown over me. One bare foot extends forward, the other still awkwardly sporting the gold heel. My dress is scrunched up beneath me, barely covering my skin.

"Hang on," he says, wrapping the thick blanket around my body again.

I flinch at his touch, but I'm afraid I might die of pneumonia otherwise, so I don't fight it. I manage to push myself into a seated position and realize we're on a small boat in the middle of the ocean. Relatively calm waves slosh us around.

Glaring at him, I try to croak out a few words, but my throat is ridiculously sore. Wincing through the pain, I try to push out my questions. "Where the hell are you taking me?" I ask.

"Just try to relax."

Anger floods through my body and I ignore the pain and scratchiness of my throat. "You have me tied up on a boat in the middle of the ocean, and you want me to relax?"

His expression turns icy and he pushes to stand. "The fewer questions you ask right now, the better."

Is he fucking kidding me? My body trembles and I'm not sure if it's from the cold or because I'm so angry I might explode.

"Why haven't you just killed me already? That was the plan, right?"

His head tilts down as if he's struggling to process something. I remember that look all too well. I also remember how I used to watch him grappling with his emotions, and desperately want to take his pain away. *What a stupid, stupid girl I am.*

"I followed you, heard you talking to your little friend. He told you to take care of me tonight. So what's the plan? Bring me out here and toss me overboard?" Nausea lances through my stomach as I realize that's probably *exactly* what he's doing.

"You should eat something," he says.

Eat? He honestly expects me to have an appetite right now?

He grabs a backpack, pulling out a paper bag. His hand slides out a small microwave cup of macaroni and cheese. "It's cold, but it's something." He offers it to me, as if the hands bound behind my back could grab it if I even wanted to.

"What is this supposed to be, my last meal?"

He audibly groans. "Just eat it, Natalie. You need something in your stomach right now."

I pull at the rope binding my hands. "Why? Because you drugged me?"

He doesn't answer, which ignites my rage even more. Tears threaten to spill down my cheeks, but I suck them back, refusing to let him see my cry.

Henry kneels down in front of me. He dunks a plastic spoon into the cup and holds it up to my lips.

I turn my face, refusing his efforts. "How do I know you haven't put drugs in that too?"

He exhales, appearing frustrated, setting the macaroni and cheese down on the floor of the boat. "Fine," he says, grabbing a dagger from his pocket.

Is that what he's planning to kill me with? I quickly try to claw together a plan. Maybe I can fight him off. I've done it before.

Henry circles around behind me and my insides coil with anxiety. If he's about to plunge that knife into my back, this is the moment I need to act.

He yanks my arms, pulling me into a standing position. The blanket drips off my body, dropping to the bottom of the boat. I flail my elbow back, cracking him right in the neck.

"Fuck!" he shouts.

I whirl around, ready to use my legs to fight him off, but he grips my body, twisting it back around to face away from him. Steadying myself, I writhe in his arms, trying to release myself.

"Stop, Natalie!" he shouts.

But I don't stop. Until suddenly, oddly, he releases me.

Sensation trickles back into my arms and I realize he used a dagger to cut the rope binding my hands. A dagger that's similar to the one Wes has. Must have scored one when he joined that creepy precog fringe group.

But he didn't try to stab me. He's freeing me, or at least my hands.

Distrust still oozes through my mind, wondering about his real plan. There's got to be a reason he's drugged and kidnapped me, and it's certainly not because he's letting me go.

I rub my hands together, breathing life back into the nerves, and turn to face him.

"Will you eat now? Please?" he asks.

My stomach wrenches with emptiness. If I want to keep up my strength, I've got to eat. And I've fought him off before, outside that prison when I ripped him away from Wes. I'm still unsure how I mustered that much adrenaline, but if I did it once, I'll do it again.

I swipe the cup of macaroni and cheese and take a bite. It's cold, as he said, but actually pretty tasty. My mind flashes to the time he offered me a bite while we were studying. It wasn't that long ago, but feels like ages. A time when I didn't know he was a precog, when someone hadn't tried to kill me yet. When I hadn't murdered not one, but two people. Though jury's still out on Amelia. And Oliver, too, I suppose.

Sickness sloshes through my gut and I set aside the cup, clenching my stomach.

Henry's eyes dance over me, and there's something in his expression. Care? Remorse? I'm not sure, but it's palpable.

"Here," he says, tossing me a water bottle from his backpack.

I unscrew the cap and take a few gulps, hydration breathing life back into me. "Thanks," I manage to mumble.

He chuckles. "I kidnapped you and you're thanking me."

I cut my gaze to him, wanting answers. "So what's the plan now? Are you going to deliver me to someone else to finish me off?"

Betrayal sinks into my pores as I release the words. I loved him, went to that prison place to save him. Then he just disappears, and this is how he repays me?

He shakes his head and grabs the cup of macaroni and cheese, swallowing a bite.

"Why did you join the Armory?" I ask.

My question is met with nothing but silence.

"Is this all because I killed your foster dad? Or tried to?" Nerves race down my spine as I ask the question. "Because he came after me first, then claimed he couldn't even be killed with that weapon anyway. That it would only kill my kind. Do you even know what he meant? Is he still alive?"

Henry clenches his jaw, still not answering any of my questions, twirling that fucking spoon around the cup of mac & cheese in a way that makes my insides curdle.

"Did they do something to you in that place? Brainwash you or something?"

His continued silence is maddening. Frustration coils around me so tight that I snap, my words bleeding over the calm sound of the ocean.

"What did I do to make you hate me so much? To make you want to kill me?"

Still nothing.

Breath lodges in my throat as I look out at the sea. I can't even see the shoreline and have no idea how far we've traveled. Thoughts of jumping overboard drift into my mind, but who knows if I'll ever find land again. I'd likely die from hypothermia before I could reach the shore. Besides, I'm certainly not that great of a swimmer. A pool is one thing, but pushing your body through freezing waves is another.

I make my way to edge of the boat, clasping the edges, watching the gentle waves lap against the bottom. The calmness of the water feels ironic compared to everything that's happened.

"Don't even think about it," Henry calls out behind me, and I realize he must think I'm about to jump.

I lift my foot up on purpose, letting the tip of my toe graze the side of the boat, testing him. Maybe this will get him to talk.

"Natalie." His voice is full of warning, and I lift my knee, resting it on the edge of the boat.

I catch him out of the corner of my eye, dropping the cup of mac & cheese and stalking over to me. He wraps his arms around my waist, yanking me away from the side.

"Get off me."

I wrestle in his grip as he takes me down to the floor of the boat, using his body to hold me down. His face is inches from mine as he wraps his hand around the base of my scalp, fisting my hair, forcing me to look at him.

"Don't test me, Natalie. Or I'll tie you up again."

And with that, he puts up an invisible wall and backs away, leaving me on the floor. My lungs are coiled so tight, I'm almost afraid to breathe.

My eyes narrow, watching him as he stands and wanders to the other side of the boat, shutting me out. I know I have to do whatever it takes to break down his walls and get some answers.

At least, before he tries to break me.

CHAPTER TWENTY-EIGHT

WES

I CIRCLE CAMPUS what seems like a thousand times, searching for Natalie, before coming to the realization that she can't be here.

Henry Thorne. That piece of shit bested me and stole her away. His name alone sends bile up my throat. I wonder what they're doing right this moment—if he's tried killing her already, or if he's taking his time. Or maybe he's not planning on hurting her, but wants her all to himself.

All of these are equally terrible options.

My insides clench and seethe as I pass by the building once again. The disgusting party thrown for Amelia rages on—a perfect decoy for Henry to steal Natalie away from me. Anxiety winds tighter in my mind as I try to piece together what to do next.

I know for sure it's got to be Henry that has her. I can feel it in my bones. And he's sucking at the teat of the Armory. The only logical way to find Natalie is to figure out a way to infiltrate their clan.

My pulse hammers out of control. There is the small issue that I'm essentially a traitor to my kind, but so is Henry. He changed a vision and the Armory still accepted him. Maybe I'm even more valuable as a traitor, more willing to take risks. Plus, I'm trained to kill. Those culty fucks should consider me an asset.

Just when a shred of optimism flickers through my body, I hear a voice call after me, like nails on a chalkboard.

"Hey! Wes! What the hell?"

It's Ciel. Cracking my neck, I let out a long groan. Saving her life is quickly becoming one of my biggest regrets.

She storms over to me with Adip tagging along not far behind. I'm certain he's going to want answers as to why I nearly stabbed him to death.

"Why did you attack my boyfriend?!" Ciel shrieks.

I volley my gaze between them. I guess they're back together, and I couldn't care less about this fact. These two are nothing more than giant pains in my ass. I really have to question Natalie's choice of friends. *If she's even alive.* No, don't think that way. She has to be alive.

Adip carries the Armory mask in his hand, and that mask certainly doesn't look like the Venetian ones the rest of us have on. Didn't he find anything creepy about wearing a plain white mask that basically covers his entire face?

"Why were you wearing that specific mask?"

"Because it was left for me. We all got masks." He shrugs as if it's no big deal. The incompetence is staggering.

"You didn't find it odd that yours looks so different from everyone else's?"

Adip shakes his head.

See? *Useless.*

"You attacked Adip because you didn't like his mask?" Ciel says. "You're more insane than I thought."

Is this girl serious? She drank my blood and came back to life. She must have a fraction of an idea that me attacking Adip had something to do with the darker parts of my life. Or maybe I'm giving her too much credit.

"I told Adip everything, by the way," she says, folding her arms over her chest in a defiant, pouty stance. "It's your fault. If you hadn't tried to basically murder him in the hallway, I would have kept your secret."

I figured that was coming—that Ciel would open her mouth. I only saved her life to make Natalie indebted to me, and now Natalie's gone, and her stupid friend is a stage-five clinger.

"I won't say anything, man. I swear. Ciel said you saved her life. I think it's cool that you're a witch, or whatever. Is that the formal name for it?"

Adip's words singe through my already frayed mind. I need to refocus. Get the hell off this island, away from this school, and find someone from the Armory. Do what I can to join them. Find Natalie. Hope she's alive. Escape with her. Just the two of us, forever.

And even more importantly, drain every inch of life from Henry Thorne.

My purpose reinforced, I fake some sympathy for Adip. "Look, I'm sorry that I attacked you. There's some weird shit going on right now that doesn't involve you."

Ciel cuts me off. "I knew something was up. It's like my skin always has goosebumps ever since, well, you know. What's going on? Can we help?"

Great. Now tweedle-dumb and tweedle-dumber want to be my sidekicks. I'd rather slice my dagger across my own neck.

"There's nothing you can do, but thanks. I'll catch up with you guys later. And I appreciate your discretion."

Before they can say another word, I'm racing back to my dorm room, the rush of vengeance on my mind.

❧

Adrenaline rips through my fingers as I sprawl out the photos contained within the file that I stole from Amelia. My eyes comb over the photos, desperate to recognize anyone besides Henry. Anyone who might be able to get me "in." Anyone I can manipulate, convince that I want to join their fucked-up little fringe army.

The task proves meaningless. I don't know any of these people, which means I won't be able to find anyone else who knows them.

My only real connection to other precogs were my brother and my uncle, and both of them are gone. Being an assassin means you're an eternal loner. Socializing with other precogs was never taught or encouraged, because any person could become your mark at any time. Befriending someone makes it trickier to when you need to strip their life away.

I comb my memory, realizing there is one other person I know. Well, I don't really know him well, but we've met.

Burak. The man who trained my uncle to become a killer. The man who gave him that book of magic to study, the one I stole, and paid dearly for that transgression. But those nights of agony were worth it to gain certain skills.

I wasn't supposed to meet Burak at all. But as a curious kid, I followed my uncle everywhere, especially when he didn't know I was trailing him. I considered it practice. If I could successfully track a trained killer, I could track anyone.

One night, my uncle ordered me and my brother to go to sleep while he slipped out. My brother was asleep, so I quietly snuck out, following him. Normally, my uncle would travel through the seedier sides of cities—back alleys, deserted corners. But this time, he went to a more upscale, metropolitan part of Seattle.

I watched from a distance as he had what appeared to be a serious discussion with a man. Some time passed and I grew bored, planning to sneak back home myself. What a stupid idea.

I'm not sure if my uncle or Burak noticed me, but Burak was the one who snatched me up and carried me to a back room, tossing me down on the hard concrete. Like a pathetic child, I begged and apologized for disobeying my uncle, but Burak didn't care about my cries. He wanted to make sure I never disobeyed him again. I'm pretty sure I blacked out at that point, either because he knocked me out, or because whatever happened in that room was so traumatizing that my brain refuses to remember.

That was the last I saw Burak in person, but he fascinated me enough that I kept tabs on him over the years. I became impressed with how visible he is as a tech investor and philanthropist while living an undercover life as a precog assassin. I figure it's his way to get easier access to people. To earn their trust. To make it so no one would suspect he's a cold-blooded murderer. In a way, I look up to him. That level of deception is admirable.

If there's anyone who could help me find Natalie, he could be the guy. He's intelligent, connected, and in the upper echelons of the authority.

If he doesn't try to kill me first.

But I do have leverage. There are certain marks who have not been successfully disposed of. One of those marks would be me.

Another is Natalie.

If I promise to deliver Natalie to him on a silver platter, perhaps he'd be intrigued enough to keep me alive and take me up on my offer. After my experience with him before, he seems the type to fuck around and find out.

All I have to do is convince him to help me find Natalie.

And then, I'll kill him and Henry. Two for one. And be reunited with her.

CHAPTER TWENTY-NINE

NATALIE

I'M NOT SURE how much time passes before the boat docks at a small, seemingly private island on the Washington coast, but it feels like an eternity. The Canadian shoreline splits to the right. I recognize the landmarks, so at least I know we're still in the United States. Not that it's much different out here in Western Washington when you're lingering right at the border.

And not that it matters much once you've been kidnapped by someone who likely wants to kill you. Someone you fell for. I gulp down the thought.

As we climb off the boat onto the shore, I think about running, but there's only one path leading into the woods. The rest of the ground is covered in thick cedar and fir trees. Dead branches with giant thorns smother the ground. It doesn't exactly seem like anyone else is on this strange, small island. No one else to help. No one to hear my screams.

Henry leads me down the sole path about a half mile. I trudge behind him, cocooned in the blanket, my feet snug in the spare sneakers he had stowed in his backpack. He came prepared for this trek, which only amplifies the unease twisting through my stomach.

We finally reach a small, somewhat dilapidated cottage. It would be charming in the right hands, but given that this is more likely to be somewhere that precogs lock you up and throw away the key, this is no rustic chic Airbnb.

Using a key from his bag, Henry unlocks the door and steps inside, turning on a small lantern by the door. I pause for a moment at the doorway, taking in my surroundings. The path appears to dead-end at this house. Nowhere to run, left or right. Henry has a key, which means I might be able to steal that from him, if I play my cards right. And there's glass on the windows, so at least if I were to break one, I'd have a temporary weapon to escape. I used glass to fend off Amelia. Maybe it will work on Henry too.

Henry's eyes lock onto mine, sending a flash of anxiety through my body. I know he can't read minds—at least, I think he can't—but he does have visions…about me.

"Come inside," he says with a warm, inviting tone, as if this is some romantic weekend getaway. Considering he's drugged and kidnapped me, likely keeping me hostage until I'm killed, I'd say that ship has certainly sailed.

I stay glued to the spot, the door still open. "Someone will come looking for me, you know."

A chuckle escapes his throat and his tone turns cruel. "Who, Wes?"

"Exactly."

He offers a dismissive shake of his head. "I should have known you'd say that. The fact that you even want him to find you is…" His voice fades into silent rage.

Wes is no prize, but he's acting like he's so much better than him.

"What is that supposed to mean? Or are you just going to keep ignoring all my questions?"

As expected, he turns away and ignores me.

Surveying the cottage, I notice a lantern. And to my left outside, an axe alongside firewood. Plenty of weapons. Plenty of options. But he has a weapon, too, so I need to play my cards right.

Before I can process another thought, Henry storms over, slamming the door to the cottage, backing me against it.

I press against the door as his hand curls around my back, twisting the lock. Snarling at him, I move my own hand, unlocking the bolt—just to mess with him.

He grabs my wrist and slams it above my head, moving so close that his hips are pressing into me. My breath whooshes from my lungs as he cages me in.

"Go ahead, Natalie. Try to escape. There's nowhere you can go that I won't be able to track you down and drag you back here."

I jerk my arm from his grip, glaring into those bright green eyes. I used to think they were beautiful. Now they just look mossy and vicious.

"Fuck you." I shove against him, trying to move him away.

He doesn't budge. "I warned you," he says.

"Or what? You're going to tie me up again? Kill me? Because you joined some shitty cult and do everything they say now? You don't control anything."

Henry grimaces, his face twisting into a rage. He spins me around before I can protest, slamming the front of my body into the stone door. He grips my wrists behind my back, tying them up again. Once he's done, he pushes me down into a chair, the rickety material creaking under my body.

He turns his back to me, shoving some logs into a wood-burning oven, lighting a match.

Fire. Another weapon.

While he's distracted, I take in the rest of my surroundings. The cabin is one small room. A kitchen with an old oven and deep basin sink. This chair and fireplace. And a single bed, off to my right.

The fire ignites and the warmth unfurls over my body, making me realize how cold I am. A chill rushes up my spine and my body shivers.

Henry wanders over to the bed, stripping off a blanket. For a second, I suspect he'll try and smother me with it, but instead, he wraps the wool around my body.

One moment, he's smashing me against a door, binding my hands. The next, he's cuddling me up in a blanket. Hot and cold. *Always.*

He stalks over to the kitchen area, clanging a few metal pots around. *Another weapon.*

"So what's your plan?" I ask, pathetically hoping for some real answers.

He doesn't reply, and anger coasts through my body.

I try again. "What do you want from me? Please, just tell me *something.* Anything."

He slams one of the pots against the countertop, turning to face me with a flat expression that's somehow more terrifying than when he looks angry. Locking his gaze on mine, he stalks over, hovering over me. Leaning down, he gets into my face, pressing his hands against the arms of the chair, nearly tipping me backwards. "Just trust me. Before we can talk, I need to…" He trails off, his sharp lack of communication causing me to rage.

Trust him?

He pushes away, and there's an instant relief when he's not towering over me.

"I'm supposed to trust you? While I'm tied up and rotting away here in this cabin? Is this all part of your plan to torture me?"

Henry snickers. "You think it's torture to have warmth, food, a roof over your head?"

I scoff. "When someone's taken me against my will, then yes."

"And yet you had no problem pushing me away to play house with Wes."

A sharp jab of anger punches through me. "You were about to kill him. What was I supposed to do?"

"He came in that place and saw me there. I asked for help and he just left me behind, probably hoping I'd burn to death, just so he could have you."

My breath cuts off, thinking back to that moment. Wes never mentioned seeing Henry inside that place. *Of course he didn't.*

Things begin to lock into place.

"I had no idea." And I didn't, but this fact doesn't seem to ease Henry's anger. "Is that what this is? Are you punishing me for what he did?"

"No, but you should feel lucky to be away from him."

My mind scrambles, trying to process that I'm tied up here, awaiting who knows what fate, and that Henry thinks I should feel lucky.

"He's no saint, but at least Wes didn't kidnap me or want to kill me. I'm not sure I can say the same for you."

Henry shoots me a gruesome look. "So you're okay with what Wes did to your mother?"

My heart spasms in shock at his words. *My mother?* Panic sloshes through my stomach, rising up to my throat.

"Are you trying to tell me that Wes killed my mother?"

"His uncle killed her. Wes's job was to track her to make that possible."

My jaw drops, reality slamming into my brain. Is this true? Of course it would be true. That was Wes's job. I just never considered that my mother could have been his mark too.

The air seems to thicken in the room as Henry digs into his backpack, yanking out a small notepad. My heart kicks against my ribs as he walks it over to me, opening up the first page.

Inside, undoubtedly, is Wes's handwriting. The date scrawled at the top: weeks before my mother's death. Underneath, it reads, *Target: Madeline Covington.*

My eyes widen, reality wrenching my stomach.

I wasn't his only mark. My mother was too. Except he let that execution play out.

And I'll never, ever forgive him for that.

CHAPTER THIRTY

WES

AS I FANTASIZE about getting rid of Henry, memories of killing my uncle float into my brain. It felt different than I thought it would. I remember the exact moment—hiding out in the woods, waiting for Henry to change his vision and save Natalie, only for Henry to strike my uncle in the head with a rock.

A fucking rock.

It knocked him unconscious, but he would have woken up, likely not long after he was struck. Henry took his sweet old time doting on Natalie, tending to her wounded knee. I nearly took my dagger and stabbed him for being so stupid and unaware. A rock won't kill a precog.

And I really should have taken care of Henry back then when I had the chance.

After Natalie urged Henry to take off, her stupid ex-boyfriend Jack came clawing through the woods looking for her. It wasn't long before he got her away from my uncle's body. That's when I was able to finish the deed.

I thought I'd feel proud, or at least delighted to watch every inch of my uncle's life drain away. But I was robbed of this pleasure. He was already unconscious and there wasn't much time before others came to check on the body. I'd hoped my first kill would be drawn out and satisfying. And while the subject of my kill was exciting, the act of it was anything but. Another thing Henry Thorne ruined.

The wind whips against my face as the ferry pulls away from the dock, making its way across the Puget Sound to Seattle. I'm situated on the upper-level outdoor deck, avoiding the crowds tucked in the seating down below. Ferry rides are a great time to reflect on regrets and plan to do things better next time. In this case, making my next kill worth it. And *oh, it will be.*

Burak was easier to track down than I'd expected, almost as if he was waiting for me. After some quick research, I discovered that he's the keynote presenter at some tech founder conference in Seattle, a short ferry ride away from Lockwood. The conference hosts parties that stretch late into the night, and Burak is the guest of honor. With thousands of hipster tech fucks smashed into one room, it should be relatively easy for me to sneak in and get his attention.

A familiar voice calls out behind me, shouting my name. "Wes!"

My hands grip against the railing, twisting my gaze to find Ciel and Adip scurrying towards me. The blood in my veins ices over. Clearly, they followed me onto this ferry. Tracked me.

"What are you doing here?" I can't withhold my contempt.

"I can feel you're in trouble. We came to help," Ciel blurts out.

Feel? How can she feel anything going on in my life? Stupid girl. These two morons think they can help, when all they're capable of doing is ruining my chances of finding Natalie.

"You saved my life. I want to repay the favor," Ciel says.

"I just want to know where Natalie is," Adip says. "Where is she?"

I grind my teeth together in frustration. What a pity that we're on this ferry with loads of people down below or I'd knock them overboard. There were many times when someone would get in the way of my uncle carrying out a hit. Unfortunate casualties, just part of the job, he'd say. Now, just when I thought this mission to find Burak was easy, these two have to go and fuck it up.

"I don't need your help," I say, hoping they'll back off and go flit off into the city and leave me the hell alone.

"Where's Natalie?" Adip asks again.

I knew it was only a matter of time before people would start questioning where she was, but I don't need anyone screwing up my own investigation. If someone has so much as touched her or looked at her wrong, they're going to be very, very sorry.

"Back on campus," I say, hoping my lie will be enough to deter them.

"No, she's not. I looked everywhere for her. That was part of the reason we went after you," Adip says.

"Well, and because I knew Wes was in trouble. Do you think when you did that witchcraft stuff and brought me back to life, something happened? Like we're connected somehow?"

You've got to be kidding me. What a mess. And one thing you learn as a trained assassin is that you cannot let things get sloppy. I should have known when I saved Ciel's life that there would be ramifications, that she'd go and blab to her boyfriend, serving up secrets like candy. *Pathetic.* Now she thinks we have some special connection. The thought couldn't be more vile.

But I can't kill them, as much as I'd like to. They're Natalie's friends, and she'd never forgive me. There are enough things she's already forgiven me for, and at least one thing that would drive her away forever—my involvement in her mother's death.

Like Natalie, Madeline Covington was nothing more than a name in my notebook. A fresh page with ink at the top. A new mark.

I knew very little about Madeline, an odd assignment. My uncle was more secretive about her than other marks, and asked me to avoid my normal research. He gave me her name, her photo, and some intel that she was meeting up with some unnamed precog who was also causing trouble.

It took me less than forty-eight hours to learn her pattern and give my uncle the perfect "in" to kill her. I didn't think much of her, didn't even know she had a daughter…until Natalie became my new mark, and I recognized the last name.

My marks don't intrigue me, just a bunch of boring, useless, clueless souls. But Natalie interested me from the moment I laid eyes on her. There's a palpable energy and heat that radiates from her, like a wildfire spreading into my skin. Something exciting and dangerous that I still can't quite put my finger on.

But Natalie can never, ever know that I tracked her mother. Or I'm certain she'll never want to see me again.

"I promise you that she's back at Lockwood. Why don't you both just enjoy the city when we arrive, then hop on the next ferry back to campus and go see her?" I say to Ciel and Adip.

They exchange worried glances, and I can tell they're not going along with my explanation. I heave out a sigh. It should be no problem to lose them once we get off the ferry, but the last thing I want right now is small talk with these morons.

Ciel takes a step closer to me with a threatening gaze. "I know you're lying," she says.

My jaw twitches in aggravation. "What makes you say that?"

"Because I told you. I can feel it. I can feel you."

My gut twists at her words. *What the fuck is she talking about?*

"You sound insane, you know that, right?" I have zero patience for Ciel to pull some mystic, aura-reading bullshit on me.

"Ever since you saved my life, I get this weird feeling when something bad happens. When you attacked Adip, my body, like, started convulsing. And then I had the same reaction when you took off and left the party. And other times too. So I know there's something going on, Wes. And I have a feeling it has to do with Natalie."

Could she be telling the truth? Did I unwittingly unlock some weird connection between us that allows her to feel what I'm feeling?

Well, I've got news for you, Ciel. Things are about to get a lot worse. And for Natalie's sake, I need to keep you quiet and out of the way when they do.

CHAPTER THIRTY-ONE

NATALIE

MY STOMACH CLENCHES and twists, and I'm worried I might vomit all over this cabin floor.

Wes tracked my mom. *Wes got her killed.*

This is something I should have figured out on my own. I know Wes is an assassin, that he was sent to track me. Why didn't I put things together that he did the same for my mom? Even though she's long gone, my heart ribbons into grief, thinking of how much I've let her down. How distracted I let myself become that I couldn't even figure that out.

What else have I been missing?

"I'm sorry," Henry says. "I didn't want to be the one to tell you that."

My chest pulls tight and nerves erupt in my stomach. I don't need his pity. His apologies aren't needed or wanted right now. Or ever.

"Wes is not a good person, Natalie."

As if I didn't know that already. When someone shows you who they are, believe them. I let Wes show me over and over again who he is, and still let myself get carried away because he was a good way to forget the pain.

And now I know he's the one who caused it.

I spit words back at Henry, and not because I want to stick up for Wes. "You don't get to act like the better guy. You have me tied up, refusing to tell me anything."

Henry scoffs, and I'm certain he's about to ignore me again, but he takes a seat on the bed across from me. He leans forward and my body instinctively curls away. If he thinks this is some moment of bonding, he's got another thing coming.

"I just told you something pretty major," he says.

"Yeah, about Wes. What about you? You haven't taken accountability for anything you've done, including kidnapping me so I can await my death."

"You're not going to die," he says bluntly.

My brain scrambles at his words and I'm pretty certain he's fucking with me.

"Please just stop with the games. I'm done."

His gaze cuts to the ground and he looks wounded. It must all be part of his act to distract from the fact that he drugged, kidnapped, and threatened me more than once.

"I'm not playing games with you," he says. He pushes up from the bed and stalks over, looming over me, circling behind my chair. His hand touches my back, sending a shockwave up my spine.

"Don't touch me."

But he doesn't listen, his hands fumbling against mine. It doesn't take long for me to realize that he's untied my hands again. I twirl my wrists, trying to get back the circulation.

"There. You think I'm playing games? You're free."

Free.

My mind races through a million possibilities. I could grab a weapon, one of the many in this room, and hit him. I could run, though I have no idea where we are or if I could find help.

He strides to a nearby chest of drawers, fishing out some clothing. "Put that on," he commands, as my eyes scan over the familiar Lockwood uniform—a blouse, a jacket, a skirt, and tights.

"Where did you get these?"

His gaze shifts away, evading my eyes. "I took them from your dorm room. It was all I could manage to grab before you came back to your room…with him."

The realization hits me like a punch. He snuck into my room and took one of my uniforms, planning for this day to come.

He turns his back to give me some privacy. My skin prickles as I slide my dress off, keeping my gaze trained on his broad back. My eyes stay locked on him, tracing the lines of his shoulder blades through his shirt.

I can't help but shiver, a mix of cold and anticipation. Slowly, I pull the blouse over my arms, my fingers fumbling over the buttons. The tension in the room is thick, a charged silence broken only by the sound of my shaky breaths.

Henry's voice cuts through the silence. "I changed a vision to save you. Do you really think I'd risk everything only to hurt you now?"

His words split through my chest. He sounds sincere, but I know the truth.

"You only saved me because Wes convinced you to do it."

Henry turns to face me, my blouse only half buttoned, my bra and underwear exposed. He doesn't even seem to notice. "Use your head, Natalie. Who cares if he encouraged me? I'm the one who lost my entire life…for you."

Anger simmers deep in my gut. "I wish you had just let me die then. It's better than being trapped here with my life hanging in the balance."

Henry flings forward, gripping my shoulders with such force

that I'm knocked off balance. I flop back onto the bed. Before I can get my bearings, he's on top of me.

"This is why I can't tell you anything, answer any of your questions. Because at this point, you'd rather die than be here with me."

I'm rendered completely speechless with his body pressed on top of mine, his words lingering in the tight space between us. The room is completely silent, other than our racing heartbeats and harsh exhales.

He lowers his head, pushing his body to stand. The mattress rises with the absence of his weight. He slumps down in the chair and my heart claws at my chest. There are so many things I want to say, but I can't. *Won't.*

Henry claims he doesn't want to kill me, yet he's got me hidden away in this cabin in the middle of nowhere. He claims I'm free to leave, but my gut tells me it's all part of some twisted test. I need to consider my next move.

"It's late," he says, his voice laced with disappointment. "You take the bed to sleep."

Feeling exposed, I yank my uniform blouse around my body. "And where will you sleep?"

"The chair. The floor. I don't know. I'm not much of a sleeper."

He's said that before, long before he changed his vision. The night we sat in his room and studied, innocently eating macaroni and cheese. A piece of me longs for that moment back. Another part wishes it never happened.

I pull on the rest of my uniform and lie back in the bed, yanking the covers up over my body, knowing damn well I won't be able to sleep myself. Henry's situated in the chair across from the bed, positioned to stare right at me. Everything is so fucked up that I can't imagine lying here all night with him just leering.

"There's room in bed if you want to lie down," I say, breaking the icy silence. At least this way, he's next to me and not just staring at me from across the room.

He pauses, considering the tension that still hangs between us, but I insist, "It's fine."

Slowly, he moves towards the bed, the creak of the mattress filling the room as he climbs in. I can instantly feel his warmth as he slips under the covers. We're close—so close that I can feel the tension radiating from his body.

I turn away from him, facing the wall, creating a gap between us. I can sense him shifting towards me, his body curving slightly as if trying to close the distance. I shut my eyes as his breath lightly brushes my neck, sending a chill down my spine despite the warmth he radiates. The silence wraps around us again, and his fingers graze up my neck, winding into my curls.

"What are you doing?"

"Your hair was on my side. I didn't want to accidentally roll over on it and hurt you."

Unbelievable.

I whirl around to confront him. "You're worried about tugging my hair, but you can drug and kidnap me without a second thought?"

"It was the only way I could get you to agree to come with me. You would have fought me otherwise. You're loyal…to Wes. I'm trying to help."

"Why do you even want to? I thought you hated me."

Henry chuckles, acting incredulous. "Hate you? Is that what you think? Don't you remember anything about our time together?"

Yes, I remember all of it. *Far too well.* But I won't give him that satisfaction.

"I barely know you. Nothing you do makes sense and it's like every exchange we have is shrouded in fourteen layers of secrets."

He reaches his hand up to my face, tracing a finger over my jaw.

I should slap it away, but the less rational part of my brain is firing to let him keep going.

"Look into my eyes," he practically growls.

I extend my hand, capturing his wrist in my grasp. My rational mind argues that I shouldn't let him touch me, and yet a much louder voice has been dying for the comfort of his touch for what seems like an eternity.

"Your eyes are bright green right now," he says.

I begin to protest, but he swipes his thumb over my lips, urging me not to fight. "There's a reason that's happening."

"Yeah, genetics. My mom's eyes turned green at my age too."

Henry closes the distance between us, inching his body closer. "There's so much I want to tell you."

My heart skips and anticipation lodges in my chest. There's a sharp ache of longing, for information. "So tell me."

"You have to promise not to try and run."

"Okay." Although I can't exactly promise that until I hear his revelations. I just need answers. Anything at this point.

"The precog authority came for me at Lockwood. That's why I left you there, not because I wanted to. I was hoping if they were able to take me, they would leave you alone. After you found me and I saw you with Wes, I didn't know what to believe. It didn't take long for this fringe group called the Armory to capture me, and I pretended to go along with their beliefs so I could gain access to some information, figure out what the hell is going on, who I am, *what* I am."

My middle squeezes as I process what he's saying so far. "So what did you find out?"

"A lot of things, about how things work. I'm not a precog. I'm a Cambion—half-demon, half-human."

His revelation burns down my throat. "You're a... demon?"

"Half. It's when a human procreates with a demon who tricked them, supposedly. Those babies are taken and raised in that facility, the place you found me. Humans can't have the babies in hospitals because we don't breathe until we're two years old. That would set off some alarms."

My brain nearly cracks from his words. He's a demon? Babies don't breathe? "What happens to the human? The mother?"

Henry shakes his head, a grave look in his eye. "I know this all sounds crazy," he says, answering my thoughts. "It's why I wanted to wait to tell you, at least until you were less angry with me, until you could trust me again. I don't know what poison Wes has leaked into your mind."

I'm not sure how much of this story time I can mentally handle, but I swallow down my fear. This is what I've been waiting for—answers.

"The facility where you found me, it also doubles as rehab centers for precogs who break the rules, like changing visions. It's all about order and control. They give you pills, but they're just placebos, just to see if you'll take them." He rolls up his sleeve, revealing his tattoo. "And this marking? Also control. There's a story going around about the psi symbol as an ancestral honor, remembering their sacrifice, but it's all bullshit. They just want to see if we'll show up on our thirteenth birthday, consent to being branded. Whoever came up with the idea is apparently Greek, and they just picked a random letter."

Shockwaves race through my gut. "So the authority is basically a dictatorship using extreme control tactics?"

"Exactly. But things shifted at the authority with the people in charge. The Armory used to operate on the fringes, wanting to bring back a more brutal, restrictive, militant way of being. Authority members in recent years were trying to change things, bring in diverse viewpoints, make things better."

My fingers white-knuckle the pillow as I take this all in. "Better?

They're still imprisoning people. And obviously killing them too. That's what Wes was trained to do."

"There's still a lot I don't know. But that shift in power meant a shift in focus, and the authority wants to change how they do things. Now they're working *with* the Armory, and the task is to find those on the outside who present the biggest threat to our kind."

"And who is that?"

"You," Henry says.

Terror wraps around my limbs. Before I can question him more, a loud bang outside shocks us both to our core, tearing us from the moment.

Henry grabs me, swooping me off the bed and onto the floor for safety.

"What is that?"

He covers my mouth, curling me into his strong grip. "Stay quiet. We can't let them know we're in here."

CHAPTER THIRTY-TWO

WES

"You're lying, Wes!" Ciel shrieks like an errant child, and all I can think about is how satisfying it might feel to toss her overboard right now. Sadly, the ferry is already gliding up to the dock and she'd be able to swim to safety.

A real pity.

Blowing out a deep breath, I continue filling in Ciel and Adip on what happened to Natalie. Or rather, my abridged (aka false) version of it.

My knuckles grip the edge of the ferry with anticipation. If we could just dock this thing, I can scramble off and find Burak. Ciel and Adip will never be able to catch me.

"So Natalie isn't at school. Where is she?" Ciel asks.

My head snaps up, so focused on getting off this damn ferry that I nearly forgot I was mid-conversation with her.

"With her father," I lie.

"There's no way Natalie is with her father. She hates him! Stop lying!" she shrieks again. Ciel stares me straight in the eye, clearly wanting answers.

"She's trying to mend fences," I lie again.

Ciel folds her arms over her chest. "Her father replaced her with a new family and didn't even tell her about it. He was obviously cheating on her mom with that woman before she died if he already has a baby with her."

What Ciel doesn't seem to realize is that I couldn't care less about Natalie's sordid family situation. Her fake father. His new wife and baby. None of it matters. The only thing that does is that Natalie is back with me, where she rightfully belongs.

The ferry docks and the speaker crackles with an announcement. Before Ciel can muster another annoying word, I race over to the deck and make my way off the ferry. A cluster of passengers swell behind me, trapping Ciel and Adip, making it easy to lose them.

With Ciel and Adip left behind where they belong, I track down Burak at some ridiculous afterparty raging inside the Seattle Convention Center. It doesn't take long for me to sneak past security, steal a badge, and make my way to the room where a DJ blares awful EDM music and coked-up tech bros try to pick up women who were clearly paid to be there.

I decide to take matters into my own hands, yanking the fire alarm and effectively shutting down the party.

As the deafening alarm rings, Burak locks eyes with me from across the room, and I can tell he recognizes me. That's right. I'm no boy anymore, asshole.

I shove my way through a sea of nerdy fucks to get outside, winding around a private, roped-off construction area. Making my way through the maze of scaffolding, it doesn't take long for Burak to catch me.

"What are you doing here?"

"I need your help."

His eyes darken and a tendril of fear starts to leech up my spine. Not much scares me, but this guy has some special way of making your insides curdle.

"And why would I help you?"

My fingers glide into my coat, tightening around my dagger. "Because you have no choice," I say. In a split second, I spin Burak around, my dagger pressing against his throat.

A chuckle escapes his lips. "Your uncle taught you well. Where is he these days?"

"I killed him. I'm surprised you didn't know."

I can feel Burak tense in my grip and I realize he must be telling the truth. If he doesn't know my uncle was murdered, maybe he's not as plugged in to things as I'd hoped. But I've already come this far. Might as well see what he does know.

"And if you don't help me, you're next," I say, threatening.

Before I can even realize what's happening, Burak manages to dislodge from my grip, twisting my body and slamming it face-first onto the ground. *Ouch.*

"Confident little one," Burak says.

Blood pools in my mouth, mixed with sawdust. I spit onto the ground. "I'm not so little anymore."

"No, but you are stupid to confront me this way. I always told your uncle you'd be a problem. You were different. He didn't listen. He cared for you."

Searing pain flares through my head, and now it's my turn to chuckle. "It really was a mistake coming here. I didn't realize you were such an idiot, thinking my uncle cared anything for me."

Clutching the back of my head, Burak slams it into the ground again. Dizziness overtakes me, but I suck up the pain and nausea.

"I'll give you five more seconds before I take that dagger and end your life. Tell me what the hell you're doing here."

"I need help finding Natalie Covington."

"Covington," Burak says, his voice haunted. He lets my head flop to the ground, backing away. "I thought both Covingtons were supposed to be taken care of," he says.

Pressing up onto my hands, I swivel my neck to face him. "Not Natalie. My uncle was sent to kill her, but I killed him instead."

Burak's face twists in what appears to be fear. "This is bad, Wesley. The Covingtons are..." He trails off, pinching the bridge of his nose. Why the hell is he so flustered by Natalie being alive? Maybe all that time playing in the sandbox with those tech dweebs made him lose his edge.

I push myself to stand, wobbling on my feet. "The Covingtons are what?"

"Not human, that's for sure. They're very dangerous to our kind. That's why they both needed to be destroyed. Especially Natalie. What the hell were you thinking?"

Confusion and anger war together in my mind. Seriously, has this guy totally lost his mind? The clock is ticking and I'm running the fuck out of patience.

"Her powers have the ability to become greater than ours. You understand that?"

Sure, there have been a few weird things happening with Natalie. She had the strength to finish off Oliver. And Amelia, although neither of their bodies were recovered. She's put me in my place a few times.

"You have no idea where Natalie is?" he says.

"That's why I came to you."

Burak shakes his head, pacing, mumbling under his breath. "Tilki. Tilki."

My chest clenches in frustration. "I don't understand what the hell you're saying."

"Tilki," he says again, like somehow repeating this phrase will help me figure it out. *The fuck?*

"You're gonna have to spell it out for me, man."

"It's not easy to explain."

"Well, can you at least try instead of babbling incoherently?" Damn, I need a joint right now.

"Tilki means fox in Turkish. That's my first language."

I can't help but burst out laughing. "Wait, are you trying to say that Natalie is like some shape-shifting fox? C'mon dude, next you're going to tell me werewolves exist."

His face screws up and it's his turn to laugh at me. "You're so naïve to think that only humans and precogs exist on this planet."

"Okay, so let's go with Natalie is a fox." I nearly lose my shit even saying that out loud. "Tell me why we're so scared of some furry critter?"

"She's not an actual fox, you stupid shit," Burak snaps. "We don't know exactly what Natalie is, but she's not human. The best way I can describe her and her mother is foxlike—tricksters, seducers, but present as faithful friends and lovers. Everything about her captivates you and you're not even sure why."

A bit of what he says rings true. I swallow back my nerves.

"Make no mistake, that girl is deceptive for her own amusement and advancement. And when she turns nineteen, it will get worse. That much I know."

"If she's so dangerous, why didn't the authority take care of her a long time ago?"

"There was an agreement, but it was broken. And it was your and your uncle's job to take care of her, which you clearly failed."

Irritation winds through my brain. "Why does everyone think Natalie is so dangerous?"

"Trust me. You'll want to kill her before you find out."

CHAPTER THIRTY-THREE

NATALIE

HENRY CLENCHES HIS hand over my mouth as footsteps crunch on the gravel outside the cabin. I can feel his warm breath against my neck as panic squeezes my chest.

Our eyes latch on to the window. The footsteps continue on, growing quieter until only the two of us exist in the silence.

"We've got to leave," Henry says, wrapping an arm around my waist and pulling me to my feet.

"Who was that?" Rivulets of adrenaline pour through my body.

Henry doesn't respond, focused on gathering up his things, slinging his backpack over his shoulder. He flings his coat in my direction, followed by a firm demand. "Put that on."

I hurriedly wrap his coat over my uniform, sliding my feet into the sneakers that he gave me on the boat. "Where are we going?"

He presses ahead, not waiting for me to catch up as I scurry after him.

"Are you going to answer me?"

He whips his gaze to mine, pressing a finger to his lips to quiet me. "They're not far from here."

"Who?"

"We'll talk about it later. There's no time." He motions for me to follow him and I resolve that he's not going to answer me again, at least not now.

We push our way down an overgrown trail that stems out behind the cabin. I guess there was another way out of this place.

We walk in silence for what feels like ten miles, but likely isn't even half of one. Henry extends his arm in front of my chest to stop me in my tracks, nearly giving me whiplash.

The faint sound of voices echoes in the distance. Henry leads me down a shorter path that switches back off the main trail. In the distance is a campsite with at least a dozen members of the Armory, maybe more, wearing their masks. We halt immediately, keeping ourselves hidden behind the forest's natural camouflage. I swallow hard as I try to count them all. Every single one of these people wants me dead.

What if Henry is one of them?

Suddenly, I'm aware of the cold reality. Henry is a member of this group. What if this is all some sick game, and I'm nothing more than an animal awaiting my slaughter? I feel nauseous, nearly delirious at this thought.

I back away from Henry and spin on my heels, about to race off to I don't even know where. Before I can make any significant movements, Henry grabs me around the waist, twisting me around and pinning me against a tree. He grips my chin, his eyes pinning me in place. "Where are you going?"

"This was a trick, wasn't it? You set me up. You're about to have me killed."

"I already told you, I'm not going to let you die. Don't you believe me by now? I'm trying to save you. Stop trying to make me the bad guy. That's Wes, not me."

He releases me and the wind bites at my skin as I feel the freedom from his grip. My body burns with indignation. My fate could lie in that Armory campsite. I don't know what to believe.

"Fine. Run if you want. Or come with me." He extends his hand, reaching out for mine.

I stare down at it, my heart twisted in confusion and agony.

I decide to trust him…to choose him.

We start backing away from the campsite, until a snapping twig pierces the stillness. Fear squeezes my chest as I catch an Armory member, their sinister mask glistening under the faint moonlight, starting in our direction.

Henry clasps my hand, pulling me away from the clearing, our feet crunching against the branch-littered ground as we retreat in the opposite direction.

Dread pulsates through my mind as we dart in a million directions, turn abruptly, switch back, and race down sharp turns, evading the trained hunters hot on our trail.

Through some combination of sheer luck and desperation, we finally lose them. Our breaths come in ragged gasps as we plunge deeper into the woods, following a snaking trail which threads through more overgrown trees.

Eventually, the dense tree line gradually recedes, revealing a dilapidated railroad track stretching into the distance.

Beyond it lies an abandoned town. Or at least, it appears to be. Boarded-up doors. Cracked windows. Everything rusted over and lifeless. As if everyone fled this place decades ago and never looked back.

In the distance, there's a lone light shining from a bakery. I guess this place isn't completely desolate and forgotten. As we charge over to it, I notice a sign for a small bed and breakfast. A slice of life in this skeleton of a town.

Still gripping my hand, Henry cranes his neck, checking to make sure no one has caught up to us. But we're alone, swallowed up by the stillness of our surroundings. A relief, at least momentarily.

Movement catches the corner of my eye and I turn my gaze to the bakery. I see the back of a woman baking loaves of bread and other pastries. My stomach wrenches with hunger.

"What is this place?"

"Somewhere we can be safe, at least for a bit," Henry says.

The sun begins to rise and I realize that it's about to be morning. A few pedestrians trickle through the town, carrying coffees and newspapers, further proof that this place feels like it's trapped in another time. I release Henry's hand and stumble back, tucking around the bakery, feeling exposed. Unsure of who I can trust.

"It's okay, really," Henry says. "The Armory doesn't come here. There's some treaty in place. They're not allowed to cross this part of town."

Confused, I look around at all the normal faces. Are all of these people precogs? Cambions? Humans? Or whatever I am?

"Do you want something to eat?" Henry asks.

I nod without thinking, hunger winning out over any of my other thoughts.

He steps into the bakery, handing the woman some cash from his pocket in exchange for two coffees, some bread, and a few pastries. I follow him to an outdoor bench and take a seat next to him. I rip off a piece of freshly baked bread, letting the warmth fill my mouth and stomach.

I catch Henry watching me eat, a smirk on his face. Eating like a rabid dog must look amusing to him, but I don't find anything funny about this situation.

"Do you trust me now?" he asks.

I meet his gaze, my heart ricocheting around. It's almost like I can feel his heart beating against my skin too.

"I don't know," I answer honestly.

His eyes flicker with disappointment, but he gives me an understanding nod.

"When are you going to tell me more about the Armory? About what's going on?" I ask.

"When you start trusting me," he answers.

Touché.

Suddenly, Henry's expression darkens. I follow his eyes, noticing a few members of the Armory in the distance, clearly looking for something. *Or someone.*

Henry grabs my hand and yanks me down an alley, covering my body with his against the hard stone wall.

"I thought you said they don't come here?"

"They don't."

Henry peeks around the corner, and I can tell by his panicked reaction that they're getting closer. "We can't let them see us," he says. "Neither of us will make it out alive, understand?"

The alley dead-ends and we can't go back out on the main street. I spot one of the Armory members crossing by, his head turned in the other direction. We are mere seconds from him seeing our faces.

"Kiss me," I say.

"What?"

I grab Henry's head and yank it to my lips. Pressing my body to his, I deepen the kiss, pouring my soul into it. If we're going to survive, this moment needs to be believable. They need to buy that we're two star-crossed lovers who can't keep their hands off each other, not Henry and Natalie.

But even I can't deny how good this feels. *How right it feels.*

Fluttering open my eyes but keeping my lips locked on Henry, I notice the member of the Armory shift his gaze in our direction.

My heart hammers against my chest, both at the notion of getting caught and being in Henry's embrace.

After an excruciatingly long moment, one that I'm internally both begging to be over and to never stop, the man passes.

We're safe. At least, for now.

I tear my lips away from Henry's and we stare at each other. His jaw visibly clenches and I'm not sure if it's from need, or longing, or fear at nearly getting caught. Or all three. He studies my parted, puffy lips, and for a second, I wonder if he's about to kiss me again.

"He's gone," I say.

"How did you…" He trails off, but I know exactly what he means. How were we able to kiss when last time, it nearly killed me?

The answer is that I've been practicing—with Wes. But it feels cold to say that right now, or to bring him up to Henry at all.

Besides, knowing that Wes was the one who tracked my mom, got her killed, makes me want to take every single sickening kiss back.

Henry's frame hovers over me and the heat between us is palpable. Abruptly, he pushes away from the wall, breaking the tension.

"They're looking for us. It's not safe here. We should go."

CHAPTER THIRTY-FOUR

WES

I'M SITTING ACROSS from Burak in a Turkish café in the middle of Seattle. I got absolutely zero sleep last night, but I'm still riding the high of finding Natalie.

Burak claims he's got a plan to find her, but all I see this jackass doing is drinking Turkish coffee and stuffing his face with pistachio baklava, like we're on some first fucking date.

"Why did you kill your uncle for her?" he asks, picking a crumb from his beard.

"You're asking me questions when you haven't answered any of mine?"

Burak lifts his chin, staring me down, making it clear he's not going to comply.

"I saved Natalie because I love her." My lips split into a grin.

"Of course you do. Everything about her is carefully planned to draw you in."

Disgust seeps through my bones. Is he really about to go on and on again about Natalie's foxlike qualities? He's never even met her.

How the fuck would he know? He must think I'm still that naïve little boy he pushed around years ago. Well, I've got news for him.

"You don't know her," I spit out.

"Open your eyes, boy. Love is just a façade."

I drum my fingers on the table, trying to leak out the aggravation building inside from this idiot's words.

He chuckles, as if this is all some kind of fun game for him—us wasting time in this stupid fucking coffee shop while he munches away on Turkish pastries. *Glutton.*

My gaze latches on to a vintage clock in the corner of the café. The long hand moves—*tick, tick, tick*—reminding me that every moment wasted here is a moment that Natalie may not survive. Or another moment she's with Henry. I nearly vomit onto his baklava at the thought.

"Can we wrap this up?" It's not a question.

"We'll go when I say," Burak snaps.

I sneer back at him, frustration slicing through my veins. "We're wasting time. Time we don't have."

Burak shakes his head at me, making a *tsk* sound. "I told you I have a plan, boy. Patience."

"I don't know what the hell you have and I'm definitely not a boy."

He shakes his head with a condescending glare. "You sure act like one. All these proclamations of love about a girl you barely know."

Irritation sputters through my chest as I try to find the words. He makes a good point, but I'll never admit it. Why am I so drawn to Natalie? Why did it feel like love at first sight?

"Don't tell me. It was love at first sight," he says.

My stomach burns as he repeats my thoughts out loud.

"Like I told you, everything about that girl is designed to make you feel that way."

Bile rises in my throat as the more rational side of my brain processes what he's saying. If he's right—if Natalie has some sort of seductive powers or abilities—is this all a lie?

No, it can't be. I refuse it.

"Wes!"

A grating voice cuts through the small café. I glance over and spot Ciel making her way to our table. Anger curls over my skin. Of all the coffee shops in Seattle, how could she possibly find me here?

"Who is this?" Burak eyes Ciel with too much interest.

"No one," I say.

Ciel scoffs, offended. She hisses at me as her gaze flicks between us. "He's lying. I'm—"

Before she can answer, I latch on to Ciel's wrist, dragging her away from the table.

She whimpers. "Ouch, Wes, you're hurting me."

I drag her through the café. Patrons skim their gazes over us as we pass, like we're celebrities and they're loser members of the paparazzi. Once we reach the back corner of a dim hallway, I whirl Ciel around against the wall, wrapping my free hand around her throat.

"This isn't a game, Ciel. How the hell did you find me here?"

Her eyes water at the pressure, and I release my grip ever so slightly. "I tried telling you earlier. Since you saved me, I can feel things. I can feel *you*."

I tighten my hand around her throat again. "What does that even mean?"

She chokes, croaking out the words. "I…sensed…you…were… here."

Releasing her throat, I keep her pinned against the wall. "How? Are you saying you had a vision?" I hope I didn't accidentally give this dimwit my powers.

"No. I just kept walking, and when I got closer to you, my body would, like, heat up. And if I got further away, it would get ice cold."

She sniffles, wiping some stray mascara dripping from the corner of
her eye.

"You're lying."

"I'm not! I'm just as confused as you. I got into a huge fight with
Adip because he thinks I've totally lost it. He said he's going back to
campus to search for Natalie. I don't know! I guess when you saved
me, something weird happened."

Well, fuck. Now I've really done it. So the consequences to saving
someone's life is unlocking their ability to stalk me and have better
tracking abilities than I do.

"Do you need help, miss?"

My gaze cuts to Burak, lurking in the shadowed hallway like
some kind of creep. *He is a creep.* This is on brand for him.

"She's fine," I say, hoping he'll leave us alone.

"I asked the lady, not you."

Glancing down, I realize my fingers are still digging into Ciel's
wrist and I've got her pinned against the wall. I release her as Burak's
eyes narrow, studying us.

"How do you two know each other?" he says.

Ciel pipes up before I can argue, and my heart rate speeds. I do
not need Burak knowing I saved this girl's life. "We go to school
together," she says.

Burak's eyes move between us. "And how did you find him here?"

"It was just a coincidence," Ciel says quickly.

Interesting. My brows dip in confusion. Ciel isn't going to sell me
out? A slight bit of admiration trickles through my chest. *Very slight.*

Burak takes a step closer to Ciel, like somehow looming over her
is going to help him read her mind. "Some coincidence." He turns
his gaze to mine. "We should go. Now." His words are pointed and
urgent. "Finish up whatever this is. I'll meet you outside," he says,
taking off down the hall.

Once Burak is out of sight, my focus goes back to Ciel. A small part of me wants to thank her for not spilling our secret to him, but I can't quite utter the words.

"Where are you going? Are you going to look for Natalie? I knew you were lying. She's not with her father. Where is she?" Ciel continues littering off her annoying questions.

I don't answer, and she puffs out a breath in frustration. Anxiety churns in my gut.

"Yes, I'm going to find Natalie." I finally spill a shred of truth.

Ciel presses. "Do you really trust that guy you're with? He seems kinda creepy. But also hot in a weird way. Kind of like you."

Please shut up, Ciel. "No, I don't trust him."

"Then let me come with you. I can keep him distracted. I'm good at that."

Hmm. It's an interesting proposition. Burak leads me to Natalie. Ciel distracts him. I save my girl. And before Natalie and I run away together, I take care of Burak, Henry, and Ciel. Three birds, one stone.

My lips curl into a grin and I extend my hand to Ciel.

"Sure. I'd love your help."

CHAPTER THIRTY-FIVE

NATALIE

HENRY AND I move at a brisk pace, barreling through the streets, away from any traces of the Armory.

He leads me to an abandoned barn on the outskirts of civilization. The ground is littered with overgrown blackberry thickets that scrape against my ankles as we walk.

He yanks on the barn door and after a few tries, manages to wedge it open. Inside is the rotting skeleton of what once may have been someone's makeshift home. A lone mattress sits in the corner. Bales of hay line the walls.

"We aren't staying long. This is just to rest our legs for a bit," he assures me.

I sink down onto the cold ground, feeling instant relief in my feet.

"I thought you couldn't do that," Henry says, his back turned to me.

"Do what?"

"When you kissed me back there. How were you able to do that?"

I know he's combing for information about Wes. My insides

curdle as his image floats into my mind. *Wes.* The reason my mother was killed. Or part of it, anyway.

"I had some practice. I'm not proud of it." There's no use lying to Henry anymore. Besides, I want more answers from him. Maybe it's time we drop this shielded game and start telling each other the whole truth.

"Practice with Wes, huh?" He twists his gaze to mine, and his glistening green eyes seem to darken.

Anxiety thrums through my veins. "Yes, with Wes. I don't exactly know any other precogs. Or Cambions, I guess. That's what he is too?"

Henry's fist tightens, and I can almost feel the rage spiraling through him.

"I did it to protect myself," I say.

That was certainly one intention, and I stand by it. Distraction was another, and I'm not proud of that choice. Now all I feel is complete disgust for ever letting his lips touch mine. But Henry doesn't have a right to feel wounded.

"Why do you care so much? You left, and I understand now why you did it, but I thought you hated me, that you'd never come back."

He shakes his head in frustration, and my lungs expand as I brace for his answer.

"I thought we…" He trails off, refusing to talk again.

Anger splits through me. "You thought we *what?*"

Henry whirls around to face me and my stomach somersaults. "I was trying to do the right thing, but you saved him that night."

My insides twist at this realization, remembering back to that very moment that I broke up their fight. How I was able to conjure some kind of inhuman strength to throw Henry off of Wes.

"I didn't know he purposely left you inside to die. I didn't know what was going on. You can't blame me for every miscommunication."

He shakes his head as aggravation weaves through my core. "You're right. I'm sorry."

My heart stills with the silence. "Are you going to tell me what just happened? Why you're even here with me?"

Henry moves closer to me, closing the distance between us. "The Armory wanted you taken care of, direct orders from the authority. They believe, for whatever reason, that you present a huge threat to Cambions. And as a new member, they wanted to earn my trust, so they gave me the job. My plan all along was to help you, figure a way out of this mess. I only drugged you, tied you up, so you wouldn't run, because I knew one of them would have gotten to you."

A sharp jab of realization punches through my gut. He was trying to help me this entire time. There's relief in that, strung along with the sickening thought that more people want me dead, that I'm a threat.

"Do you know what I am?" Part of me doesn't even want the answer.

Henry's worried gaze rests on mine. "I don't. Just that you're not human."

My stomach turns, not because it's the first time I've heard or considered that I'm not human. But somehow, coming out of Henry's mouth, it just all seems more real.

"There's something else. I'm not completely sure, but I think… there's a chance… your mother could be alive."

My body shutters violently, then comes to a stop. A deafening, *heartbreaking* stop. No. My mother is dead. Wes tracked her. His uncle killed her. Henry said so himself.

Henry locks his eyes on mine, and I hold his stare, my heart cracking in half. The words barely croak out of my mouth. "My mother… is alive?"

No, that can't be. We had a funeral. There was a casket. A closed casket, but a casket. Someone would have known if she wasn't the one inside of it. *Right?* My stomach twists and bile burns in my throat. Is this some kind of sick joke?

"I got some information when I was with the Armory."

His words make my heart leap into my throat, choking me. My insides clamp down, waiting for more.

"There was an order to have her killed. That went to Wes's uncle. Wes tracked her and his uncle was supposed to pull off the job, but rumor is, he was paid off not to."

I'm frozen still, heart rapping against my chest. "So then, where is my mom? If she's alive, she would have come to find me. I know she would."

"I snuck through some of the Armory captain's documents and I found information about a new regime change. Apparently, there are certain people who are being held at the authority headquarters on the outskirts of Vancouver. These are people that the authority has a vested interest in, and instead of killing them, they keep them."

My heart jerks and slams into my chest. "So they're holding my mom prisoner?"

"Her name was on the list. And there was a date—a recent one—what seemed almost like a psychiatric report. I don't know for sure, but I think she might be there."

My mind spins in a sickening loop, trying to process this information. "But weren't you ordered to kill me?"

Henry slowly shakes his head no. "I was ordered to take you alive."

Terror unfurls in my gut. They didn't want to kill me, they wanted to take me, keep me as their prisoner.

If my mother is alive and held captive, I have to save her. "How do we get to that place—the authority headquarters?"

Henry opens his backpack, pulling out a crumpled, yellowed map. He unfolds the document on the ground. We both sink to our knees for a better look.

"I stole this from the Armory. There's a tunnel system here."

Henry motions to the section of the map showcasing a winding tunnel.

I point to several squares situated on the winding, sketched path. "What are those?"

"I think they're cells."

Disgust prickles along my neck. *Cells.* Is that where my mother has been held all this time?

Henry's knee brushes against my thigh and a rush of warmth skates up my body. His gaze drifts over to meet mine. He's taking a giant risk, continues to take risks, over and over, for me.

"Why are you doing all of this?" I ask, because selfishly, I need to hear him say it.

His words splice through my heart, and my emotions tumble down. "Because I'm in love with you."

CHAPTER THIRTY-SIX

WES

THIS IS NOT how I saw my day going, but here we are. Stuffed into the back of a tiny rideshare car. Me on the left, shifting around to find comfort in this creaky old back seat. Burak on my right, Ciel practically draped on his lap.

She was right, though—about keeping Burak occupied. His hand cups her knee, inching up her thigh after she willingly placed it there. Maybe I've underestimated Ciel. I'm not attracted to her. Not one bit. My eyes are completely reserved for Natalie. But Ciel has proven to be a cunning girl. A worthy opponent? Perhaps. Which could make things complicated later. When I eventually have to kill her.

Burak received intel about a sighting of Natalie and Henry in some unincorporated community of Washington with a population of 300. He wouldn't tell me how, or who alerted him to this information. Burak has proven to be somewhat useful to me so far, if not a complete ass.

Anticipation blows through my brain as we drive closer to where Natalie might be. *My Natalie.* Knowing she's with Henry, that he took her away from me, causes violent disgust to claw through every inch of my body. My muscles grow taut, imagining the despicable things he may have done to her.

If he touches her…

The driver slams to a stop right before a set of train tracks, the impact reverberating in my brain. How is it possible that none of these fucking rideshare drivers know how to actually drive?

I peer over at Ciel and Burak and my vision blurs. The sick wail of a horn emerges in the distance and the train barrels down the tracks, moving closer. A vile undercurrent of nerves washes through me before a vision smacks into my brain…

Natalie and Henry walking down a dark tunnel. I don't recognize this place. Where are they?

The loud clomping of footsteps follows, startling them. They quicken their pace, Henry grabs her hand. Who's chasing them? And why the fuck is he touching my girl?

Henry pulls Natalie around a corner and they disappear from my view, but the hallway is still very much visible. Where did they go?

Like a camera following a mark, my vision tracks Henry and Natalie to their hiding spot. He crowds her against the wall, caging her in with his hands, his face dangerously close to her lips. Rage burns through me. What kind of sick fucking joke is this vision?

Natalie leans up, pressing her lips—what are supposed to be *my* lips—*to his.* Betrayal lodges in my mind.

No, this can't be real. This can't ever happen.

She pulls away, twisting her face so it's in my full view. "Sorry, Wes," *she says.*

Wes? Am I the one chasing her, chasing them? Am I the one in this fucking vision? There's no way… because I never would have let them walk down a hallway together in my presence, much less touch at all. I would have snapped Henry's neck, even if it had to be in front of her, before that could happen.

Ciel's voice cuts me off mid-vision. "Wes!"

My vision clears and my fists are clenched so tight, I think they might shatter. "What the fuck do you want?" I yell back at her. Irritation vibrates through my core.

Ciel and Burak cut their gazes to mine—cataloging every inch of me, sizing me up.

"We're here," Burak says, still studying me. "You just had a vision, didn't you?"

Fuck this guy. Technically, he's right. But what does he know? Anger seizes my brain, clouding my thoughts, and I try to shake off what I saw.

My original goal was to find Natalie. Now I have a new goal: find her before Henry has the chance to claw his way back into her heart... or her mouth... or any other part of her body.

"No, I didn't have a vision. Let's go," I say, blood crackling as I shove open the door to this shitty little rideshare car.

Burak and Ciel exit on the other side, blissfully unaware that I had a vision that cut like a dagger, slicing my entire existence in two.

"Stay here," Burak orders us, leaving me alone with Ciel. There's a dilapidated general store ahead with a chipped sign. We're in an average small town, but to a trained eye like mine, every detail matters.

In front of the shitty, worn-down store, an older guy sits on a bench, sipping his morning coffee. There's a familiarity about a dude just sitting and drinking his coffee in the morning, yet something seems off. He's too relaxed, too unconcerned. I narrow my eyes, instinctively unsettled.

Burak strides over to the guy, their conversation appears light, casual even, but I can tell it's marred by tension. People think they're good at wearing a mask, but I always notice when it slips.

"He was right," Ciel says, interrupting my thoughts, her doe eyes watering with concern. "You had a vision about Natalie. I know it."

What does she know? I shake my head at her like an errant child.

"I felt it," she says.

I'm growing real tired of Ciel pulling the "I felt it" card on me, like she's a human lie detector test and I'm her only subject.

"You have no idea what you're talking about."

"Yes, I do. And you know it."

I pluck a fresh joint and lighter from my pocket, letting the flame singe the end for a moment longer. Taking a deep inhale, I blow a cloud of smoke into the air, waiting for that first hit to calm my system. It doesn't.

"You can't smoke your way out of this, Wes," Ciel says. What, is she trying to give me therapy? Make me talk about my feelings?

"What? Did you pay for one of those spiritual coaches or something?"

"Excuse me. Coaches are awesome. I've had four. You should try it sometime—maybe it would help with all this hostile energy you're putting out into the world."

"Hostile energy?" The words spike against my throat.

Ciel shuffles her hands around in the air, like she's trying to conjure some magic powers. This girl is a trip. "I spent three months in Bali when I was fifteen, and this shaman taught me about energy work."

"No," I say, cutting her off completely, taking another hit off my joint. My stomach wrenches with anticipation at the moment I can finally get rid of her and Burak. The moment I'm finally reunited with Natalie.

"Okay, fine, you don't want my help. I get it. Whether you like it or not, we're connected. You're the one who saved my life. This is all your fault."

Yes, Captain Obvious, *and you never fucking let me forget that.*

Burak marches over to us, ending the onslaught of Ciel's torment I'm having to endure. "Word is your girl and I guess her other boyfriend skipped town already."

Rage rolls through my bones. "Then why did we waste time coming here?"

"You asked for my help. Maybe we'd have a clue where they went if someone would just share their vision." Burak challenges me with his gaze, and I practically hiss back at him.

Ciel folds her prissy little arms over her chest. If my vision was clearer, or longer, maybe I could find Natalie myself and just slaughter these two right here in this Podunk town.

"The only thing I saw in my vision was a hallway, more like a tunnel. The lighting was shit."

"A tunnel?" Burak scratches his head, seeming intrigued. "What did it look like?"

"I don't know, man. A dark-as-shit tunnel."

And with my smart-ass comment, Burak smacks me upside the head. The gesture rattles my mind like earlier, snapping me into another vision.

I'm shouting at Natalie, unable to control my temper. "You're sorry? You're fucking sorry?"

Her lips split into a grin. Is she liking this, torturing me?

Every step I take closer to her, she's able to dodge—Henry blocks her way.

"Get away from her," I threaten.

A ringlet of light forms around Natalie, her eyes blazing green. Where did that come from? *Behind her sits a painting of a woman with horns and wings.* The woman looks like an older version of Natalie. Wait, the woman looks exactly like Madeline Covington, her mother.

The vision slips away and I clasp onto the details. "I saw a painting."

"What was it?" Burak asks.

Glancing down, I try searing that painting to memory. "It was of Natalie's mother. But she was painted as like a mythical creature or something."

"What do you mean?"

"She had horns and wings. I don't know, it was like one of those paintings of a Greek goddess, but maybe more sinister. She's dead, so did some creep memorialize her or something?"

Burak eyes me. "The authority knows how dangerous she is. If anyone would paint her that way, it would be them."

"So, what? You think Natalie is with the authority? Or will be when my vision actually happens?" My insides tighten as I practically answer my own question.

"It's possible that's where she is headed," Burak says. "The closest headquarters is just over the border."

"You know where it is?"

Burak nods. "But it would be very dangerous to try and get in there. Impossible, even. I'll take you, but there's no way you'll make it out alive."

I drop my joint to the ground, crushing the end with my shoe. "Show me the way."

❧

Burak's driver drops us near some gaudy establishment stretched just far enough beyond Vancouver BC that no one could hear you scream.

I'm guessing that was the intention.

The three of us slide out of the car and trek over to the building closed off by iron gates. Disappointment bleeds through my gut when I don't see Natalie anywhere. Not that she'd be lounging outside this dank place, but a guy can hope.

"Let me take a look around. You two wait here," Burak says, as if he thinks I'm going to chill out in the fucking forest with Ciel while he figures out how to get inside the building undetected.

"Yeah, okay, you do that," I say, having no intention to wait out here with her. I've got my own plan to find Natalie, and it doesn't involve either of these two idiots.

A large shadow moves in the distance, followed by what sounds like a tree cracking and falling to its death. Another shadow passes, making it clear we're not alone.

"Run," Burak says, taking off through the thick forest, dodging trees, ducking under the twisted branches. I'm on his heels not far behind, darting through the woods to get away from whatever or whoever doesn't want us to be here.

Ciel lags behind me, trying to keep up as we round the corner and burst into a clearing, slamming to a halt.

Before us stands several members of the Armory, in their signature uniform of all black with white masks. There's at least a dozen of them, as if they knew we were coming and waited patiently for their prey.

I reach my hand into my coat to clutch my dagger, preparing for war. My uncle trained me to fight in groups, and I know Burak is even more skilled than me at this, but the Armory may be skilled in an entirely different way.

The first thing you do in this situation is assess what's at your disposal. A tree you can use to gain momentum, a spot on the ground where your opponent can slip, a way to use your weapon and the surrounding elements to your advantage. My eyes dart to each member, the ground, the leaves, the surrounding trees—but it's near impossible to see well through the thick mist.

The Armory stares us down in a pyramid-type formation, I assume an alpha member at the front. I study each of their silhouettes, trying to determine which one is Henry. If any.

Ciel presses into my back, hiding, and I pull her around to my side. On cue, one of the Armory members darts forward as if they sniffed her out, swinging their dagger. I shove Ciel back, sending her crashing into a tree.

"Go!"

She obeys and takes off, which distracts her opponent long enough that I get the upper hand.

I'll try and remember to thank her later for letting me use her as a pawn.

He pitches forward to go after Ciel, and I easily block his advances, slicing my dagger into his chest. He crashes back, smacking down on the ground hard enough to knock the wind out of him. Before he can scramble to his feet, I jab my dagger deep into his stomach—ending his life. As I rip the dagger from his body, a surge of excitement pumps through my veins. There's nothing like watching someone take their least breath.

Nothing, except being with Natalie.

My kill sends the rest of the Armory into a frenzy. It's a blur of blood and fog and death—Burak and I stab through members with relative ease. Sweat glides down my back as I circle around yet another member, clanging his head into another, and swiping my dagger into their necks one by one. If you hit the right spot—the carotid artery—you can hear a refreshing popping sound. Music to my ears. The perfect appetizer before you hit them with the final blow to the gut.

We're winning until another figure steps out of the shadows, followed by another. There are more of them, but still only two of us. My feet fly over the grass and dirt as I attack another member, wishing I had enough time to rip all of my victim's masks off and see which one, if any, is Henry.

Just as I take out another one, a burning pain erupts through my forearm—blood spraying out onto the ground. I twist to face the asshole who gouged my skin with his dagger, ripping and shredding at him with my good arm. He's a worthy opponent, knocking me back so hard, I slam into the frozen ground. I scramble to my feet as six more Armory members close in, holding the line.

Earth-shuddering pain leeches up my arm and an unfamiliar pang of worry enters my mind. What if I can't defeat these assholes? What if I never get to Natalie? *Defeat.* It's not something I can accept.

My eyes pin to the tree over to my right. Yanking every last ounce of strength from my core, I use it to jump off and wipe out a half-dozen Armory attackers, knocking them down to the ground. I rip a dagger from one of the dead bodies and double-fist my attack, wincing through the severe pain lancing my forearm.

I completely lose sight of Burak as I finish off the rest of the Armory. It's not a competition between us, but I can't help feeling a surge of satisfaction with each opponent I defeat, hoping my number of kills is greater than his. A feeling of triumph washes over me as I land the final blow, until a chilling scream slices through my mental victory.

Is that Natalie?

I follow the scream just a few paces in, but unfortunately, I don't find Natalie. I find Ciel. *Who was supposed to fucking run.*

She's on her back, fending off a member of the Armory. She slams her foot into him again and again as he stabs down with his dagger, missing her every time.

"Get off of me!" she screeches as I creep up behind him and take him out with a slice to the neck, then a stab to the gut. I throw his body down to the ground, helping Ciel up with my other hand—the arm that was injured.

She clasps my arm and pain gouges through my skin. "You're hurt," she says, her eyes watering with concern.

"I'm fine," I spit back at her, though it's not true. I know it will heal, but fuck, does it hurt.

"Are they all gone?"

"You mean did I slaughter them? Yeah."

"Where's Burak?"

I lead her back to the break in the trees, looking around for him, but there's nothing left except the wreckage of dead Armory members. A few steps more and I find Burak among them, blood seeping from his stomach where one of one of those Armory fucks plunged their dagger, his shocked face frozen in time.

"Oh my god. He's dead?" Ciel asks.

"Appears so."

"Can't you bring him back to life, like you did for me?"

Technically, I should be able to, but I won't. He's no use to me now. But Ciel doesn't need to know that. She also doesn't need to know that this is the last time I'll come to her rescue.

"Witchcraft only works at night," I lie.

"Really?" Ciel shivers in place.

I start down the path back to the building, shrugging off my coat and wrapping it around my wound while Ciel stumbles to keep up behind.

"Now what? Shouldn't we go get help or something?"

"Who is going to help us, Ciel? We need to get inside that building. Find Natalie." I've thought about whether or not to bring Ciel inside or kill her and leave her body out here with the rest of them, but I think she'll be an asset. A perfect distraction while I comb every last fucking inch of that place for what's mine.

My Natalie.

CHAPTER THIRTY-SEVEN

NATALIE

My body rumbles with his admission and heat skates along my skin. I'm suddenly very aware of how close I am to him. The air is thick with suffocating heat.

I know I really shouldn't focus on this right now. Resistance drains from my body and a familiar urge begins to swell in its place.

Henry lowers his gaze—I can't tell if it's disappointment, anger, or fear. Maybe it's none of those things. I still can't bring myself to utter a word in return.

He loves me.

He looks back up at me and we both swallow together as I study the curve of his lips, remembering the last time—

"Is it because of him?" he asks. His eyes narrow, flickering with anger. No mistaking that. "You can't say it back."

"No." It's the first word I can manage. The *only* word I can manage in this moment.

My breath thickens against the air as he twists away from me, pacing, running his hand through his unruly brown locks. He takes a few intentional steps to the far end of the room, heading to the door. I should let him go, though I don't want to.

Before I can protest, he spins back to me, barging over. He clamps his hands around my arms, tugging me against him, causing my breath to snap in half. He moves me back until I'm pressed against a bale of hay, the edge digging into my lower thigh.

"It *is* him, isn't it?" His voice is raspy and unforgiving and coated with jealousy. "You can't be in love with him." His fingers flex over my wrist, tightening his grip. He must already have a clear picture in his mind of Wes and me.

"I don't love Wes," I say. "Trust me."

He cups his hands around my face, his emerald-green eyes melting into mine. His voice trails off and he backs away, my heart racing with his absence.

"I was playing him for information, just like he was manipulating things for what he wanted."

"And what was that?"

"Me," I answer.

Henry's face tightens, trying to mask his feelings—and doing a terrible job of it. "And then?"

"I hated him. I was attracted to him. He made me furious. You left. I didn't think you'd ever come back. I'm not really sure what else to say."

Henry's chiseled face slices through the shadows of the room, fraying apart. "Do you still want him?"

"No, of course not." I swallow, my throat dry with pain and desire.

The words shift the room and Henry closes in, wrapping his hand behind my head, gently fisting my hair. He cranes my head back, causing my spine to arch and my chest to graze his. He's silent, studying my face, and all I want to do in this moment is kiss him.

As if he's read my mind, his lips crash down on mine and he releases a growl that causes my insides to throb. I'm lost in his embrace, pressing into him, rotating my hips into his, causing another growl to erupt from his throat. All of my practice with Wes seems to fly out the window as my throat begins to close.

As if he can sense what's happening, Henry pulls away and we're both panting for air. His eyes flame, drinking me in, and he places his hand over my chest, nuzzling into my neck. "I can feel your heart pounding."

A small moan escapes my throat as oxygen fills back into my lungs.

"You're shivering."

My senses pour back in, and I realize my hands are trembling with neediness. I look up to the ceiling as he trails kisses down my neck, suppressing a moan. He swallows a choppy breath.

"I love you too." The words bubble out of me. I couldn't stop them even if I wanted to.

He looks at me with those hooded green eyes, drinking me in, breath escaping his parted lips. I press my mouth against his, slowing the pace to savor every drop of his kiss. Oxygen leaks out once again and disappointment climbs through every cell in my body. Stars begin to swirl in my vision and my body tingles and numbs.

Weak, I pull back from his kiss, nearly falling back onto the hay bale behind me.

Henry catches me, steadying me in his strong arms. "You okay?"

I nod, unable to catch onto a breath and speak. He lifts me into his arms, setting me down on the soft, hay-coated ground. He lays next to me, propped up on one elbow, tracing his finger along my collarbone, up my neck, and through my hair. His touch feels incredible and oddly healing.

Am I losing the ability to make our kiss last longer? Maybe it's like a muscle—practice every night is necessary. I'm wildly curious, but there are far more important questions that need answering right now.

"As much as I'd love to stay here with you, I want to go to the authority. If there's a chance my mom is there, I have to go."

Henry nods. "It's not going to be easy to get in there. We need to get your strength back."

He lies down completely next to me, curling me into his arms. I drink in his warmth, wishing we could stay like this forever.

Maybe someday.

Maybe when I find my mom.

Maybe when I finally know the truth.

⸽

The authority building is on the outskirts of Vancouver BC, and it's nothing like I imagined.

I expected a sort of sterile prison. This place looks more like the Basilica of Saint-Denis in Paris—a gothic jewel resting on beautifully manicured grounds. It's somewhere you might expect to take a luxury vacation, not be held against your will.

The compound is closed off by ornate iron gates, not unlike Lockwood. There are no guards or cameras visible, but you immediately get an eerie feeling of being watched.

There's nothing but forest stretching out from the authority building. It's completely enclosed, private, with nothing around.

Perfect for hiding things. *Or people.*

Henry managed to find this place on the map that he stole from his time with the Armory. My lungs continue to cramp from our kiss earlier and we move at a much slower pace than I'd hoped, but we've made it. We're here.

Now we just need to sneak inside.

We study the gate together, circling the property to keep watch for cameras and for any places we might be able to sneak in or climb over.

There's a slice in the gate near the back of the property that appears to be a maintenance entrance. Several unmarked trucks are parked outside. The opening is wide enough that I might be able to sneak through.

"I think I can crawl through there."

"Really?" Henry sizes it up, skepticism all over his face.

"It's worth a try. If I can do it, I'll just unlock the gate from inside and let you in."

Henry pulls the map from his coat, studying the placement. "If we enter through that door to the left, we can hit the back staircase, which leads to the cells."

Cells. Where my mom could be. What if she's been held there all this time? What if they've done things to her? My eyes fill with hot tears and I swallow them back. There's no time to cry.

I just need to get her out.

CHAPTER THIRTY-EIGHT

WES

MY FUCKING ARM is killing me.

I'm not one to whine and I've certainly sustained enough injuries in my day. Especially when my uncle thought it was funny to slice into me with his dagger when I least expected it. I remember seeing kids with clowns and balloons and parties, and there I was, just trying to sew up my wounds.

My uncle claimed it was part of the training—a way to toughen me up. Guess it worked.

Joke's on him now.

That moment of taking my uncle's life away is singed into my brain. Crouching over him, knuckles twisted around my dagger. He never thought I'd do it, that I'd even be capable of defeating him. I assumed his death would bring me some sort of peace, but surprisingly, it didn't. It felt good to do it, but it was a momentary high, much like a hit of weed that fades just as quickly as it arrives.

Pity that he wasn't even conscious for it.

A surge of pain spikes up my arm, rattling my bones—this damn wound relentlessly creeping through the rest of my body. Typically, my wounds heal fast, another bit of magic I've been trying to perfect.

But this one.

This one…

"Fuck." I lose my footing, stumbling against a tree as another onslaught of pain slices through my body.

Ciel puts her hands on my shoulders. "Hey, let's chill here for a minute."

"We don't have time for that. Natalie is inside that place." My vision blurs as I determine how far away we've gotten from the authority building. We're surrounded by thick forest—the building no longer in sight. In all the chaos, it seems we've lost our way.

I wrap my palm around the wound, blood trickling out everywhere on the ground.

"That looks bad," Ciel says.

Yeah, no shit.

I huff out a breath, bracing as another stab of pain jumps over my arm and right into my skull, knocking at my brain, causing a vision.

Natalie's locked in a cell. Bare cement walls. Dirty concrete ground. She's pacing, but doesn't seem scared. More determined.

They've locked her up in that building. *My Natalie.* They've caged her away from me.

She turns to face someone. She's not alone. *Henry creeps over.* Bile rises in my throat. *Get the fuck away from her.*

He traces his hand over her hair, cupping her chin. My hair. My face. My Natalie. He's touching what's mine.

He lifts her chin so they're gazing into each other's eyes. His lips move as if he's reassuring her of something. She lifts onto her toes, pressing her lips to his.

I'd rather lose an arm than be trapped in this nightmare-ish vision.

They kiss for what feels like an eternity. A worse pain stabs and twists in my gut, watching this horror story play out before me.

They finally break apart and turn... as if they're both facing me. Staring right at me. Taunting me.

A guttural scream escapes my throat as my vision cuts out. Ciel's voice smashes through the empty space between vision and reality.

"Wes, you are seriously creeping me out. Are you like dying or something?"

I blink my eyes open as something wet presses against my face; gravel swishes in my mouth. It takes me a moment of Ciel's shrieking to realize I'm face-down on the ground, eating dirt. I must have fallen over during this fucking vision.

Pressing to sit up, I spit the dirt out, expecting to feel another slice of vomit-inducing pain. But there's nothing.

Glancing down at my forearm, I realize my wound is completely gone.

"Woah, did you just pass out and like magically heal yourself? Because that's pretty cool."

Blood ices over my veins. I'd take a thousand wounds over watching Natalie wield her betrayal over me. How could she trust him? Choose him over me? After everything I've done. I saved her. I orchestrated all of this... for her. I loved her... *still* love her... despite her obvious flaw of letting Henry Thorne manipulate her.

I grind my teeth at the vision of them kissing. My mind flickers with a vivid fantasy of hunting him down and cutting off his hand for touching her... then cutting out his tongue for taking what's mine.

That's my face. My mouth. *My Natalie.*

My draw to her is unexplainable, but I know we're meant to be together. I've never had a purpose in life other than killing, and that's not a purpose I chose. But I'm crystal clear on my purpose now—it's Natalie. And even though she's betrayed me by going back to him, I can forgive her.

She's not perfect, but I love that about her.

A pulse of excitement thrums through my body as I stand,

rationalizing my vision. It will all be okay once she's back in my arms. I'll nip away any trace Henry has left on her lips, her body, or wherever else his vile hands and lips have been since he ripped her away from me.

Momentum surges my body ahead and I'm moving swiftly through the trees, Ciel trailing not far behind.

I've got to get to that building now.

If my vision is correct, Natalie's alive. Good news.

But if my vision is correct, it also means Henry is with her, leeching himself into her heart and everywhere else.

I can't wait to kill him. Ending his life will surely be more satisfying than watching my uncle take his last pathetic breath or any of those idiotic Armory members I just took out.

Picking up speed, I'm through the forest in less than twenty minutes, scanning the authority property for a way inside, Ciel trailing behind.

"How are we going to get in there?" she says.

Shhhh. I press my finger to her lips. Her mouth opens again in protest, but I glare at her, which keeps it shut. *Finally.* I can't have this budget Kardashian screwing things up, not when we're so close. My only hope is that I can use her as a distraction, and while they figure out what to do with her, it will buy me enough time to get to Natalie.

Scanning the property, I make my plan. In the back of the building, the gate is cracked just enough to slip through. It seems like an egregious error on their part and gives me pause. Are they attempting to lure me in?

Maybe they are, but that's why Ciel is here as a backup plan.

"Slide through there," I order her.

Her mouth drops open. "You want me to go in there alone?"

Internally, I'm begging that one of these authority fucks finds us so they can take Ciel away and shut her up for good.

"I'll be right behind you," I say in my most reassuring tone.

Ciel nods and slips through the gate, turning to face me, extending her hand and reaching back through the gate. "C'mon."

My eyes dart around, checking. No alarms. No cameras. At least not so far.

Then Ciel's eyes widen in horror. "Wes, watch out!"

Before I can find out what she means, everything in my world goes black.

The first thing that hits me is the pain.

An insistent throb, knocking at my brain. Something gurgles in my throat and I spit a glob of metal-tasting substance on the floor. *Blood.*

My eyes adjust, clocking my surroundings. I'm in a cement dungeon. No windows. A door at the far end. This place looks exactly like the one in my vision. The one where Natalie was being held… *with Henry.*

Pressing onto my hands, I wobble and nearly collapse again as my head pulses with pain. Someone must have knocked me out and tossed me in here like a rag doll.

There's something green in the corner of the room. I crawl over to it, immediately recognizing it—Natalie's green hat.

She must have been in this cell.

Where the hell is she now?

I wrap the fabric over my knuckles and huff in the scent of her, allowing it to give me strength.

What have they done with her?

The pain, the dizziness, seems to disappear, and all that's left is a primal drive to find her. Instinctively, I reach my hand into my coat, surprised to find my dagger still there. Why would they leave me with a weapon? Unless they were stupid enough to not even check.

I head for the door, wondering if I can use my dagger to pick the lock. Likely not, but it's worth a try. My palm folds over the knob, and as I try to insert my dagger into the lock, the door suddenly pushes open.

Unlocked.

The question is: why?

CHAPTER THIRTY-NINE

NATALIE

THE FLUORESCENT LIGHTS in this hallway are blinding.

Henry and I snuck into the building with surprising ease. Maybe too much ease.

Anticipation simmers in my chest as we move down the hall—nothing but white walls, white concrete floors, and rows and rows of the brightest lights covering the ceiling. There's nowhere to hide here, and I'm guessing that's the point.

But there also doesn't seem to be anyone watching.

There are no doors, no other halls, just one direct path ahead—which worries me. What is this leading to?

"I thought the map said that the cells were here?"

Henry yanks the map from his pocket, checking again. "It does, but clearly, we're in the wrong spot."

I peer over his shoulder, gripping onto his strong back to get a better look. "This place doesn't seem to be on the map at all." Dread swirls through my gut. Are we even in the right building? At the right place?

Suddenly, a deafening wail cuts through the silence. The lights on the ceiling flutter and shut off one by one, leaving us standing in a pitch-black hallway.

A chill scratches up my spine and Henry curls me into his arms. Then a warm glow stretches out of a doorway at the end of the hall—a room that wasn't visible to us seconds ago.

"What the hell is that?"

Henry shakes his head, curling my body behind his for protection. "Follow me. Stay close."

We slowly creep forward, Henry clutching the dagger in his hand. Casting our glances around, we enter the strange room. Exposed brick walls, buttery-leather furniture in coppers and mustards, and ornate sculptures fill up the space.

"What is this place?"

I turn and face a full-length mirror, bizarrely placed in the center of the room. My stomach tightens as I notice my face looking a bit different. My body shivers as I walk to the mirror—my eyes have shifted from muddy brown to emerald green. I blink a few times, expecting it to just be my imagination, like that time in Henry's bathroom at Lockwood.

But the color remains. Bright, emerald green.

"My eyes."

Henry walks behind me, wrapping his arms around my body.

"They changed again. Just like my mom's."

Henry lifts his gaze and fixes on something beyond the mirror. "Natalie, look."

I follow his eyeline, spotting a large painting leaning against the wall. I don't recall that being there just seconds ago... just like this entire room. It's as if we're locked in some bizarre video game and objects are just randomly appearing.

Tremors race through my body as I step closer to the painting.

A woman with horns and wings and stars projecting from her body.

And not just any woman.

This painting…

"That's my mom." Tears cause the words to choke in my throat. "Why is that here? Why did they paint her that way, like she's some kind of devil?"

I have no time to think about these questions when the loud clomping of footsteps startles me from my thoughts. Someone must know we're here and they're coming for us.

Henry grips my hand, leading me out the door at the far end of the room, away from the footsteps.

The warm glow disappears as we quicken our pace down a dark tunnel. Dampness fills the air and our feet splash through small puddles covering the ground. Once again, this place seems entirely different than the sterile, asylum-like white hallway and the warm, inviting room with that painting of my mom.

The footsteps behind us grow louder and I'm terrified to turn back and see who's chasing us. It's definitely not a single person—the steps drum in rhythm, as if there could be a small army behind us.

Henry pulls us into a dark corner, the hallway still somewhat visible if you squint enough. He crowds me against the wall as the strangers grow closer, my heart thumping so loud, I'm afraid it will give us away. Fear swells in my brain like oxygen filling a balloon and I wonder how long this will go on before I pop.

Within seconds, the strangers march past us, one by one. They're all wearing military-like uniforms and hats, and are fixated ahead. Luckily, none of them seem to know we're just inches away, hiding.

I must count a dozen of them before the final person walks by, carrying someone who appears to be unconscious. I squint, wondering who they have captured. Just before they walk completely out of view, the arm of the unconscious person flops down, revealing a gleaming gold bracelet with a dangling, square-shaped sapphire.

Ciel.

I'd recognize that bracelet anywhere. Adip gave it to her on the first day of school at Lockwood. I'd known Ciel peripherally through society events and other bullshit over the years, but didn't know much about her at that time, other than what she wanted as an engagement ring one day—an emerald-shaped sapphire. I don't even remember how we got into conversation about engagement rings, but Ciel was very clear. Adip definitely wasn't about to propose, but he certainly wanted to impress her.

My breath speeds and panic rises in my gut. Ciel is here, and she's either already dead or soon to be, from the looks of it.

Once the authority army—or whoever the hell these people are—are gone from our view, Henry faces me.

"Ciel. Why is she here? What did they do to her?"

Henry cups my face in his hands. "We'll find out, okay? We can save her."

"But she might already be dead." I can barely breathe, my throat constricting into a panic attack. My vision starts to blur as I desperately try to catch my breath.

"Look at me. Look at me," Henry says, trying to calm me down.

I try focusing on his eyes, but it's too difficult.

"Don't think about that right now," he says.

The sight of Ciel claws endlessly through my brain. It's my fault she's mixed up into this. I did this to her.

Everything crashes down on me at once. The attack on my life. Killing Oliver. And Amelia. Not even being sure they're dead. Henry. Wes. Mom. Ciel.

"Natalie, please, look at me."

Henry's eyes are full of pain and I know he's doing everything to help. I make a greater effort, sucking in air, but my lungs refuse to fill.

"Do you know the first time I saw you?"

The question catches me off guard and suddenly, my breathing slows, little blips of oxygen passing through.

"No."

Still cupping my face, he traces his thumb along my chin and up into my hairline. "You were in the hallway, talking to Ciel. Your arms were crossed over your body, and you looked very bored."

A giggle escapes my throat. Resting bitch face has always been my downfall.

"Your hair. Your lips. I couldn't take my eyes off you." He strokes his hand over my hair, gently tugging the back.

"That's because you had a vision of me dying and it freaked you out."

"No. My first vision was just your face." He strokes his hand over my lips. "This beautiful face. And then I saw you in person and my heart stopped. It still does… every time I see you. Every time I'm with you."

My eyes latch on to a shadowy figure setting into view, and I squeeze Henry's arms, alerting him that we're not alone. I squint, trying to make out who is standing in front of me, watching us.

They take a step forward, the warm light from the other room illuminating their face. A gasp erupts from my throat.

Wes's menacing eyes stare back at me.

CHAPTER FORTY

WES

NATALIE. *MY NATALIE.*

My vision plays out right in front of me, wreaking havoc on my insides. At least I got here before they kissed and I can make sure the rest of this disgusting scenario plays out much differently.

I'm particularly looking forward to snapping Henry's neck, making him feel the pain of taking what's mine.

Fury rips through my bones as I stride over to him, but before I know it, Natalie's blocking my way—her palm smacking against my cheek with a sharp crack.

She glares into my eyes. "You asshole."

A chuckle escapes my lips as I graze my hand over my cheek, feeling her mark on me. What did he tell her? What lies did he spill?

And most of all—what did he do to convince her?

"You have nothing to say to me?" Her throat scratches out the words, eyes blazing with rage and pain.

She raises her palm again, but this time, I block the blow, gripping tightly onto her wrist. She attempts to wriggle free, but I squeeze harder, unwilling to let her go. Not now. *Not ever.*

Cutting my gaze to Henry, I try to fix this little mess. "What lies has he been feeding you? Huh? After he kidnapped you, took you away from me?"

"Let her go now," Henry says. He's attempting to sound dangerous, but his demand sounds like a pathetic little whimper.

He takes a step forward before Natalie stops his advances. "I can handle this."

There. That's my good girl.

I tilt my head to catch her eyes, then let my gaze drop to the heavy rise and fall of her chest. "Everything's going to be okay. It's just you and me now," I reassure her.

She rips out of my grasp. "You were the one who tracked my mother."

My chest cramps and the truth slowly decimates my insides. *She knows.* A secret I'd hoped to take to the grave because I knew it would be hard for her to forgive me… to move past it.

But I can fix this.

"I didn't know you back then. It was just a job."

A thick tear glides down her cheek—*that perfect cheek*—causing the breath to freeze in my lungs. She has to understand, it had nothing to do with her.

I can fix this.

"If I had known it was your mother, I—"

Her nostrils flare and I feel her anger sliding into my bones. "You what? Wouldn't have tracked her? With the intent of having her killed?"

"It was only a job. My uncle was responsible for what happened."

"But you were a part of that! And you kept it from me this whole time!"

Irritation claws through my veins as my patience wears thin. Why doesn't she see that I kept this from her for her own good? I was trying to protect her, save her. Like I always do.

"You're a monster." The words float so naturally from her lips.

"Yes, I know." My mouth splits into a grin, hoping we can put this all behind us and get back to our life together. I'll take care of Henry and get us the hell out of this place.

But she doesn't fall into my arms or give any indication that we've moved past this little issue. Instead, she turns her back on me…

…and walks over to him.

Rage coils through every inch of my body, watching her step closer and closer to Henry Thorne.

"You're choosing him." It's not a question but a statement, intended for her to argue back, but she doesn't behave as I'd hoped. She just sidles up next to him, pressing into his body—as if she needs his protection. *From me.*

"He left you at Lockwood, Natalie. All alone. You were in danger and he left you."

Henry's jaw tightens and he makes a move toward me, but she clasps his arm, stopping him.

"Tell me—who was there for you, huh? Who never left you? Who saved your life?"

"I saved her," Henry cuts in, acting like some valiant knight.

"Bullshit. You only did that because I talked you into it. Otherwise, you would have let her die."

Henry grunts and lowers his eyes as Natalie's stare locks onto mine, sending adrenaline up my spine. I've got her attention, and soon, she'll be back in my arms where she belongs.

"Get out of my life, Wes."

Her words slice through my heart and I study her face, searching for the lie. She can't mean that. We're meant to be together. I've done everything to create that reality.

"I never want to see you again," she says.

A disgusting level of desperation erupts from my core—followed closely by simmering rage. "Really? You don't want me? Someone whose entire life is consumed by death, and wants nothing more than to have a life with you? You make me feel alive, Natalie. Don't you understand?"

She opens her mouth to answer when a deafening alarm blares, silencing her words. My hands fly to my ears, trying to drown out the noise. Several shadowy figures move into the tunnel, heading right for us.

Before I can make a move, someone grabs me from behind, whirling me around and smashing my cheek onto the ground. A searing pain leeches from my jaw into my head, sucking away my consciousness.

❦

A burn radiates up my spine as dizziness overtakes my body.

My eyes blink open and I register that I'm back in a concrete cell. This one is a bit different—there's a small window in the corner. I force myself to stand and grunt with pain as I move over to the glass, realizing it looks through to another cell. An empty cell.

Just great.

Before I can process another moment of this fucking mess, the lock clicks and the cell door creaks open. Someone is shoved inside wearing a black hood that covers their face. Anticipation simmers in my gut as I squint, trying to see if it's Natalie. Hoping it's her. The door is shut and locked within a split second.

The person wobbles around on their feet and I quickly come to the conclusion that it's not Natalie at all, but a man.

"What the hell?" he croaks out, gripping the edge of the hood, trying to maneuver it off his face. A quite amusing display, if you ask me.

"Pull it up to the left," I say.

"Who are you? Someone here?" The hooded person whips their

head left to right, as if they can see anything with that ridiculous face covering.

"Dude, here." I'm not much of a helper, but if this guy has some information on what happened to Natalie, I'll take what I can get.

I rip off his mask and a chill scratches up my spine.

It's my uncle.

But… I killed him. *I know I did.* Is this some kind of nightmare? What is this place doing to me?

My uncle blinks his eyes open as I suck in some oxygen, trying to get rid of the wave of nausea roiling through my stomach.

His eyes grow wide, then narrow. "It's you." And I can already tell he's not happy about that.

Instinctively, I back away from him, fisting the dagger in my coat. Not that it will do any good. That's how I killed him last time, and look how that turned out.

"How are you alive?" The memories of killing him surge forward in my brain. Did someone resurrect him using magic? And why?

"I don't know. I woke up in this place," he says.

Bile rolls in the back of my throat. "So did they revive you, or…?"

"You're asking questions I can't answer, kid. I woke up strapped to some operating table. They put me in one of these cells and the only person I see is the guy who drops off my two shitty meals a day."

Why is my uncle here? Why is he alive? What the fuck is going on?

I have no time to come up with answers when my uncle grips my jaw, squeezing so hard that my lips deform. "Don't think I forgot what you did to me." He releases me just as quickly and shakes his head. "All for that stupid girl."

"Don't call her that."

He chuckles and eyes me like a useless slab of meat… no different than the way he's always treated me. "You always were worthless."

"Then why did you waste time training me?"

"Because I answered to Burak, and he thought you had potential."

"Well, Burak's dead and I'm still alive, so I guess he was right."

His eyes lower and I can practically feel the fear surging through his body. I killed him once, I can do it again. I blow out an amused breath—there's something so gratifying about watching the weak-willed, the people who are scared of you. It's an especially welcome distraction right now.

"How did you kill him?" he asks, squeaking out the words.

"I didn't do it myself—but I did slaughter a ton of those Armory members. One of them got to him."

His gaze cuts back to mine. "You killed members of the Armory?"

"Guess you trained me well." It's a joke, not a compliment. Though I suppose there's some truth to it. All of those days he beat me senseless when I messed up in our training sessions. Even then, in the darkest of moments, I could sense my uncle's weaknesses, plucking them out and searing them into my memory.

The sound of the lock clicking again cuts through the silence. What mysterious person from my past are they shoving into this cell now? A door creaks open, but it's not the door to this cell.

They're putting someone in the cell next door.

Rushing over to the glass, I spot Henry getting shoved inside the cell next to me by a guard. I glare at him, tossing him the middle finger, but he has no reaction. In fact, he doesn't seem to see me at all.

Before the guard shuts the door, they shove one more person inside with him… *Natalie.*

The guard leaves, locking the two of them inside that cell, together. A most disgusting sight. I smack my palm against the glass to get her attention. But she also doesn't seem to hear or see me.

"Natalie!"

Nothing.

She rushes into Henry's arms, and anger rises through my body like lava. Are they just locked in there, pretending I don't exist?

"Hey!" I shout, but there's no reaction.

"You're wasting your time," my uncle says. "It's soundproof. They can't hear you."

My fists clench at my sides. "There's a window right here. They can fucking look right at me."

He shakes his head. "One-sided glass. You can see them, but they can't see you."

My chest throbs with rage. What kind of torture is this? Am I supposed to just stay trapped in this cell and endure watching them?

My uncle sidles up next to me, staring through the window. "Ahh, the girl. Makes sense now."

"What does?"

"One thing I've suspected since I've been here, this whole place is designed to break you. And you, kid, don't break easily. But that girl might do it."

CHAPTER FORTY-ONE

NATALIE

HENRY WRAPS ME into his arms as my heart seizes in my chest. We're locked up in some cell together. What have they done with Ciel? Is my mother even in this place?

Being in a panic isn't going to help. I have to stay calm… focus. That begins with figuring out a way to get the hell out of here.

Icy tendrils of anxiety coil up my spine when I spot a small window in the corner of the room. "Look, there's a window. Maybe we break it."

Henry studies the glass with me, squinting to get a better view, both realizing it's completely dark on the other side.

"Is that a window on top of concrete?" I ask.

"That's what it looks like, but why would that be here?" he says.

Who knows? In this creepy place, anything's possible. A chill reverberates through my body. "Okay, so if we can't get out through the window, how do we get out of here?"

A click sounds from the opposite side of the room and our heads whip in the direction of the cell door. Henry shields me with his body as a guard enters, setting a tray down on the concrete ground without speaking a word. The guard exits and we stare at the tray, covered with a cup of coffee and a mug of tea.

I sink down to my knees, picking up the mug—breathing in the cinnamon scent. "This is cinnamon tea… my favorite. How do they know that?"

Freaked out, I let the teacup clatter to the ground, boiling water spilling over the cement, the scent of cinnamon wafting through the room.

"And black coffee for me," Henry says.

"Don't drink that. They could have poisoned it." My empty stomach lurches and my throat scratches from dehydration. The tea seems to have ignited my hunger and thirst, making me woozy. My body begins to tremble until Henry wraps me into his arms.

"You're freezing."

A chill sinks into my bones, as if someone has cranked an air conditioner to an unbearable freeze. Despite the frosty cell, Henry's body is boiling.

"Come here." He shifts us down to the ground and pulls me into his lap, attempting to cover every inch of my body with his. His warmth caresses my heart that's swollen with enormous amounts of pain and dread.

"I would have saved you after I had that vision, you know. It wasn't because of Wes," he says.

His words slick over my body. "I know. But it doesn't matter."

"It *does* matter. Don't you understand? You're the only thing that matters to me." He tips my chin so my eyes meet his. I can see him coming unraveled as he eats me up with his gaze.

Maybe it's the chaos or the danger or the sheer mayhem of the last few months all circling into this cell, but I lunge forward, crashing my lips into his, needing a distraction. Except, he's more than that. Much more.

His fingers tangle into my hair and his body shudders, putting delicious pressure on my scalp as he devours my mouth. I'm not sure when, or if, I'll ever be able to do this again. If we'll even make it out of here alive. I pour every inch of my soul into this embrace, lapping up the heat searing between our bodies. I know, with Henry, our kiss can't last long before I lose consciousness, and I don't want to miss a second of the pleasure I only feel when I'm with him.

He tears his mouth away from mine, studying my face to make sure I'm okay. I'm desperate for more, aching with a rabid need for him. My legs are shaking and flames dance on my skin.

"Don't stop." I barely etch out the words when his lips are back on mine, our desire and emotions spilling over.

He traces his lips over my cheek and down onto my neck, taking me all the way down to the ground, the concrete suddenly feeling like it's burning with heat against my back. He grinds his hips into mine as I stretch my leg around his body, aching to feel more of him. My eyes flutter open and closed at the sensation of his teeth nipping at my skin.

My consciousness begins to blur and I know it's time to stop, but I don't want to. Letting out a small moan, I promise myself to give it just ten more seconds.

Ten more seconds of pleasure. Before we need to stop.

Ten…nine…eight…seven…six…five…

My eyes drift closed and Wes stampedes through my mind. He's standing in a cell just like this one, banging on the other side of the glass window, *watching us*.

Panic claws at my chest and I shove Henry off of me, trying to smooth out my choppy breaths.

"What's wrong?"

"It was…" My words trail off as my gaze drifts to that small window in the corner. Is it possible that Wes is really on the other side, watching us? Anxiety slices up my skin like paper cuts.

"What is it?" Henry covers my hands with his, gently rubbing my knuckles with his thumbs. I can't unlock my gaze from the window, and he notices. "Why are you looking at that?"

"I think we're being watched. By Wes." A sharp ache pummels against my chest. I don't want him watching me or to be anywhere near me.

Henry stands, storming over to the window, rapping his fist against it. "There's still nothing there."

"We can't see him, but I—I'm pretty certain—he can see us."

Henry's confused eyes dance over my face. "Why do you think that?"

"Because I just saw… I had… maybe a vision."

Henry's eyes widen in horror, and I get it. Do I suddenly have precognitive abilities? The idea of it pools in my nerves and I start trembling again.

"We can't stay in here. There's got to be a way out."

Henry leans against the wall and his gaze dips down in deep thought. "When I was locked in that place, that precog rehab, I was able to make things happen."

My heartbeat leaps into my neck and my ears begin burning. "What kind of things?'

Henry runs his fingers through his thick hair, twisting it at the end, as if he's struggling to tell me. "I think when I was in there, I was able to unlock other powers."

Swallowing a breath, I scramble to my feet. "What kind of powers?"

"Do you remember when you and I were in the woods at school and we made the leaves float up around us?"

How could I forget? It was the first time he kissed me. I nod, letting the memory glide over me, bringing a surge of heat to my body.

"I was able to do that again—but I created a storm. A few of them. One even caused a flood. And you were there."

My stomach jerks with confusion. "I was?"

"You weren't physically there, but maybe energetically? When I thought of you, really fixated on my memories with you, I could shift things in the atmosphere."

The knot in my stomach comes undone. "If you were able to do that before by just thinking of me, then what can we do now?"

Henry's brows furrow in confusion. "I don't understand my full powers. What they are. How to use them."

My mind snaps the pieces into place. I rush over to Henry, clasping his hands into mine. "There has to be a reason this is all happening to us. Me and you. What if all of this is because of us, because of the powers that unlocked when you changed that first vision? Because of whatever I am? And who I am when I'm with you."

Henry tightens his grip on my hands and a shiver coasts through my body. His eyes squeeze shut as if my touch is too much to bear right now.

"Look at me," I say.

He blinks open those blazing green eyes, coiling them into mine.

"We want to get out of here, right? So look at me. Hold me. And think about that."

We lock together, fingers intertwining, facing one another. Energy pulsates between us, slowly beginning to churn and stir like the beginnings of a tornado, reminiscent of that day back at Lockwood.

Goosebumps surface on my skin and my breath hitches as my hair lifts in the wind…wind that we seemed to conjure.

With a sudden jolt, the ground beneath our feet starts to tremble and shake. The smooth cement floor begins to crack, tearing apart like pieces of brittle glass, shards flying up and ricocheting off the walls. Fragments of cement pelt against our skin.

Henry pulls my body to his, shielding me from the onslaught. "This is too dangerous!" he shouts over the chaos.

A sharp gust of wind coils through the room and I can taste freedom on the outside of the cell. "Don't let me go!"

The concrete pieces beat against our bodies and I squeeze into Henry, bracing for the impact. A loud crack rips through the cell and gravity gives out. We both lose our footing, and my gaze drops, realizing the floor has broken in two—nothing but miles of darkness below.

Another quake hits the cell, knocking Henry into the open space in the ground. I catch his hand before he falls, trying desperately to pull him to safety.

"Hold on!"

The concrete batters my arms, but I harness more energy, tightening my grip on his hand. He steadies his body, climbing back up and nearly making it onto the flat ground with me, when a beam of light shoots up from the ground—sucking Henry down with it.

His hand falls away from mine as I lose my grip, screaming after him…

…watching him plunge into the darkness below.

CHAPTER FORTY-TWO

WES

SATISFACTION SURGES THROUGH my veins like some delightful pill.

Although I wish Henry Thorne's demise was taken care of by my own hands, I can't deny how pleased I am that he's gone—regardless of how it happened.

A sharp thrill chases up my spine as I watch Natalie on the other side of the glass, staring down into a black hole after him. The anticipation of our reunion has all my nerves firing. My lips twist into a grin, thinking of my hand fisting into those curls, pulling her close to me, and making damn sure she never thinks about Henry Thorne again.

"What are you smiling about?" my uncle grunts behind me.

"None of your business."

Natalie appears frozen in time, unable to move her gaze from that dark hole. Her body's not moving either—not trembling, not crying, not screaming, not smiling. I rap on the glass with my fist, hoping it will get her attention but knowing it won't.

Shifting the atmosphere, causing a tornado-like storm contained in a single spot. I remember that from the book of magic I stole. The question is, does Henry know how to wield magic now too? Does Natalie? Or was that someone else's doing? The thought sends shards of disgust through my mind.

"Your obsession with that girl will get you killed."

A chuckle escapes my throat. Didn't he hear me? I defeated the Armory while Burak met his death.

"You're just bitter that I'm better than you now—stronger than you," I say, refusing to unlock my eyes from Natalie's frozen demeanor.

My uncle's laugh cuts through the concrete silence.

I whip around to face him, wanting nothing more than to carve that laugh right out of his throat. That'll teach him to respect me.

"What's so funny?" I say, sliding the dagger from my coat, white-knuckling the handle.

"You're nothing more a pawn getting played here. You'd be a fool to think otherwise."

I'm the fool? He thinks he's untouchable, but I've gutted my uncle once and I'll happily do it again. I wonder if the authority will come save him a second time. His blood would certainly liven up this concrete cell. If anyone's a fool here, it's him.

He steps forward. "I'm not scared of you, Wesley."

The use of my full name makes my blood ice over. I trace a finger over the sharp blade of my dagger.

"I'm not your enemy. They are." He points up to the ceiling at some invisible force he thinks is hovering above us.

Aggravation stabs into my hands and I grab my uncle by the collar, shoving his weak body against the wall with such force that the glass window rattles. I press the tip of my dagger into his neck, pricking it just enough to let a trickle of blood flow out.

"Who is *they*? The authority? Let them try their best. I'll defeat every single one of them."

"And how do you plan to do that?"

"I studied you when you didn't realize I was watching. I found your book of magic, remember? You couldn't beat that information out of me for good."

Before I can register what's happening, my uncle has the upper hand, lifting my body into the air and slamming me down on the concrete ground. The dagger rolls out of my grip as nausea climbs up my spine.

"What did you do?" he shouts.

My mouth fills with the familiar taste of metal and I cough out a splotch of blood. "I brought someone back to life. Amongst other things."

My uncle shoves off me, putting space between us. "You should have never done that."

"I don't answer to you. Not anymore." I press to stand, getting my bearings.

"There are reasons I trained you the way that I did. Reasons we don't use magic, that it's forbidden. I always knew, deep down, you were going to be a problem. But I figured I could harness that menace inside of you the right way."

My teeth grind together as aggravation dances on my tongue. I remember being a young boy, watching my uncle in awe, mesmerized by how he moved so quickly, so fearlessly, controlling everything and everyone.

What a farce.

"The people you work for locked you up in a cell and you still want to follow their rules?" I ask, not even bothering to suppress a laugh.

"They saved my life after you took it."

My mind clouds with fantasies of gutting into his pathetic waste of a body. I can't believe I used to think my uncle was so powerful, only to discover he's just a sad, pathetic little sheep.

"I don't follow anyone's rules. You should know that by now."

He continues pleading with that ear-piercing whine. "When we use magic, it throws everything off balance."

I heave out a bored sigh, cracking my neck. "Whatever. I'm just a precog using a little magic."

His body jerks forward with rage. "We're not precogs. Clearly you haven't worked that out yet, smart guy?"

My gut twists, not wanting to listen to this pathetic excuse of a man, but also dying to know more about who we are—what I am. "What are we then?"

"Demons."

I burst into laughter, unable to help myself. "Demons? Like the devil?" I have to admit that would track, though.

"Half-demons. Cambions. Centuries ago, the authority realized the only way to keep us in order is by suppressing our true powers. They had to make us believe we didn't have any. They were successful in suppressing everything but our visions, so they rebranded our kind from Cambions to precogs."

My fingers scratch against my temple at this warped tale. Maybe when they brought my uncle back to life, they broke his brain. Or fed him a bunch of lies so he wouldn't go even more insane.

"My job was to get rid of any Cambion who defied the order, who could get anywhere near discovering their real powers. That was supposed to be your job too."

"So when were you planning to tell me the real story?"

"When you were old enough to handle it and not abuse things. Which clearly, I was right—you weren't ready. You still aren't."

Excitement flares in my chest at what this could mean. As a half-demon, I must have even more powers to unlock… to use to my liking. The ability to destroy what doesn't serve me is the best news I've gotten all year. Hell, even my lifetime.

This inevitably means that Henry is also a half-demon. The idea that he may have discovered this fact, unlocked certain powers before me, sparks a wave of repulsion in my gut. I dismiss the feeling, clinging on to my excitement.

My uncle studies me with a disappointed glare. "Why do you seem so thrilled with this information?"

"Because you just confirmed to me that I am more than a simple precog. Visions are bullshit. This is a fantastic turn of events for me."

"No, Wesley, you don't understand. The authority has all-consuming power. They won't allow you to unleash your powers. They can defeat you. They *will* defeat you. Especially under this new regime."

Unable to wipe the grin off my face, I lean back against the wall, feeling more comfortable than ever. The only thing that will complete this moment is having Natalie by my side. I wonder how she'll react to the news that I'm a devil—or at least half of one.

Heat rushes into my groin as I imagine those brown eyes widening, shifting to green in fear, and the pure delight of doing whatever necessary to convince her that she's safe with me.

Only with me.

But if Henry already knows, then she does too. Why must he ruin everything?

I shake off my fantasies of Natalie and disdain for Henry for a moment. Just a moment. "If we're all Cambions, what makes you so sure the authority can defeat me? We all have the same powers. Plus, I know some magic."

My uncle inhales a sharp breath. "You are incredibly stupid."

Annoyance snaps through my brain. "What about Natalie? What is she? Is she a Cambion? Fairy? Wait, how about a mermaid?" I can't stifle my laugh.

My uncle doesn't seem to take too kindly to my teasing. "She's none of those things. But what she is—it's far more dangerous. You should have let me handle things when I had the chance."

"You mean I should have let you kill Natalie rather than turning the tables on you." Tragically, that didn't work out as planned.

"I was never going to kill her. I was paid to keep her alive, to deliver her to the authority, until you had to fuck it all up."

A wave of wrath sweeps through my bones and I snatch a fistful of his shirt. "Bullshit. If you weren't planning to kill her, what were you doing in the woods?"

He chuckles, that sickening, deep sound that's looped through so much of my life. "Didn't mean I couldn't have a little fun."

I shove his body down to the ground. How I'd love to kill him again, slowly this time, make him suffer for every single second he touched Natalie.

"If the authority didn't want her dead, what were they planning to do with her?"

"She's here now. I guess you'll just have to see," he replies in an ominous tone.

I make my way back to the window, dying to catch another glimpse of Natalie after listening to this blithering, revolting idiot.

As I step closer to the glass, I realize something looks different. The room on the other side is no longer a cell with the floor bottomed out.

An inferno of rage spikes through my chest as the nightmare in front of me plays out in real time.

Natalie is gone, replaced by a single painting. The colors wind and twist into a sick sort of tribute to Henry and *my Natalie*—on what appears to be their wedding day. My insides cut open and sharp pain whips against my chest as I study the painting—her curls swept into a veil, his gaze locked on her face, and her hand pressed against his chest, revealing a diamond engagement ring and gold wedding band.

My body trembles, fury unlocking in the deepest parts of me. All of my rage funnels into the room and I let out a guttural scream, so forceful my lungs could collapse. The room quakes along with the noise, knocking my uncle off balance and sending his body tumbling to the ground.

"Wesley, stop!" my uncle shouts over the chaos, but I've already lost control.

All that matters is that I destroy that painting and get my Natalie back.

CHAPTER FORTY-THREE

NATALIE

A CONCOCTION OF rage and despair swells in my heart as two guards drag me down a never-ending hallway, far away from the cell—from whatever dark abyss Henry dropped into.

I refuse to believe I've lost him, that he's been ripped away after whatever it is we did with our collective powers.

There has to be a way out of this mess. For Henry, for Ciel, for my mom—if she's really here. Hell, even for Wes.

No one deserves to be under the iron grip of this authority. My body becomes feral with adrenaline, allowing my mind to refuse the pain leeching up from my limbs as the guards squeeze and twist and drag my body ahead.

My frustration escalates and survival kicks in. I refuse to go wherever these people are taking me. My memory flickers to the time I fought off Oliver, shoved Henry away from Wes, stabbed Amelia. Untapped powers whir inside me, bursting at the seams to escape.

I don't need to be saved. I'm the one who needs to save them.

Up ahead is a rusted steel door and I'm certain that it's the next place these guards are about to cage me in—or maybe end my life altogether. The closer I get to the door, the more manic I become.

I can't let these guards put me in there. I can't let them win.

Energy spikes up my core and I focus on the guard to my right, clenching on to my bicep. Focusing mind on muscle, I drag my arm into my body and then smash it against the guard's face.

The impact is stronger than I realized, sending him toppling back against the wall. The other guard—the female guard—rips into action, reaching out to contain me. I kick my foot into her knee, hearing a sickening snap as her knee breaks and she flops to the ground in agony.

Groaning with pain, she reaches up for a single button on the wall—something I didn't notice before. I lunge ahead, fisting her hand before she can press and alert someone. She tries to wriggle free from my grip, but her strength is no match for mine right now.

The other guard crashes into my back and I shove into his body, sending him flying against the wall. His head smacks against the concrete and he flops down onto the ground, unconscious.

The other guard seems as disarmed by my strength as I am. She yanks away, managing to get to her feet while clutching her wounded knee, hobbling to the steel door.

A sharp chill envelops my body, like it's whispering to me: *go after her. Don't let her get away.*

She inches closer and closer to the door, perhaps to get herself to safety or to find help and destroy me. Or both.

My feet slap against the concrete, reaching her just before her hand can crank the knob open.

She turns to face me. "I know what you are," she says with disgust.

My gut twists and I'm dying to ask what she knows. But before I can wrench out a word, her hands dart out, strangling my throat. I choke and sputter, desperately trying to pry her hands off as she squeezes tighter and tighter—as if she's sucking power away from me.

"You will destroy all of us," she says as my consciousness starts to crack under the pressure of her grip.

Panic lodges into my brain, but I swipe it away. This is no time to freak out. No time to back down.

With my vision growing fuzzy, I muster every last ounce of my strength to shove her away. Her head clangs against the steel door and she flops forward onto the ground. I scramble away from her body, still wildly confused by my own strength and powers, but no time to process it all.

My head whips around the empty hallway and the unconscious bodies of the guards crumpled on the ground. I'm not sure if they're passed out or dead—and I don't want to stick around to find out.

There are two directions to go—back to the cell where I just came from, or attempt to get through the steel door ahead. My instincts fire, warning that I don't want to meet what's on the other side of that door.

I charge down the hall, back to the cell, the place where I lost Henry. A chill spider-crawls through my body as I twist down the dark halls, like a hamster trapped in a cage. Are they watching me right now? Laughing at me? Delighting at my panic?

Focus, Natalie.

I pause to suck in a few deep breaths when the sound of gunshots shatters the silence. Terror rips through my chest as I run as fast as my legs can go without stumbling. Footsteps trample close behind and I know I'm running out of time before they catch me.

My eyes freeze onto a door to the left. I don't know where it leads, but I need somewhere to hide. I crank open the handle and thrust my body inside the dark room, shutting the door behind me just in time for the guards, or whoever it is, to stomp past without noticing where I've gone.

My legs give out and I slide down against the door, gulping down oxygen.

A women's voice slices through the darkness. "Who are you?"

I'm upright in an instant, trying to slow my breathing, to remain calm. A lamp flickers, illuminating the person behind the voice.

My heart freezes when I see my mom standing before me.

"Mom?" My heart unclenches, hammering in my chest as I race over to hug her.

She backs away from me and I slam to a heartbreaking stop. Her gorgeous green eyes appear vacant as she stares me down. "Who are you?" All the light has been ripped from her voice and she sounds almost robotic.

"It's me, Mom, your daughter."

I try to contain my horror, not wanting to upset her. Who knows what these people have done to her since she's been here, what kind of trauma she's endured. They've broken her, that much is clear.

A tear trickles from my eye. "Mom, it's okay. I'm going to get us out of here."

She shakes her head, backing even further away from me. "Why would I leave? I'm happy here."

A shiver of fear digs into my bones. *Happy?* They must have brainwashed her into their precog cult—something I didn't even consider.

"No, Mom, listen to me." I reach for her hand, but she swats mine away. My stomach cramps with longing and I squeeze my eyes shut, trying to remember what she must have gone through to forget her only daughter.

"They told me you were dead, but they kidnapped you, held you prisoner here."

She turns, taking a few paces away from me to a door on the far side of the room, each step bouncing off the walls and stabbing me in the heart.

"I'm happy here," she repeats. It's the second time she's uttered that phrase in that same robotic tone.

Her hand reaches for the knob, twisting it open.

"Mom, wait!" I call out, hoping she'll hear the desperation in my voice. She pauses in the doorway and time seems to stand still.

I'm not sure how long we've been fixed in that position before I try once more. My words ball in my throat and I choke out a sob. "Please, Mom, these are bad people. They're trying to kill me and others I love. They must have done something to you."

She turns to face me with that same blank expression, causing my heart to claw against my chest.

I'm about to creak out another plea when her eyes flick to the ceiling. I follow her gaze, noticing a tiny blinking red light lodged in the corner. *A camera.*

My insides coil as I realize my mom's not trying to push me away—she's trying to warn me.

CHAPTER FORTY-FOUR

WES

RAGE UNFURLS FROM my bones and I'm unable to move my eyes from that painting. Henry and Natalie together. Married.

That fucking painting.

My vicious thoughts drown out what's happening behind me… around me. The window blocking me off from Natalie's cell shatters and explodes, sending shards flying, narrowly missing my scalp. My uncle's garbled pleas are drowned out completely, leaving nothing but silence.

Beautiful, perfect silence.

My eyes move from the shattered window to the rest of the room, realizing that my uncle has completely vanished. Whatever power I was able to conjure managed to break the glass, make him disappear, and leave everything else—most importantly, me—intact.

Seems things are taking a turn for the better.

Now if I can just find Natalie…

I climb through the window into the next cell, a few broken shards scratching into my arms as I work my body through. My feet smack onto the concrete and I move to the painting—that disgusting painting of Henry and my Natalie's wedding, acting like some kind of premonition.

Over my dead body.

Clutching my dagger, I rip into the canvas, sweat dripping over my brow as I slice every last remnant of their union apart.

Anger burns through my soul as I saw away the final piece, leaving a large gash in the center of Henry's neck. Sadly, it's not the real Henry, but this will do for now. When I've got him at my mercy in real life, I'll be sure to slowly cut him open, one slice for every moment he's kept me away from Natalie.

The painting now sits like a rotting corpse on the ground before me—allowing the burning to ease in my chest. I back away, feet crunching on broken glass, as I squeeze my eyes shut in satisfaction, allowing the rush of destroying something to wash over my skin.

I blink my eyes open, realizing there's someone standing in front of me.

My brother. *Timothy.*

Is everyone I thought was dead, now alive?

"What are you doing here?" I ask, a small pang of something creeping into my heart. I suppose because I care.

"Waiting for you," he says.

I draw my brows in. "Don't talk to me like some cryptic asshole. How are you alive? You looked very dead the last time I saw you. And how did you know I was coming here?"

Timothy heaves out a sigh, the same thing he used to do every time my uncle sent him back to the house because he was useless in training. Which was basically every day, until he gave up on him entirely.

"They gave me some pill and I blacked out. No one tried to kill me, at least not that I know of. And when I woke up in here, I apparently unlocked another power—reading your thoughts," he says.

My gut churns at his revelation. I don't want anyone

knowing the thoughts that twist around my head, especially not my do-gooder brother.

"Where's your girlfriend?" I ask.

"You mean my fiancée, Willow?"

"Whatever, yeah, her. Did they bring her to this place too?"

Timothy lowers his eyes, clearly upset, and I think I already know the answer. "I asked one of the guards about her when I woke up in here. They just said there was no use for her anymore. All I remember is being inside that rehab place and then I took pills, the same ones they made me take every day. Now I'm here with you. And I can apparently read your mind. Lucky me." Timothy's eyes drag to the painting, or the carcass of it, anyway. "Wes, c'mon, do you really think that girl is ever going to love you?"

I swallow the disgust in his words. "She does love me."

"No, she doesn't. You just don't understand what love is because our uncle fucked you up so bad."

In my mind, my knuckles swipe over his words and crash into his face. What business is it of his? But memories halt my impulses—all the times he tried to help me—the nights when my uncle's temper reached a boiling point and his only satisfaction was to take it out on me. Timothy would hide me in his closet and lie, claiming I'd gone out into town. Sometimes he even took the brunt of my uncle's rage… for me.

I tuck my fist into my pocket. "Don't comment on things you don't understand."

Fear coasts across my brother's face. He opens his mouth to say another word, but I click my tongue in warning. If he can read my thoughts, he knows what I'm capable of.

A small part of me feels sorry for him—reading my mind while locked in this odd supernatural dungeon must be torture for him. I'm sure he wishes he'd died in that rehab place.

"No, Wes, I don't wish I died there," he says, answering my

thoughts. "Is this the way your brain has always worked? Since we were kids?"

"Pretty much."

Timothy shakes his head as if he's disappointed in me, but I don't really care that much. He's my brother, not by blood, and my allegiance to him only carries so far. Out of sight, out of mind, I suppose.

Now that he's in my head, he should understand my limits.

His face flushes crimson, his anxious tell. He twists away from me, as if that will be enough to shove my thoughts from his brain.

"How can you judge me? We were both dealt a terrible hand in life. I'm just trying to take back control," I say.

Timothy whirls around, letting his frustration unfurl. "You can't do that, Wes! We aren't the ones in control here! Don't you get that?"

"Really? Then who is? The authority? You know we're not even precogs, right? We're apparently half-demons and have incredible powers that these people are trying to suppress. They're only doing that because they're scared of us. All we need to do is use our full powers and take them down."

Timothy scowls. "You're so naïve. What do you think this is? They drew you here on purpose. You took the damn bait."

"I came here for Natalie, on my own terms. I gutted most of the Armory and made my way in here. The authority can't beat me."

With a sigh, Timothy starts pleading. "What makes you think they're dead? You thought I was dead, and I'm standing right here. You thought Uncle Warren was dead." He paces the room. "I over-heard the guards this morning. They said they were expecting you."

My jaw clenches so tightly, I think my teeth might crack. "So you're saying these people can read my thoughts too?"

"I don't know, Wes. But you're not infallible. You can't defeat these people. You can't make Natalie love you. You can't control things!"

His words wrench up my spine, spiking my brain with adrenaline.

He's challenging me—but no matter what he thinks he knows about me, he's wrong.

I'm going to see my plan through.

Because people like me don't unravel.

They win.

CHAPTER FORTY-FIVE

NATALIE

MY STOMACH SWIRLS with the aftershocks of seeing my mom—*alive*.

She's trying to help me… to warn me. Is she acting so distant to keep up appearances? Does the authority want her to pretend she doesn't remember me, her own daughter?

Or do they think she's brainwashed and she's been playing them the whole time?

I attempt to follow her, but as my hand reaches for the knob, the door warps and twists, fading out into a beige-colored wall. I scan the rest of the walls as they flood into that same nothingness, the door I entered also disappearing, imprisoning me even further. No, this can't be.

I slam my palms against the frustrating beige space walling me off from my mom. From the truth.

I spin my head to the camera, anger snaking up my spine. Someone, or several people, are watching me on that camera right now, delighting in my pain. Probably laughing as they study me, an animal trapped in their cage.

My heart pounds and rage stampedes through my brain as I try to come up with a plan. I'm now stuck in this beige room. The doors have disappeared, and there's a camera watching my every move.

Something inside of me snaps and I whip my gaze back to the camera. If they can see me, can they hear me?

Let's find out.

"Hey!" I call out. I give it a moment, but there's nothing but silence in return. Let's see if I can get their attention.

"You think you're smart, but I know what you're doing. I'm locked in here because you're scared… terrified of what I'm capable of. You can try your best, but keeping me in a room with no doors won't be enough to stop my powers. Some authority you are. Instead of facing me, you're hiding behind a camera, thinking this room will be enough to contain me. You're weak. But unfortunately for you, I'm not."

I suck in a shaky breath, steeling myself for their response.

The sound of a door clicking open startles me. I whirl around to face a guard, standing in the doorway that just disappeared moments ago. "Come with me," she barks.

I swallow the thick knot in my throat and follow her, my thirst for answers overriding the savage pounding of my heart.

The guard grips onto my arm, leading me into a room that should belong inside a castle. It's even faintly reminiscent of some parts of Lockwood. The room is framed with lavender panels, antique furniture that seems to drip with money, and modern gold accents, like some gothic revival. There's even an air of whimsy, which feels like a sick, twisted joke in a place like this.

The room is oddly decorated with a stage-type area with three mahogany chairs perched on top. Except they're not really chairs— more like thrones, the middle one more sizable than the others.

There's no one else here but me and the guard. The room is enormous but feels even smaller and more stifling than that horrible cell. Time moves differently with anticipation, and the moments crawl on.

But I'm willing to wait as long as it takes to get the people I care about out of here.

Footsteps pad into the room and a tall, thin man enters. He doesn't seem to notice me and just moves to one of the chairs, taking a seat on the throne to the left, drumming his bony fingers on the sides. Is he here to determine my fate?

Let him try.

Another person enters, this time, a woman with wild salt and pepper hair. She also ignores me and makes her way to the throne on the right, taking a seat. I can only assume these two are members of the authority. Maybe it's just the adrenaline, but they don't seem so intimidating.

The loud clack of high heels stomps through the silence. Something hot spikes through my stomach when I turn and notice Amelia enter the room.

Unlike her colleagues—if that's what they are—she *does* look at me, her gaze spitting venom right into my soul. Panic coils around my body, not understanding what's happening, yet already knowing things are about to get worse.

Amelia takes a seat in the center throne as I gulp down a breath. I knew deep down she had to be alive, but it's still jarring to see her here. Especially after I tried to end her life.

My eyes flick back and forth between the three of them, my body tightening with unease.

"You said we are weak. But you are not, correct?" Amelia says, her voice dripping with amusement. "Let's see just how strong you are."

A large metal door creaks open at the far end of the room. My eyes widen in horror as two guards drag my father inside. My pretend father, anyway. He's beaten and bruised; his eyes flare with desperation.

"Dad?" My words creak out without thinking. Was he a jerk to me? *Yes.* Is he not my real father? *Also yes.* But he doesn't deserve this twisted fate.

The guards shove my father down in front of me and he yelps in pain when his knees crash against the ground. Blood trickles from his head and I note more cuts and bruises. How long has he been here and what have they done? Is this why he didn't return my call? When did they take him?

Amelia and her cronies stare down at us from the platformed stage. "This man lied to you, treated you like property. He couldn't even bother to keep up appearances as your father. A weak person would let that go. A strong person would make him pay."

My heart jumps into my throat. What do they expect me to do, torture him more? Kill him?

"I'm not going to hurt him."

Amelia rises from her chair, stalking over to us. "Interesting."

My spine stiffens as Amelia steps closer. "What do you expect me to do?"

Amelia watches me, her voice like vicious silk bouncing off the space. "Well, I guess if you're too weak to do it…"

Quick as lighting, Amelia's hands lock onto my dad's neck, snapping the life from him. A sickening crack echoes off the walls and the room bleeds together.

She's taunting me. Every inch of my body is shaking, but I don't back down. I don't retreat. I meet Amelia's glare, my expression neutral and my breath shallow and even. I can't let her know she's gotten to me. I can't let her win.

Amelia's brows lift, as if she's impressed. The air grows thick around us as I narrow my eyes like ice picks. I'm not sure how to claw out of this mess, but I'm going to make damn sure Amelia doesn't spot a weak bone in my body.

"Very interesting," she says, her words souring in my stomach. She shakes her head, her lips curling into an amused grin. "What are we going to do with you next?"

"Despite what you may think, I'm not a toy."

She lets my words linger in the air before continuing, her expression morphing from amused to ambiguous. "Perhaps we can play a game then."

My heartbeat rages. "I have no interest in playing some sick game with you."

"We won't be playing each other."

Before I can respond, nausea floods my stomach, and everything goes black.

⁂

My eyes adjust to the dark hallway, a single light flickering from a sconce on the wall. The image of Amelia snapping my father's neck lingers in my brain.

Muffled voices cut through the silence, crowding out the painful memory. I move forward, pressing tightly against the wall, unsure of what nightmare I might endure this time.

The hallway grows darker the farther I walk toward the voices. I squint, trying to make out the details. The voices get clearer and my stomach flip-flops at the familiar giggle.

Ciel.

I race down the hall, tripping over something that's too dark to make out. Scrambling to my feet, I move ahead, following her laughter. She sounds happy. But how can that be? Worry climbs through my brain as I get closer.

Turning the corner, I'm in a different block of cells—each has a full wall of glass making it easy to see inside. I frantically look left and right into each empty cell until I hear yet another familiar voice.

My gut wrenches at the deep sound of Henry's words.

My insides seize as I spot Henry and Ciel inside the last cell in the block. Ciel is pressed against the wall, Henry watching her like an animal hunting his prey, his eyes wild with desire.

I bang on the glass, but they don't see me, or at least they're pretending not to.

Henry moves to her, curling Ciel into his arms and smashing his lips down on hers. Betrayal stomps through my insides. This can't be happening. Why? *How?* I squeeze my eyes closed, refusing to believe this is real. Amelia is surely toying with me—she said so herself.

Slowly, I open my eyes, but Henry and Ciel are still there, now deepening their kiss. He lifts her up, her legs wrapping around his waist as a moan escapes his lips.

I think I might vomit when an arm winds around my waist. I fight back, desperate to wrestle free from whoever it is. They pull me flush to them, pressing their palm against my mouth.

"Shhh. It's just me."

Wes.

I shove away from him, looking back into the cell, but now it's empty. No Henry. No Ciel. Maybe it wasn't real after all.

"Did you see that?" I ask Wes.

He shrugs in his typical bored way. "Yeah, so?"

I huff out a breath. If he saw it, then it was real. "You saw Henry and Ciel?"

He knits his brow, taking a step toward me, backing me against the wall. His arms cage me in. "Maybe you had a vision, and your precious Henry is nothing more than a guy who wants to fuck your best friend."

"Get away." I shove him off me and stride down the hall.

"Where are you going?" he calls after me with an amused tone, like he's also playing some twisted game.

"Anywhere but here!" I shout back.

"Jealousy doesn't look good on you, Covington." His words leech through my skin and stop me in my tracks. "There are things you should know," he says.

I refuse to turn around. "As if I'd believe anything you say."

"If you don't want your mom to end up like your dad, you should listen to me."

CHAPTER FORTY-SIX

WES

THE AIR THICKENS between us as Natalie pushes me away yet again.

Liar.

I don't trust you.

I don't believe anything you say.

Her words gash open my heart. Doesn't she know by now that everything I've done is for her? I've lied, sure, but only for her own good.

I take a step closer and she jerks back. "What do you know about my mother?"

Not much. But I can't exactly tell her that. It's the only bargaining chip I have to make sure she doesn't run away from me again.

My brother proved fairly useless as I tried to pry information out of him, but he did have one intriguing tidbit about this place.

"My brother said—" I start to say, but I'm cut off as Natalie's words thrash out.

"Your brother? I thought he was dead."

"So did I. But he's here, along with my uncle."

Natalie braces herself against the cell, and I figure it's probably a good time to reassure her that I'm here, that she's safe... with me.

"Don't worry, my uncle won't try to hurt you again. Not when I'm around."

Her eyes narrow, blazing green with anger. "I don't need your protection, Wes. I don't need you."

My heart cracks under the weight of her rejection—spitting venom through my limbs. I try to squeeze her harsh words from my mind.

She's just scared.

She's out of her mind.

She'll come around.

"Tell me everything you know." Her demand coils around my spine like a snake. I have something she wants—information. I need to remember that I have the upper hand, and if she wants to know what this place is, she'll have to stick it out with me.

I can barely wipe the smirk off my face when she shouts out my name, growing more frustrated by my silence. I take one more step closer and her back presses harder against the wall of the cell—attempting to put more distance between us. Excitement ripples through my chest at the sight of her pressed against it.

"You have thirty more seconds to talk," she says.

"Or what?"

She's about to protest, but her lips smack closed. Realization passes through her eyes—she needs me. Although I'd like to hear her say those words, knowing that the thought is looping through her mind is enough. *For now.*

"I'm going to tell you."

"When? You just said my mother is in danger and you're here playing pointless games."

My stomach tightens, wishing we were back at Lockwood right now, having fun playing our games. The ones we used to play in her bed, or mine. "My brother thinks the authority is performing experiments." As much as I'd like to focus on visions of our future, I stay on task, giving her the information she craves.

Her eyes stray from mine. "What kind of experiments?"

"He wasn't sure. But my brother isn't exactly the brightest crayon in the box, so…"

She scowls at me in disgust. I want nothing more than to clasp my hands over that scowl and swallow her lips with mine. Sadly, this isn't the time for that.

"Does that mean they're experimenting on my mother? Or us? Or both?"

Nerves weave through my chest. Of course we're not part of it—we broke into this hellhole. They couldn't have drawn us here, right? The thought hadn't occurred to me before, but now that it's lodged in my brain, I can't get rid of it.

"Wes!"

Natalie stops my mind from spinning and I suck in a deep breath as I continue. "My brother said he overheard some things from the guards here—about how important it is to keep people contained. It makes sense. I was told my entire life that I'm a precog, but it turns out I'm a half-demon. A Cambion. You believe that?" I can't help but chuckle.

"I know." Natalie glares at me and fury sinks into my bones. Henry *does* know what we are and he told her. The idea of the two of them sharing anything makes me want to shred this entire place into a thousand pieces.

"Where is your brother now? Maybe he can help me find my mom."

"I don't know." And that's the truth. "We were together in the cell—the one you were in with Henry." Disgust seeps through my chest at the memory.

"Wait, were you really watching us?"

"Yes. It was clear you didn't see me or know I was there. Or you wouldn't have done what you did." Betrayal slices through my words. I've already resolved to forgive her for this little stint with Henry. It meant nothing. *I know it meant nothing.*

Natalie chews on her bottom lip. "If they're doing experiments, they must be messing with us. Things keep appearing and disappearing. We're locked in places and then we're not. We're out in an open hallway right now, but no one's come after us. Amelia said this was a game..."

Amelia? Fuck, so she's here too, and alive. Maybe Natalie's right—this is all designed to toy with us until we shatter. My uncle alluded to this as well—this place serving as our personal torture chamber. The authority certainly has an interesting view on entertainment.

Well, good luck to them, because they'll never be able to break me.

"Is this whole thing just about taking away every person I love?" Natalie says.

Aggravation splits and weaves through my brain. Sure, this place took Natalie away from her mom. Ciel. Henry, though she can't really love him—it must be Stockholm syndrome causing those confused feelings.

"That can't be true or we wouldn't be here together right now."

Her face morphs and shifts into disgust. "I don't love you, Wes."

Her words send fury through every inch of my body. How can she say that? My stomach spins and drops. This feeling is familiar... it's the same feeling I get when tracking most people, knowing their death is just around the corner. Rage bleeding away all reason, followed by an unexplained darkness—as if I'm mentally blacked out and something else takes over my body.

Before I even realize what I'm doing, my hands grip Natalie's arms. I twist her around and smash her body against the wall—pressing my body against hers to hold her in place.

"I don't love you. I never did," she says.

My mind fires, wanting to break every single thing in sight—including her—for trying to hurt me like this.

Then something wraps around my throat, hurling me away from

Natalie. My body crashes against the concrete wall, crunching to the ground. It takes me a moment to get my bearings. My head feels like it's split in two, and I'm not even sure I'm still alive.

I focus on the rise and fall of my chest. At the very least, I'm still breathing. My brain clouds and I blink furiously, trying not to lose consciousness.

"Stay away from my daughter."

My gaze traces the smooth voice to Madeline Covington, now standing next to Natalie, curling her daughter into her arms like I'm some kind of monster.

A sea of vicious thoughts rips through my mind.

You left your daughter in danger while you traipsed around here with the authority.

You knew your daughter had powers—that she may not be human—and you never bothered to tell her.

You failed her again and again while I was here to pick up the broken pieces.

I try to etch out my thoughts but my throat lodges, jamming the words down into my chest. My muscles scream in protest as I try to move, but my body feels like it's trapped in a vice.

"Don't bother," Madeline says. "You won't be able to speak or move until we're out of your sight."

Fury rips through my body as I try to writhe and fight and scream, but my body remains glued to the ground. My eyes are the only thing able to move—watching Madeline drag Natalie away from me.

As soon as they're out of sight, my heart ramps up in my chest and the blood rushes to my limbs. Their silhouettes still visible in the distance, I fight to stabilize my legs, attempting to chase after them, but they disappear into the darkness ahead.

My nostrils flare, knowing she's going to turn Natalie against me, even more than she already is. Natalie thinks this place is designed to torture her. I think she's got it wrong.

It's designed to torture me.

"No, *you've* got it wrong." A familiar voice rings out behind me and I spin around, meeting the cold gaze of Amelia, who was clearly reading my thoughts, just like my brother.

"Did you like the visions I showed you?" she asks.

Realization slams into my body. Did Amelia somehow plant visions into my brain? Is this actually all some grand experiment, and I'm one of the subjects?

"I left Natalie's hat for you in the cell. Did you like that as well?"

Natalie's hat? Wait… Amelia put it there?

"Yes, to all of your questions." She answers my thoughts. Like my brother, she's reading my fucking mind.

"And I have a proposition for you," she says.

CHAPTER FORTY-SEVEN

NATALIE

WARMTH FLOODS MY insides as my mom tucks us inside of a dark room. It's the first time I've felt safe since I got here.

Honestly, it's the first time I've felt safe since Mom died. Or since *I thought* she was dead.

My eyes try to adjust to the darkness as I hear the click of the door close and lock. As soon as Mom turns to me, my thoughts clear and I wrap myself into her arms. I have so many questions, need so many answers, but all I want to do is hug her—something I never thought I'd be able to do again.

As I squeeze her tight, I notice an absence—her arms limp around my body, not exactly hugging me back. A small sob escapes her lips against my shoulder and I pull away.

"We don't have much time. Natalie, honey, I'm so sorry. For everything." What is she apologizing for? These people faked her death and locked her up in here. Why would that be her fault?

"I don't understand, Mom. They kidnapped you, put you in this place. Why are you sorry?"

She shakes her head, and a sinking feeling lodges into my heart, my breath getting caught in my throat. Tears begin to float down her cheeks and I get the distinct feeling she's about to say something I don't want to hear.

"That's not what happened, honey."

Her words carve into my heart. So they didn't take her? Is she here willingly?

I move away instinctively, the back of my thighs bumping into a desk behind me. A monitor shakes alive, filling the dark room with light. I spin to face the screen—noticing that it's security footage… of the Lockwood campus.

My skin slicks with cold sweat as I look over at my mom. "Mom, what is this?"

"It's you," she says in a quiet murmur.

I whip my gaze back to the screen, realizing she's right. It's me, standing backstage with Jack, right before he's about to go on and accept class presidency.

"Why do they have this? Why is this playing? I don't understand." Confusion rips my mind to shreds.

"That's when this all started," she says.

Frustration roars through my bones. "Mom, just please, tell me. I know I have some kind of powers. That I'm not human. I think this whole thing is happening because of me, but I don't know why."

"Not just you. It's happening because of *us*. You and me. And your real father."

"Is it because you were working on a story to expose precogs? Or Cambions? Whatever they really are."

Mom shakes her head with confusion. "I was never working on a story about them. Is that what they told you?"

I nod, my insides clenching, awaiting the truth.

"Honey, I had a specific agreement with the authority for my entire life. I became quite close to a few members, progressive members who imagined a new way of doing things. A way that supernatural beings could live peacefully amongst humans without risk of harm. It was idealistic but possible, we felt. Until Amelia rose in the ranks, banished any forward thinking, and unseated anyone who didn't agree."

My thoughts scramble together as reality smacks me in the face. "So what are we? Cambions too?"

My mom lowers her eyes with a deep exhale, causing a sharp throb in the middle of my stomach as Mom explains. "I'm part Cambion, part Astral."

Astral? I squeeze my eyes shut as the term gnaws at my mind. This is all so bizarre and incomprehensible.

"What is an Astral?" I ask, leaning against the wall, feeling faint.

"I draw part of my bloodline from humans and demons—that's the Cambion side—and the other part from the cosmos."

I rub my forehead, my mom's words locking together the puzzle while so many pieces are still missing.

"So why didn't you ever tell me?"

Mom swallows, braiding her trembling fingers together. "When I was brought into this world, my parents handed me over to the authority, and they initially wanted me dead. They didn't understand the full scope of my powers because I'm part Astral, and apparently took a vote. It was decided that as long as I was raised under their rule, I could live. They took me in, and right before I turned nineteen, my full powers unlocked. Certain physical characteristics, like my eyes turning green, aligned me with Cambions, but other things, like my spectrum of powers, didn't. I always cooperated with them, and they discovered I had a talent for investigating and gave me a job. It was supposed to be a track and report, that was it. But I met someone, fell in love with him, and got pregnant with you."

My eyes blink in surprise as I take in a deep breath. "So where is my real father? Is he human?"

"No. He was... *he is...* a God."

My insides fracture, feeling more lost and confused than before. "What? I don't understand."

Mom swallows. "Your father is an immortal God. I didn't actually know that until I became pregnant with you and he revealed everything."

"So where is he?"

"Right now, I don't know. But I'm pretty certain he's very far away, likely not even on this plane of existence."

My stomach flips and falls, bottoming out.

"Your father got into a lot of trouble for getting involved with me. He had to leave for his safety and for ours. The authority didn't want you to be brought into the world. It was too risky—you have immortal blood and a power construct they don't understand. But I begged them to let me keep you. They took a vote and agreed that you could live as long as I fabricated a marriage for appearances, didn't tell you anything until you were eighteen, and allowed them to keep a close eye on you, dictating what you did, where you went to school. I didn't want to agree to that, but it was the only way for you, for both of us, to live. I'm so sorry, honey."

I can feel the anguish pouring out in her words. If she didn't agree, I would have never been born. She would have been killed. It was an impossible situation.

"But I don't understand why the authority faked your death. And you left that note with Ray so I would find you, right?"

"What note?" she says, genuinely.

"The note that led me to the box in Dad's house."

Mom stares at me with a blank expression. She really has no idea what I'm talking about. So who sent me that note? Who planted that box? Who was Ray?

As if something clicks, Mom begins pacing the room. "That must have been another part of Amelia's plan."

Heat surges through my veins. "What do you mean?"

Mom wanders over, clasping my hands into hers. "There was a regime change at the authority and Amelia manipulated her way into power, found out about the agreement between the authority and me. I knew Amelia many years ago—she was a friend of mine, the one who helped me when I was pregnant and alone. I lost touch with her and then she turned up, completely different, and changed the terms of my agreement. Her first order was to force me back here—she faked my death so there were no questions asked by the police. I begged her to let you live free. I couldn't imagine a life where you had to be locked inside these walls, under her rule. She had me drugged and when I woke up, it became clear that she believed she'd wiped my memory. But whatever she attempted didn't work. So I've pretended that I don't remember you to keep the peace… to keep you safe. But I was wrong, and I just put you in more danger."

My hands begin to shake, and my mom clenches them tighter. "So does Lockwood exist as a holding cell for Cambions and people like us? Are the other students not human?"

Mom shakes her head no. "The authority owns Lockwood. It's the perfect place to fly under the radar, especially as people like us grow into adults and gain more agency into our powers. There aren't that many supernatural beings in the world, so only a few a year attend Lockwood. The rest of the students are humans—very wealthy humans, who are too self-involved to notice any of the kids have powers. The school is also under constant surveillance—easy for the authority to keep watch and take care of things."

My mind is ready to collapse from sheer exhaustion and the weight of all of the revelations. I try scooping out the parts that still don't make sense, the questions I have.

"Is she watching us right now?" I ask, shivering at the thought, scanning my gaze around the room.

"There are no cameras in here."

I look back at the surveillance footage looping on the screen behind me. On the screen, I'm standing backstage next to a nervous Jack, waiting for him to accept the title of class president, wanting to be anywhere but in that moment.

"You said it all started here. What does that mean?"

Mom releases my hands, her eyes glistening with fresh tears, causing nerves to claw up my spine. "Amelia decided that the best way to deal with your existence was to figure out a way to keep you and your powers contained."

My stomach splinters at the mental image—me as a puppet and Amelia pulling the strings.

"And how is she doing that?"

"By performing an experiment. She had Oliver send Henry to Lockwood and implanted that vision of you in his brain—just to see how it all played out. The authority suspects Henry is something else as well, something more than a Cambion. Amelia ordered a false hit on your life, sending Wes's uncle there after you, and paying him off to capture you instead. The goal was never to kill you, just to observe you, Henry, and to a lesser extent, Wes. Amelia has some interests in his true nature too. Honey, all of it is a test. And I didn't... *I don't* know how to protect you from it."

My mind clouds and my ears feel fuzzy with nerves. "Mom, how do you know all of this?"

"Because Amelia thinks my memory was wiped. So she tends to speak more freely around me. I'm not a prisoner here. They treat me as a guest, as long as I stay in line, under their control."

My heart hammers so loudly, I think I might collapse. "I don't understand—what is Amelia trying to accomplish? Is she trying to figure out my full powers? And then what?"

The strain on Mom's face sends ice through my veins. "Honey, she wants to see how far she can push you, how much you will come unraveled. And she's going to keep doing it again and again unless we find a way to stop her."

CHAPTER FORTY-EIGHT

WES

I FEEL ODDLY calm as Amelia leads me inside some haughty chamber full of colorful vintage furniture. Ice isn't surging through my veins. There's no pounding in my chest. Just a calm, cool stillness.

She didn't breathe a word as we wound through the maze-like halls of this place, which was a good thing, because it allowed me to work out how these halls crisscross together. To help me carve a way for Natalie and me to eventually escape.

"You won't escape, just so you know," Amelia says. It keeps slipping my mind that she can read it.

But she underestimates me.

"I can warp these grounds to my liking. There's no way out unless I want you to leave."

My knuckles tighten and that calmness begins to dissipate. "So is that another one of our powers? To change space?"

"No, it's magic. Which I realize you've used already, despite it being forbidden and punishable by death."

My bravado spills out. "You're using it. Does that mean I can kill you?"

She looks at me with an inquisitive stare, ignoring my question. "You are quite entertaining. And surprising. I didn't initially want you to be part of this, but here we are. Would you like something to drink?"

My throat is so dry, it feels like a thousand paper cuts when I swallow, but if she thinks I'm going to consume anything from this place, she's more insane than I thought. I shake my head no, wondering what she means by me being a part of this. I set that thought aside, my interest tugged in a different direction.

"I'd like to hear about this bargain you want to make," I say.

"You're quite confident for a child." She turns away, pouring herself a drink from a dark wooden bar cart.

"I'm not a child. I'm eighteen. That's considered an adult, in case you weren't aware. You seem to spend a lot of your time locked away here in your evil chambers, plotting."

A chuckle escapes her throat. "So the girl you brought back to life, Ciel. She must mean a lot to you."

Ciel? Mean something? Now it's my turn to laugh. "No. I only saved her because of Natalie."

"Ahhh, the illustrious Natalie. I imagine you didn't think through the consequences of saving Ciel then."

Irritation floods my veins. "What consequences?"

"You're bonded to her now."

Bonded? What the hell does that mean? I try my best to keep my cool, but it's impossible when Amelia has clawed her way into my brain, reading and relaying every thought like it's some nursery rhyme.

"Ciel can feel your energy, sense when you're in danger. It's been torture for her here, which has honestly been delightful to watch."

Frustration whirls through my mind. So Ciel is alive. A strange hint of relief floods through my veins and I swat it away. What is that about? Why would I care about her? Before we got in this place, I was seconds from killing her, leaving her out in the woods.

Amelia laughs. "You can try to deny it all you want. The truth is you easily could have killed Ciel before you entered this building, but you didn't."

I suck in a deep breath, but the knot in my stomach refuses to loosen. *Bonded.* No. The only person I want to be bonded with is Natalie. *She is mine.* She is who I'm supposed to be with.

"Your desperation for Natalie isn't your fault, you know." There's a slice of compassion in her voice and I wish I could wipe my mind clean so she can't read and morph and twist my thoughts any longer.

Disgust coils in my bones. "I'm not desperate for her. I'm in love with her."

"Trust me, you're not."

Trust Amelia? I may have made a lot of fucking mistakes in my life, but trusting Amelia won't be one of them.

"Everything about Natalie is designed to draw people like you and me in. Trust me. I've been in your shoes. I'm trying to help you, Wesley. I'm extending an olive branch."

Anger swells in my chest, lodging in my throat, making it feel even drier, scratchier than before. I'm growing sick and tired of listening to this conniving asshole when I should be finding Natalie, getting us out of here.

Amelia sighs, her face softening into an empathetic gaze. But all I see is the pure manipulation in her mannerisms. "Natalie is something very powerful and extremely dangerous. She is part Cambion, part Astral… and has other parts to her genetic makeup that are designed to draw you in and never let go."

My fingers twist together and I nearly crack my knuckles in two. So Natalie is some cosmic crossbreed who is made to lure in guys like me who would do anything, even kill for her?

"Exactly." Amelia answers my thoughts. "Like I said, in the past, I've fallen prey to someone like her too."

I don't want to believe her, and yet irritation winds around my skin, poking and prodding at every nerve. I was raised with purpose—as an assassin. I had one mission: death. Every inch of my training and life was carefully calculated. Find the mark. Track them. Kill them.

Until Natalie came along, blinding me with obsession. I'm not like this, I've never been like this—so consumed by someone. I thought this was love. Isn't that the definition? Someone you care for so deeply, your bones ache in their absence? Someone you would shatter the earth for?

"I know this can't be easy to hear." Amelia talks down to me like a mother nurturing her child. It makes my insides curdle.

My gaze sweeps over the tacky space, scanning every corner, assessing each detail. At the far end of the room, a weird looking device catches my eye. Perched on a table, it resembles a colossal crystal ball with two levers on its sides. The core is filled with an array of metallic spikes, a design as intriguing as it is odd. A flicker of recognition sparks within me, the sensation of having encountered a photo of it before.

Where have I seen it before?

Amelia answers my thoughts once again. "You recognize it?" She points to the contraption, a tinge of anxiety in her smooth voice.

"No." I shove the thought from my mind. No need to give her more ammunition. "Look, if your plan is to kill Natalie, you can't really think I'm going to participate. I saved her once and I'd make the same choice, over and over again."

"We don't want her dead. We just want to understand her better, know the threat she poses. The only way to do that is to experiment, push her to the brink, and unfortunately, that includes testing things on the people she cares about most."

Nausea sloshes through my stomach at the idea of being a pawn in her sick little game. Though the thought of finding out what Natalie would do, how far she would go, to save *me* is intriguing. She denies her love for me, but I see right through it. Her body will always betray her words, harsh as they might be.

"So you're trying to hurt me to see if Natalie will lose it?"

"No, not you. Ciel. Her mother. And most importantly, Henry. The one she loves."

Rage burns through every inch of my body and my mind splits with fury. Within seconds, I'm inches from Amelia, my hand wrapped around her throat, wanting nothing more than to squeeze every last drop of life from her.

Through choked breaths, she whispers, "If you want Natalie to change her mind about you, I can help."

My grip loosens and I shove her away. "I don't need your help."

Suddenly, something solid but invisible blasts against my chest, tossing my body against the wall. My skull cracks as I flop down to the ground. I try moving, but I seem to be completely frozen, everything except my racing thoughts.

I can hear the clicking of Amelia's shoes until she's looming over me, cutting her darkened gaze to mine. "I tried doing this a different way, but you refuse to cooperate."

The words get caught in my throat as oxygen leaks from my lungs. Frantic, I gulp down air, but it doesn't seem to help.

"You want Natalie, despite the fact that she doesn't want you. And you're bonded to another girl. I know you're special—there's a level of darkness burning inside of you that very few possess. If you help me, I'll help you."

Reality crashes through my insides as I croak out a "yes" to her bargain.

She releases her invisible grip on me and my body wrenches to the side, every inch of me sweating with agony. I suck the life back into my lungs as heat and adrenaline pumps back into my veins.

"What the hell do you want me to do?"

Amelia's face softens into that fake compassionate expression that I wish I could slap right off. "I have a plan. Until then, a bargain's a bargain."

Before I can say another word, everything in my world goes black.

CHAPTER FORTY-NINE

NATALIE

"**Mom, if the** authority is scared of us, of me, if I have these special powers, can't I defeat them? You said I have immortal blood." I try to pepper bravery into my voice, even though panic nearly sears open my bones.

Mom shoots me a cautious glance, the same look she would give me when I played too close to the street as a kid, or swam out too far in the ocean. "Honey, the authority is a centuries-old, strategically designed government. We can't just take them down. I don't know how your genetic makeup works. Yes, your father is immortal. I don't know if that passes on to you. And Amelia is beyond just the power of authority. She's wielding magic, and there's a reason it's forbidden."

Adrenaline pummels my heart, nearly cracking it in two. "But we have to try, right? I just need to figure out how to use my full powers. I've already used them before."

Mom's eyes widen and she backs away, as if she's suddenly terri-fied of me. "What did you do?"

I'm worried about frightening her, but there's no time for

concern. Who knows what fresh hell Amelia still has in store for me and the people I love.

"Once, when I was with Henry, we made the atmosphere shift somehow. It's hard to explain. And then I had the strength to kill both Henry's foster dad and Amelia. Or at least, I thought I did. And when I was locked in that cell with Henry, we caused the whole floor to collapse under us… but then…" My voice trails off and pain slices through my mind as I try making sense of all this.

Mom is silent, her face frozen into a grimace.

"Mom?"

She seems to shake off her disturbing thoughts. Or at least she tries to. "You likely have other powers, different than mine, from your father's side. But again, no one knows how that all cycles together. Which is why Amelia is so hell-bent on finding out."

Tears well up in her eyes again and I race over, wrapping into her arms. There's a part of me who wishes I could rewind back to childhood, when nothing felt as safe as being with her. But even then, at least for her, every one of our interactions must have been laced with some kind of fear of what the future—*now*—might hold.

Our moment is broken when something fires in the distance—it's more of an explosion than a gunshot. The sound is muted, but loud enough to make an impact.

"What the hell was that? Where did that come from?"

Another blast. My eyes dart to the security footage on the monitor, realizing the sound is coming from the speaker. Racing over, I notice the screen has switched to Henry.

Alive.

He's running down a hallway, dodging an explosion to the side, concrete rubble shattering around him. I take a frantic second to analyze his surroundings.

"Mom, do you know where he might be?"

Mom looks at the monitor, shaking her head. "It's impossible to know, especially when Amelia knows how to wield magic. She can warp this space, change things. She can implant visions, like she did with Henry. She can read minds, though she hasn't been able to read mine. It's a huge point of contention for her—that some of her magic may not work on me… or you… or others. I believe she can also shift space and time, make things appear not as they are."

My brows knit as I look back at Henry on screen, darting down another hallway, the camera seeming to magically track and switch to showcase his every movement.

"So what's happening to Henry might not be real? Is this part of Amelia's plan—to make me to see this? Does she know we're in here?"

Mom shrugs, but the grave look in her eye screams "yes."

Clenching my jaw, I weigh the possibilities. This could be a setup, but it could also be reality, and I can't take that risk. "I have to try and help him. And clearly, being with Henry unlocks some kind of powers. Maybe we're stronger together."

Mom grabs my wrist as I pass, stopping me. "Honey, you might be doing exactly what Amelia wants. She could be drawing you back into her web."

"But this is never going to stop. She's going to keep trapping us like hamsters in a cage, trying all different ways to torture me. I'm not her chess piece. I'm the whole fucking game. So from now on, I make the rules."

My fear dissipates as the words erupt from my body—even I'm surprised by the force in them. Mom seems terrified…for me. *Of me.* But I can't stick around to reassure her that everything will be okay. I'm not even certain it will be—but I sure can't wait around for Amelia's next move.

"I'll come with you," she says.

"No. You already said that Amelia doesn't want me dead. But she does want me to crack, and she'll use you to do it. She can't read your mind, right? She thinks you don't remember anything? So just play dumb. Deny."

"Honey, now that you're here, I'm afraid I won't be able to pull that off."

"You did a really good job keeping things a secret from me my entire life." My gut twists at the words. I don't blame her for not telling me about what I really am, but it does prove she's a damn good secret keeper.

Mom nods as a heaviness blankets the space between us. This time, it's my turn to protect her.

∽

Trapped in a maze of halls and caves and locked doors, I wind my way through the authority building, having no idea where I'm going, but trusting that Amelia must be watching me, luring me somewhere.

It really doesn't matter which direction I turn. At some point, she'll maneuver things so that I find Henry, and likely trap us into some other impossible situation intended to break me.

But this time, I know what she's up to and will do everything in my power to stop it.

I hear sudden movement and duck into a dark corner. A guard walks past, craning their neck, probably searching for me. I'm not sure what role these guards play here. Do they know about Amelia's experiments? Do they even care? Questions ricochet inside my mind like gunshots, but I need to focus. I need to find Henry. I need to figure out a way to put a stop to all of this.

As soon as the guard disappears out of sight, I'm moving again, until my feet slide out from under me and I crash down onto the ground.

There's something wet underneath my body. I press myself up, my hands sticky with the substance. Squinting through the darkness, I rub my fingers together, realizing I just slipped and fell in blood.

Whose blood is this?

Panic claws up my spine and I shove it back down. This is Amelia's game, which means she's trying to rattle me. She *wants* me to panic. Wants me to think this is Henry's blood.

I follow the sticky red trail to a winding staircase that seems to descend forever into the earth. Gulping down my nerves, I carefully make my way down, hearing a soft groan in the distance.

Henry.

Quickening my pace, I move swiftly down the stairs, taking them two by two. As my feet slap down onto the concrete below, I spot Henry across the room, curled into a fetal position.

I race over to him. "It's me. What happened?"

He's hurt, bloodied, but in the darkness, I struggle to tell where the blood is even coming from. His eyes land on mine and he reaches out, clasping onto my hand with a weak grip, his breathing heavy and labored. He places my hand over the blood on the front of his shirt.

My mind races—is this real? An illusion? Part of Amelia's game?

I tear open his shirt to get a better look at the gaping wound on his stomach. Henry chokes and blood trickles out of his mouth. His body starts to shake. Terror wreaks havoc on my insides. He's dying, right here in my arms.

Think, Natalie, think.

Ciel snaps into my brain. Wes saved her life with magic. He detailed every second of it to me, five times over. I made him.

Wes is a Cambion, but so am I. Partly, anyway. And apparently, I'm even more powerful than him, so maybe magic will work for me too. Maybe it will work even better.

The last breath whooshes from Henry's lungs. I reach my hand into his pocket, relieved to find his dagger there.

Slice into the side of the wrist, not over the vein. Just a little. Not too much.

Replaying Wes's words in my head, I jab the tip of the dagger into the side of my wrist, making a vertical slice.

Please let this work. Please let this work.

Using my other hand to open Henry's mouth into an "O," I lay my wrist over his mouth, letting the blood slowly drip inside.

Count backwards from ten. *Ten, nine, eight, seven, six, five, four, three, two, one.*

Nothing. Henry doesn't stir or make any movement. Panic rips through my muscles and the pain registers in my wrist. What if this doesn't work?

"Please. C'mon, Henry, please."

More seconds pass and hope floats out of my body, crashing down on the cold ground, taking my heart with it. Maybe I can't use magic, I'm not capable. I'm sure I followed all the right instructions. A storm of emotions crashes into my brain and a sob escapes my lips.

I can't let Amelia win, can't let her break me.

But I'm afraid she's already done it.

Just as I'm about to pull away my wrist, Henry chokes to life.

"You're alive." I put my hands on his cheeks as his watery green eyes stare up at me, his lungs filling back up with air. The wound on his stomach begins to close, like magic.

It worked.

Relief breathes into every inch of my body, until…

Henry's hands snap around my wrists. His eyes turn feral.

Something's not right here.

I try to pull away, but he tightens his grip, flipping me over onto my back. His strength seems to have doubled, tripled even. He studies my face, almost like he doesn't recognize me.

"Henry, it's me." I whisper the words, hoping he'll snap out of this, but my words don't seem to matter.

His lips crash down onto mine, prying my mouth open with

his. He feels different somehow, like an entirely separate person, someone I'm desperate to get away from.

My consciousness begins to slip as I attempt to shove him off me. My vision blurs and my limbs begin to go limp. The weight of Henry's body disappears from mine as he stands, looming over me.

I blink, desperate to regain my sight, but my head is spinning out of control. A slice of my vision clears just long enough for me to notice it's not Henry standing in front of me.

It's Wes.

CHAPTER FIFTY

NATALIE

"**What the hell** is going on?" I shoot Wes a vicious glare, horror bubbling through my veins.

"It was the only way to break the bond with Ciel and secure it with you," Wes says, his lips curling into a disgusting smirk.

No, this can't be. Everything in this place is an illusion. This is just Amelia, wielding her magic again. I can hardly feel the pain from the cut on my wrist when rage is slicing into every other part of me.

The dagger lies on the ground, and as I reach for it, Wes snatches it away, tucking it inside his coat.

"What do you want?" I keep my hand coiled around my wound as I stand.

"You. I thought I made that obvious already."

Revulsion floods my body like thick, burning lava. "You're truly a psychopath, you know that? Are you working with Amelia to torment me? Have you been working with her the entire time?"

"No, she just made me an offer I couldn't refuse. Now you and I are bonded together. Forever."

He can't be serious. Bonded with him? Over my dead body. My mind twists around his words—not about the weird bond, but about the fact that *Amelia made him an offer.* It's unsurprising that she's chosen Wes as her confidant. But that means they've talked. That means he has information.

"Okay, fine then, we're bonded." I play along, hoping to seep information from him. "That means nothing if Amelia wants me dead."

Wes takes a step towards me. Instinctively, I back away, then stop myself. If I'm going to get information, I need to stand my ground. Maybe even give him a hint that I might be delighted with this fake bond he's rattling on about.

"Amelia doesn't want you dead," he says. "She just wants to get to know you better."

No new revelations here. I'm aware Amelia is testing me. Let's see what else he's got. "What does that mean?"

"She can't read your mind, and that's the only way for the authority to understand your kind."

"And what is my kind?" I'm aware already, of course, from my mom's revelations. But how much did Amelia tell him about me?

"You're some combination of Cambion and something called an Astral, which is apparently some kind of cosmic being, and other things too. Like someone mixed you up in a supernatural cauldron. They definitely did a great fucking job making you."

He rakes his eyes over me as my stomach twists and churns. I don't believe a word he says. Bile rises in my throat at his pure delusion. Was there ever a time I wasn't so disgusted by him? I can hardly remember now.

Memories snap into my brain like nightmares, reminding me of all the long nights we spent together, his hands exploring my body, his lips on mine. I'd be lying to myself if I were to admit every moment was a game. A part of me—*a part I'm not proud of*—wanted him then and liked that he wanted me. A part that felt grateful for his distraction after all the pain and loss.

But not anymore.

Now when I look at him, all I see is a monster. A monster who was trained to kill. A monster who ruthlessly tracked my mother with every intent of having her murdered. A monster who manipulated things for his own gain. A monster who is now working with Amelia.

Cambions are supposed to be half-demon by definition. Maybe Wes should check his lineage because if anyone is the full devil— it's him.

He must notice my sheer disgust because he starts pleading. "Natalie, I'm doing this all for you. I hate everyone but you. I love you. Don't you understand?"

His delusion shoots at me like bullets, and the worst part is, I think he's actually sick enough to believe his words.

"I'm right here. What could you possibly want with Henry Thorne?" he says, more delusion pouring from his mouth.

I want to scream how much I hate him, how much I wish I could erase every last touch, every last kiss, every last drop of time with him. But I can't. I have to stay the course.

I have to play the game.

My eyes trail to the droplets of blood trickling out of my wrist and onto the floor. Letting the tension loosen from my spine, I try and avoid the loathing coursing through my veins. "How were you able to appear as Henry?"

Wes gulps and darkness passes through his eyes. I practically smell the rage sizzling in his chest that I dared to ask about Henry. "Amelia used magic, knowing that you'd only come running if Henry was in trouble. Aren't you ever going to get tired of wanting to save him?"

Anger drums through my veins. *No, I won't tire of that.* But hopefully, soon, it will be the last time I need to.

"So what's the plan? You're going to drag me back to Amelia?"

Wes scrunches his brow. "Why would I do that?"

"Because you're making deals with her, happily becoming her pawn just to play me."

Wes takes another step forward and my stomach cramps. His gaze searches mine, like he's trying to figure me out. I'm certain he is. The last thing I want is for him to be anywhere near me now, or ever.

But this is the only way.

"What's your plan?" I ask.

He doesn't breathe a word—his usual smirky expression is strangely blank. An icy shock coats my mind. *Something's not right here.* Not that it ever is.

"You have nothing to say?"

My question is met with more silence. It's as if Wes is a character in some video game and he just started glitching.

I can hardly stand to look at him, but my curiosity keeps me glued in place for the time being—dying to know… *what he knows.*

He extends his hand for mine and my teeth grit, refusing to touch him.

"Your wrist. Let me help." Without waiting for my approval, he reaches out, grabbing my wrist and cupping it in his hand. Within seconds, the wound closes.

Detached from whatever magic he's wielding now, my eyes lock on to the handle of the dagger peeking out of his coat.

He doesn't release my wrist and his eyes search my face, probably wanting a reaction, some gratitude for his healing.

"You healed me. It's only fair I return the favor," he says, his head dipping closer to mine.

"I guess now it's back to my turn," I say.

"Your turn for what?"

Before he realizes what's happening, my hand reaches out, ripping the dagger from his coat, and plunging it into his stomach.

Something deranged thrums through my mind as I stay on him, twisting the dagger deeper as agony erupts from his throat.

"She... will... bring... me... back... to... life," he croaks out.

Yes, asshole. I'm aware Amelia can use magic and bring you back. I only need to buy enough time to get away from you.

I shove him away, letting his body slam to the floor as I race away from his screams, still holding his dagger.

CHAPTER FIFTY-ONE

HENRY

THE FIRST THING I notice is the smell. *Bleach.* So strong, it burns my throat as I suck in some much-needed oxygen.

Blinking my eyes open, I'm nearly blinded by the fluorescent lights, the white ceiling and walls. *Where the fuck am I?*

Memories slowly ripple back into my brain. The cell. *Natalie.* Trying to conjure our powers. The floor crashing in. Plunging into the darkness.

And now I'm here in this sterile room, not unlike the room in that precog rehab where my foster dad nearly burned me to death, and Wes left me to die.

But I got free then. And I can damn well do it again. I attempt to move, but my body is strapped down to the bed—thick, rubber-like straps cover my chest, arms, stomach, and legs, rendering me completely immobile.

There's an IV jammed into my vein, pumping some clear liquid into my body. Probably something to keep me drugged and unconscious. How long have I been out?

The door to the room swings open and my mouth gapes in shock at the sight of Iva, the guard from that fucking place. The guard who was shot when she tried to help me escape. Not only is she here, but she looks completely different. Long, red hair cascades down her back—a wig maybe? She's wearing scrubs, pink with small flowers. The only thing that's the same is her tattoos.

"Iva?"

She doesn't look at me, just peers down at the clipboard she's holding. "You're awake." She scribbles something with a pen.

"You're here. Alive and well."

She doesn't react, just keeps writing. Wandering closer, she checks something on the monitor hooked up to my IV. "Things will be confusing for a while. That's normal. Just follow our instructions. And if you have any visions, please buzz us immediately." Iva points down to a remote with a red emergency button attached to the side rail of the bed.

"Iva, it's me, Henry. Don't you remember?"

She shakes her head. A bemused smile sneaks onto her lips. "As I said, confusion is normal."

This must be some kind of twisted joke. "Did you ever find your sister?" I ask.

Her brow knits and she pats my arm. "I don't have a sister. The medicine you're getting is very strong. It's common to have delusions."

She turns away and begins to leave as I struggle against my restraints.

"If you want to pretend you don't know me, fine. But at least tell me what I'm doing in here and what fucking drugs are being pumped into my system."

Iva doesn't face me again, just calls out as she swings open the door, "Someone will be in to speak with you shortly."

The door slams closed, as if I'm a patient awaiting some fake fucking doctor. If they think I'm going to listen to anyone in this place, they've got another thing coming. I stretch my limbs, gritting my teeth as my muscles strain against the straps. Every inch of my body and mind feels weak. If I could just get this fucking IV out of my vein.

Squeezing my eyes closed, more memories flood in. Joining the Armory, faking my belief in them, getting information about Natalie, her mom, rescuing her. *Losing her again.*

Where is she now? How long have I been away from her, drugged, trapped in this sterile hell?

The door swings open again and Oliver steps inside. Shock freezes me in place. *He's alive.*

"What the hell do you want?" I twist and writhe, trying to free myself from the restraints. It's a losing battle.

"Calm down, Henry."

"Calm down? I'm locked up again, drugged, and you're supposed to be dead. And that woman, Iva, she was shot. And now she's acting like she doesn't even know me."

Oliver smiles, which only ratchets up my fury. Does he really think this is funny?

"Iva's memory has been wiped—a successful and impressive experiment, if you ask me. Something we'll be able to use to our advantage moving ahead. And as far as me, your girlfriend wasn't successful in taking me down."

Nausea lurches through my gut and I'm not sure if it's from the drugs or this fucked-up situation.

"Henry, please understand. This is my job. And it's all in your best interest."

Anger and confusion war inside my brain. *His job? My best interest?* I didn't know much about Oliver's work growing up, only that I was told he was an investor—in businesses, properties. I certainly wouldn't have guessed his job entailed experiments, kidnapping, and torture.

Disgust drips from my tongue. "Some career you picked. You must be real proud."

"I work for the authority."

My body tightens, my knuckles gripping the metal edges of the bed so tight, they lose all color.

"I'm one of the people in charge of control and order. Natalie is a wild card for us, and we must figure out how to contain her. And you—there's something special about you that we struggle to understand."

Fury bleeds through my bones. "This doesn't make any fucking sense. You told me I could finish senior year somewhere else. If I'm part of this, why would you want me to leave Lockwood?"

"I had to act the part. Wouldn't you find it odd if your father ignored things? Besides, that was part of the experiment. I wanted you to leave Lockwood and you refused."

"No. This can't be real. At the rehab place, you said you thought Natalie was dead."

"Again, I was playing a role. It's my job."

A heatwave of rage rises through my core. "You tried to kill me."

"No, son. We don't want to kill you. The only thing that can kill you is a dagger. The holy oil was a lie."

"I heard the guards when they took me. They said I was to be executed. The plan was definitely to kill me. I joined the Armory. They told me…they killed precogs using all sorts of ways."

Oliver shoots me a compassionate look that makes my stomach churn. "All part of the experiment. The Armory too. I know it's hard to understand. These things are very complex, a lot of moving parts. We just need to understand Natalie's full capabilities and whatever bond she has with you—a bond that was never sealed in blood, and yet exists anyway."

Blood bonds? My nostrils flare and every inch of me wants to crack this room in two. If he thinks we're about to have some heart-to-heart regarding how I feel about Natalie, he's got another thing coming.

"If you think I'm going to tell you anything, you're more insane than I thought."

"Oh son, you don't need to tell me. We're watching it all play out right now. Natalie will eventually find you in here and try to free you, attempting to kill everyone in her path along the way."

Disgust decimates my insides at the thought of these assholes using Natalie—and me—in their sick power play.

"But you all seem to come back to life, so what does it matter who she tries to kill?"

Oliver sighs. "Henry, I know it's difficult to process right now, but Natalie isn't like us. If we don't learn the extent of her powers, how she operates—we won't be able to contain her. Our interests will be compromised."

"What do you mean contain her?" Blood ices over in my veins at his cavalier attitude about Natalie's existence, as if she's an animal locked in a testing facility.

"These experiments are new for us. It was Amelia's brainchild when she stepped into power—to learn about the unknown through vigorous research and testing. It's no different than any crisis plan done by a human government or corporation. Or university research project. In my opinion, what we're doing here is innovative, ambitious, but not without fault, of course."

Fire surges up my spine. "Last I checked, humans don't torture and experiment on each other to get information."

Oliver shoots me a look, the same as when he'd scold me as a child. "We're not human." Oliver pauses, likely weighing whether or not he should open up to me. I'm nearly certain he won't, until he croaks out a vague explanation. "We need to see how far Natalie is willing to go, because she is the only one who is truly capable of wiping out the authority, destroying us... and anyone else she wants gone."

Disbelief coasts through my body. Everything Oliver's saying sounds equally possible and batshit insane. Is Natalie truly that powerful? Of course she'd want every one of the authority members dead. They're spending every waking moment torturing her. But Natalie, wanting to wipe out our entire kind? No, she wouldn't do that.

What she would want to do is take down Amelia, along with whatever sick experiment she's running here.

"Seems very risky and pretty stupid of Amelia. You say Natalie has the capability to kill you, destroy all of us, and you're doing everything to poke the bear."

"That's why we have a failsafe," Oliver says.

"So you're saying Amelia has some safety switch for this ridiculous experiment?"

Oliver begins to walk back to the door. "Historically, that is how testing works, at least when it's done well. There must be a way to reset, start over, try again." He states this in such a matter-of-fact manner, talking down to me, like I should have a master's degree in human experimentation and torture.

Rage splinters my stomach. "Why is Amelia really doing this? It can't just be some sick power play. She must have a personal vendetta."

Oliver replies in a soft, reasonable voice that makes nausea climb up my throat. "I told you, Henry. This is all for our protection."

"Protection?" A laugh escapes my sandpapered throat. "Kidnapping, imprisoning, torturing—you call that *protection*?"

"Son, I know it doesn't seem like it, but I'm doing what's best for you. For all of us. Trust me."

Trust him? *Trust him?!* What a delusional piece of shit. Wow, how lucky of me to have been raised by some evil dictator's lackey. Fuck my life. Truly.

Oliver twists the knob, the door creaking open. "All I ask is that you try to trust in the process here. You're doing something for the greater good. You won't see it now, but in time, I hope you might."

My stomach rolls over in disgust. "If you're trying to brand this whole thing like I'm some hero, willingly being tested for some greater good, then you can at least clue me in on what the hell is going on."

"I'm sorry. We can't remove the element of free will. That would ruin the experiment. Besides, it's already apparent that no matter what I say, or anyone says, you're going to side with Natalie Covington. What good would it do if I gave you more information?" Oliver shakes his head, as if I'm some great disappointment. "I knew deep down that I shouldn't have taken you in. You didn't come into my care like the others. You were different than them. I could always tell."

I swallow down his bitter words. He's certainly not the only one who wishes things were different.

Oliver shuts the door behind him, leaving me more fucking confused. If precogs, Cambions, whatever we really are, have a knack for something, it's being so cagey that no one knows what the hell anyone is talking about.

I suppose that's on purpose, keeping us all so confused that we just give up asking questions altogether.

A level of rage I've never felt before unfurls through my body—like every slice of anger from my entire life has been bottled up under my skin, ready to burst.

If I know anything in this moment, it's that I'm not waiting around for whatever fucked-up climax Oliver or Amelia has planned for us.

CHAPTER FIFTY-TWO

NATALIE

Twisting and turning. Racing. Stumbling. So much confusion.

This place is a never-ending haunted house of horrors. My mind spins in violent whirls. I need to get Mom, Henry, and Ciel—find us a way out of this hell. The thought that Amelia is able to manipulate everything in sight, that she's wielding magic on top of her powers, coils at the base of my neck, sending shockwaves through my skin.

My brain shatters into a dozen shards of glass, my mind combing over her plan to imprison all of us just because she wants to entrap me. Knowing that this is all my fault, that my existence has put all these lives in danger, sends bile up my throat. I quickly swallow it down, trying to keep up my courage.

I have to remember that all of this is because the authority is scared of me—of what I'm capable of. Which means I have powers. I just need to figure out how to unlock them, and use them against Amelia and her cronies to break us out of here.

My shoes slap against the concrete floor, tearing around yet another corner, realizing every hallway in this damn place looks exactly the same. Endless concrete—stretching, winding, twisting, all designed to keep me trapped.

Lifting my eyes, I notice a blinking red light in the corner of the room. Amelia must be watching right now, taunting me, laughing at me.

Staring directly into the camera, I scream out, as if I'm a soldier going to battle, "What are you waiting for?" Spit flies from my mouth as anger surges out of my pores. "Why don't you just face me, huh? I know why. Because you're scared of what I am. Because you know I can defeat you."

My entire body quakes with pure rage, and I refuse to take my eyes off that camera. Taunting her worked before, so let's hope I get her attention again. My grip tightens on Wes's dagger when a jolt of electricity shoots up my arm. *I've felt this before.*

I try squeezing the handle again, but nothing happens. The electricity must be related to something. It can't be random… can it?

I feel a hand catch my arm and I whirl around, stabbing the dagger into the air. There's nothing physically present, but something, or someone, is attempting to slither through my head.

"Who's there?"

There's no answer. Just darkness, endless concrete, *and that camera.*

What feels like an arm encircles my waist, attempting to drag me out of the hallway. Except, when I lower my eyes—there's no arm at all. Something is trying to pull me out of this hallway—something I'm unable to see.

I thrash around, gulping down ragged breaths as I try to get free. There's nothing physical to push away, and yet something strong is dragging me across this floor. Power coils through my arms, and with one hard push, an electric shock bursts from my hands.

Whatever was holding on to me loses its grip, giving me enough time to scramble away. A deafening clap of thunder rings out above the building and rain pummels down on the roof. Panic floods through my bones and I begin running, but that invisible thing grabs onto my coat, flinging me back. I lose my footing, come crashing down to the ground.

A pair of fingers trails up the nape of my neck, into my hair, tugging gently. I roll onto my knees, jumping to my feet, stabbing the dagger once again into the air.

Words float into my ear. Words that are undoubtedly in Henry's voice.

It's me. I'm trying to help.

Shock clashes into my body like a lightning bolt. I whip around, still enveloped in nothing but darkness and silence. Henry's nowhere to be found, but there's no mistaking his voice. Is this just another one of Amelia's tests?

Natalie, it's me. Turn to the right, then walk straight.

My heart wrenches at the sound of his voice. This must be a game, a farce, Amelia once again trying to lure me where she wants me to go. She's already tricked me once with Wes. I'm sure she won't hesitate to do it again.

I turn left instead, moving in the opposite path of the directions, my chest loaded with a heavy sense of purpose. Another crack of thunder rattles the entire building.

Natalie, don't go that way.

Nerves claw at my skin as I white-knuckle Wes's dagger. Nightmarish fragments pummel my brain one by one. Amelia slaughtering my stand-in father right in front of me, as if she's disappointed I wouldn't seek revenge on his lies and do it myself. Ciel's limp, unconscious body being dragged into this place. Henry plummeting into the darkness. Bringing Wes back to life when I thought it was Henry, and apparently creating some vomit-inducing bond.

Natalie, please listen to me. Turn around and I'll guide you to me. Please.

Henry's words spider-crawl along my spine. What if it really is him? What if he's found some way to talk to me? We both have powers that seem stronger together. And if Amelia knows how to wield magic, we can learn too. Maybe he's figured some of that out already.

My mind wars at the possibilities. I can keep looping through these hallways, on a road to nowhere. Or I can follow the voice to either find Henry or claw my way out of Amelia's next challenge.

Either way, I don't see a better next step.

My eyes snag onto the camera as I turn, heading in the direction of Henry's voice.

"This better be you," I say, my blood chilling as I wait a moment for his response. Unfortunately, I don't get one.

Moving ahead, I question every footstep, fear ramming against my gut at what lies ahead.

Take a right. Then a sharp left.

His words keep slipping inside my ears, but Henry hasn't made any attempt to reassure me that this is, in fact, him. Inhaling sharply, I continue on, making the right turn and a sharp left at the end of the hallway.

As I curl down the next path, the dark hallway vanishes into a blinding white area—fluorescent bulbs rain down on the space. A single metal rolling cart sits outside a door at the far end.

I'm inside the room.

I follow his words, bracing myself for whatever truly awaits inside. I clutch the dagger in front of me, moving slowly to the door. I twist the lever handle on the solid metal door, pushing it open.

My insides pull tight when I find Henry inside, strapped to a hospital bed.

His eyes seem to flood with hope. "You heard me," he says.

Panic stabbing into my chest, I race over to him, taking a moment to inspect if he's hurt... and that he is, indeed, *Henry*. Not that I'd exactly be able to tell, given how easily Wes seemed to shape-shift into him.

"Is it really you?" I ask, studying his eyes for the truth.

"Yeah," he answers, matter of fact. "It's me. I swear." His gaze probes into mine, begging to believe him.

"Why didn't you answer? I was talking back to you."

"I couldn't hear you. I was just hoping against all odds that you'd hear me. And clearly, you did."

I go to work using Wes's dagger, slicing away at Henry's binds, careful not to cut into his skin. "How were you able to do that—talk to me, telepathically?"

Henry winces as I release one of his arms. "I'm not exactly sure, but I seem to be able to conjure powers if I'm pushed far enough, past my limit. There's this rage and then I just think about connecting back to you—like we have some kind of unexplainable bond."

I swallow down that word as I release his other arm. *Bond.* I really hope Wes is full of shit—like usual—because I can't imagine a fate worse than being bonded to him.

Henry rolls out his wrists, stretching the life back into his body. He rips out the IV from his arm, blood spurting from his vein onto the white bed. I hand him a cotton pad from the metal tray next to his bed and he presses it onto the wound.

"What were they injecting you with?"

"I have no idea. I'm guessing something to keep me weak because I feel like absolute shit right now."

"Well, being strapped to a bed unable to move might do that. Also, falling into a giant hole might be a culprit," I say.

Henry manages a laugh, and for a brief moment, it's like we've left a storm and fallen into sunlight.

"I can cut off the rest of the binds," he says, reaching out for Wes's dagger.

Instinctively, I clutch onto it. "I've got it," I say, working into the straps on his legs. It's not that I don't trust him, but I also don't want to release the one weapon I have right now.

"Oliver paid me a visit."

My blood chills. *So he is alive.* And I'm certain he'll want me dead after what I did to him.

"He's working for Amelia, apparently."

Great. So he'll delight in my slow, painful undoing at the hands of Amelia.

I free Henry's legs and he swings them off the bed, pressing them to the floor. As he tries to stand, his legs wobble and give out. I place my body under his torso, helping to steady him.

"Take it easy," I say, gazing into those green eyes filled with a glazed, wearied sadness.

He traces his hand along my cheek, down the nape of my neck. "I tried pulling you out of that room, you know, but you kept fighting me."

My stomach drops. "Wait, that was you? I thought it was some shadowy creep or Amelia. Or both."

His lips curl into a grin. "I just envisioned tugging you from the room and leading you here. I could feel your resistance, so I started thinking of what I'd say to you."

"But how did you even know where I was? Or where you were?"

"I had a vision."

An uneasy feeling claws at my chest, like we're back at the beginning of our story together, when Henry had his first vision of me. Or at least the first vision I knew about.

"Oliver said this is all some kind of test. The authority is trying to figure you out, me out, and they're pushing our limits in this fucked-up place to do it."

"I'm sorry you got dragged into this mess."

He cups my cheeks in his hands. "This isn't your fault. It all started when I got involved and changed my vision. They're aware of our connection. Oliver seems to think I'm different than the others somehow."

My mind coils, remembering back to the beginning, before me and Henry. Everything seemed normal back then, at least somewhat. Getting to Lockwood. Being annoyed with Jack. Listening to Ciel's latest relationship drama. Laughing with Adip.

My heart drums into my throat. "This didn't start with you, Henry. It's who I am. I had a mark on me ever since I was born. Not a mark like yours." I motion to the branding on his forearm. "But a worse one, an invisible one. I didn't even see the danger coming."

I inhale deeply, squeezing my eyes shut and letting the oxygen simmer in my lungs for just a moment. It's like ever since I met Henry that day, I haven't stopped to think. Haven't breathed. Haven't processed any of the truly fucked-up things going on.

There's a click at the door and my body surges into fight mode. My head snaps to the entrance, noticing two guards entering the room. I stand in front of Henry, pushing us both away from them, holding out the dagger.

"Don't come any closer," I threaten.

But the dagger is ripped from my hand by some invisible force, sent flying across the room, right into the hands of Amelia, who glides her way through the middle of the guards.

"Glad to know there are still some things you can't do." Her slippery voice sends a chill through my veins. "I'm struggling to figure out how you managed to find him. And why I'm unable to read either of your minds," Amelia says, studying us both as if that will mentally unlock our secrets.

A spike of power travels up my body. Henry and I don't understand our connection, but neither does she. It's an even playing field until we can figure it out. *And we will.*

"This is between you and me. Let everyone else go," I say.

Henry puts a protective arm in front of me. "Natalie, no."

I bat him away, standing firm in the face of Amelia and her grand experiment. My heart leaps into my throat, but I refuse to let her see me weaken. "They have nothing to do with this," I say. "I'll do whatever you want. You can keep me here, study me, just let the rest of them go."

"I'm not leaving without you," Henry says.

I flick him a look to stay quiet.

Amelia gives me a bemused smile that makes me immediately want to kill her. *Again.* Not that it would do any good.

"You seem to have a good heart, Natalie," she says. "But there's a darkness inside of you. I know it."

"You mean because I stabbed you—after you tried to kill my friend and were about to kill me? I'd hardly call that darkness. It's self-defense."

"We can argue semantics all day, but I know what you really are. And I have something else for us to do. It involves your mother and your friend Ciel. Henry too. You can come willingly, or we'll take you against your will, and it won't be painless."

I take a step ahead and Henry grabs my arm, twisting me back. "What are you doing?" he grunts at me under his breath.

"Trust me," I say, squeezing his hand back.

An electric jolt shoots up my arm, and from Henry's reaction, I can tell he felt it too. That's what we have when we're together—*power.*

CHAPTER FIFTY-THREE
NATALIE

HENRY KEEPS A tight grip on my hand as we follow Amelia through the maze-like halls—a plank walk to whatever she has in store for us next. She leads us inside the same gothic revival room we met in before, where she ended my fake father's life.

Her same two creepy counterparts are in their chairs—the tall, thin guy and the woman with the salt and pepper hair, both expressionless. I wonder if they're Cambions too. Or some other supernatural being. Right now, they look like robots—cold and empty.

Wes stands behind them, very much alive—which isn't a surprise. I figured he had Amelia on speed dial to bring him back to life. His eyes spit daggers at Henry and at me. More like, both of us together.

My stomach tightens as Ciel is dragged into the room by a different guard. It's the first I've seen her since she was unconscious, being carried into this place. Now she's awake, barely, the light completely drained from her eyes, her body slumped, unable to stand.

"What the hell did you do to her?" Tears brim in the corner of my eyes.

"The drugs make it more amenable for her to be here. When she was bonded to Wes, she wouldn't stop calling out for him. But since he's broken that bond and reinstated it with you, we're just waiting for the drugs to wear off," Amelia says.

My chest cramps and nausea claws into my brain. Does that mean the bonding thing is real? No, that can't be. My eyes dart to Wes, whose expression is now horrifically smug.

"What does that mean, bonded?" Henry demands, his entire body visibly frozen in tension. He's gripping my hand so tight, I'm afraid he might crack my palm in two.

"Jealousy. Now that's one way that things get out of control," Amelia says to him.

Another guard leads Mom into the room. She appears disheveled, her eyes glassy and swollen.

A stab of pain vibrates through my heart, thinking of what they've done to her. "Please, just let them all go. I'm obviously who you want."

My pleas once again go unanswered.

"Natalie, I realize you're an unwilling participant here, but it's imperative that I see the moves you make, the decisions, your triggers, all of it," Amelia says with a calculated glimmer in her eye.

Before I can protest, large, glass-like cubes rain down from the ceiling, appearing out of nowhere, walling off Mom and Ciel.

"What the hell are you doing?" I cry out, before realizing that I'm no longer holding Henry's hand… and that he's also been encased in one of the glass cubes.

Henry smashes his fist against the cube. "Let me out!" His voice is garbled, almost incoherent inside the thick glass.

Ciel collapses to the ground, her lifeless eyes staring right at me. Mom falls to her knees, sobbing. Wes fixates his eyes on Henry, clearly getting a sick kind of satisfaction from watching his downfall.

Everyone I love, trapped in fishbowls, made to watch whatever horror Amelia has in store next.

I smack my fists into the glass of Henry's cage, hoping I can conjure our collective powers and smash each one of these cubes open, one by one. As my limbs connect with the glass, it does nothing but send pain shooting up my wrists, rattling my brain.

"Let them go," I say, knowing deep down that my demands will do nothing. "What do you want from me? Stop playing games and just tell me."

My words are met with nothing but silence.

The sound of trickling water cracks through the room. The trickling turns into gushing, as if a faucet has been twisted all the way on. I turn in the direction of Mom's screams. Inside her glass cube, water rains down, already reaching up to her kneecaps.

Terror rips through my bones. "Mom!" I race over, bashing my fists against the glass with every ounce of strength I can muster. What good are my powers if they don't even work when I need them most?

"Stop this!" Henry shouts. "That's enough!"

I continue pummeling the glass encasing my Mom—kicking, punching, trying anything to break it open. The water reaches chest level and soon, it will close off her oxygen.

"I think we've had enough, Amelia," I hear Wes say from behind me.

"You don't get to have demands," Amelia says back to him.

Hysteria climbs up my throat and I belt out a deafening scream, kicking, clawing trying everything to break the glass—but nothing works.

The water travels up Mom's face, covering her nose, then lifts over the top of her head. Bubbles escape her throat as she mouths, "I love you."

No. This is just some sick experiment. Maybe even an illusion. And if it is real, Mom can be brought back. *I can bring her back.*

"Oh look, she remembers you. Guess we weren't able to wipe Madeline's memory after all," Amelia says, her voice growing louder behind me.

Wes argues, panicked. "Wait, no, that isn't what we agreed on. You can't do that!"

Out of the corner of my eye, I notice Wes moving ahead, right for me. Before he can take another step, a glass cube smashes down from the ceiling, encasing him. He screams my name from inside the glass, pummeling his fists in frustration.

Mom floats inside her water-filled cube, barely conscious. Adrenaline swallows me whole and morphs into something different, a burning sensation encircling my stomach, scraping against my skin.

I look over at Henry, at first locking eyes with him, then watching the rise and fall of his chest—matching his breath. We need to merge our powers again, break my mom free.

Seconds pass before his thoughts slip into my mind. *Punch the glass again.*

In a split second, I race to my mom and smash my fist into the glass. This time, my fist shatters through the glass, sending shards flying everywhere.

I drop to the ground to avoid the onslaught of glass as a scream rings out behind me—the tall guy, one of Amelia's cronies, trying to yank a huge shard of glass out of his chest.

Mom's body flops out onto the floor, water draining around her.

"Mom, Mom!" I crawl over to her, shaking her limp body, but she's not breathing. I pump my hands on her chest.

"It's no use, Natalie. She's already gone," Amelia says.

My eyes blaze as I peer over at her with pure, feral hatred. This must be what it feels like to be Wes. What it feels like to deeply want to strip the life away from someone, make them feel that same level of pain that you do.

"You forget that I know about the magic. I know how to bring us back to life," I say.

I'm on my feet, darting across the room to the woman with the salt and pepper hair. I fling my body into hers, sending her crashing to the ground, and grip the dagger from a leather sheath on her pants, ripping it away from her in one swift movement. The woman seems terrified of my strength, not even bothering to put up a fight.

Just as I'm about to slice the dagger into my wrist, feeding Mom my blood to bring her back, Amelia's words freeze me in my tracks.

"It doesn't work on your kind, Natalie. Anyone with Astral blood can't be brought back that way."

My heart stalls as I swallow back tears. No, this can't be true. I refuse it to be true. I drop down next to my mom, slicing into the side of my wrist, letting the blood drip down into her mouth. My tears begin to flow, giant salty droplets mixing with the drips of my blood.

"Mom, please, come back. Please." I can barely speak through my sobs.

Moments tick by… nothing happens. Of all the things Amelia's lied about, this is the one time she's telling the truth. My heart shreds into a million pieces and I leave it on the floor, along with my mom's body.

I don't have a heart anymore.

My hands press into the ground as rage coils around my skin and I let out an agonizing scream. The walls begin to rumble, rattling Amelia's normally unshakable stance.

If she wants to treat me like an animal in a cage, I'll show her what it looks like to be locked up with one.

I let another scream rip through the building, the foundation reacting to my rage. Lights unhinge from the ceiling and crash onto the ground. The floor splits, swallowing up Amelia's cronies, sucking them into the abyss below.

Wind whips through the room, knocking Amelia to her knees, but it doesn't seem to have any impact on me. Ciel presses her terrified face against the glass cube, watching this all play out, mouthing my name.

Amelia begins crawling to the far corner of the room, away from me. She tries to stand, but another gust of wind knocks her down.

My palm tightens around the dagger. Killing Amelia didn't work last time, because any Cambion can bring her back to life. I could destroy this entire building, but even then, how long before someone breathes life back into her?

The wind stalks Amelia like prey as she crawls ahead. Wes bangs on the glass, trying to get my attention, but I ignore him. Is he going to ask me to save her?

Wes calls out through the glass. "Natalie, destroy that! Over there!"

Wes points over at some odd, crystal-like contraption sitting on a table. It almost looks like a giant crystal ball, but has two levers on the side. The middle is filled with various metal-type spikes.

And Amelia is heading right for it. Another onslaught of wind encircles her body, holding her back.

Wes bangs on the glass and screams. "Natalie, I know you don't trust me, but please listen. She's going to reset the experiment. She's going to keep making you endure this, over and over. If you want things to end, you've got to stop her now."

His sharp warning leeches through my brain. *Experiment. Reset.*

I peer over at Henry as he slides another message into my brain. *I can't believe I'm saying this, but listen to Wes. Oliver said it. That's the failsafe.*

Rage surges through me as I propel ahead. Amelia somehow circumvents the wind, managing to get onto her feet. I reach deep into my mind, searching for my uncovered powers. Please let me stop this before she locks us into a never-ending loop of pain and torture.

Amelia reaches out for the lever and I lunge at her with the dagger. She turns just as the blade is about to connect with her skin, electricity shooting from her body, sending me tumbling backwards, knocking the dagger from my hand.

Her hand reaches for the lever of the crystal contraption as I press up onto my feet. Hurling my body at hers, I grip onto her hand…

But it's too late.

She smashes the lever down as lightening encompasses the room, stripping everything to white.

Suddenly, I'm standing alone in a void, shivering uncontrollably. Henry is gone. Ciel is gone. Mom is gone. So are Wes and Amelia. Everything is bright white, empty.

Something rips into my chest, like an imaginary dagger tearing me in two. I scream out in agony as black, tar-like liquid leaks into the room. The room begins to spin faster and faster as everything turns to darkness.

Then the floor gives out.

And I'm falling… falling… falling…

Lungs seizing… heart stopping…

CHAPTER FIFTY-FOUR
NATALIE

Nausea.

That's all I feel in this moment, like I'm about to barf up ten pails of puke. It takes me a second to register where I am.

Oh, right. I'm backstage at Jack—my boyfriend's—inauguration. And by that, I mean he's about to become class president of Lockwood, the way-too-expensive school we attend on a private island in Washington state. 175 rich kids smashed into posh purgatory for our senior year of high school.

My stomach sloshes and churns. I must have eaten something earlier that didn't agree with me. I probe my memory. I had tea. Oatmeal. The normal stuff. Maybe it's just nerves or general annoyance because Jack is being a level-ten douche today.

As I look out from backstage at this ridiculous spectacle, I knock my head against a twelve-foot flower tunnel of white roses and wisteria. Petals shower to the ground. My eyes scan the room and I scoop up the stray petals, wanting to barf again as I shake a few from my hair.

Frankly, everyone is so distracted with their own drama at Lockwood, I don't think they'd even notice these petals mixed with puke.

A strange image claws its way into my brain, like someone's plugged a USB cable into my forehead and started playing a movie—starring me.

I see myself in a darkened corner of a hallway, my back pressed against a stone wall. I'm wearing a silky red dress and a Venetian mask and there's some guy caging me in that spot. He rips off his mask, looming over me. I definitely don't recognize him. He says in a raspy whisper, "You're in danger."

The image disappears and I'm once again looking at the inauguration— students shuffling into their seats. A live orchestra readying in the corner.

What the hell was that? It felt like a daydream, but certainly not one that I conjured on purpose. My wool uniform jacket suddenly feels itchier, hotter than normal.

"You look like a ghost," Jack says, surveying my appearance. "What's the matter?"

"I don't know. I feel sick," I reply, nausea creeping into my chest again.

"Well, I'm about to go on. Can you pull yourself together?"

Oh, Jack. Always so understanding. How I wish I was ballsy enough to slap him right here in the hallway, watching the shock and embarrassment on his face.

Suddenly, another image fires into my brain.

It's the same guy that was in the last one. *We're in the hallway at Lockwood. He grabs Jack by the shirt and shoves him—sending his body clear across the hall like some superhero. Or supervillain. Jack's body smashes into the lockers so hard, one of them springs open from its lock.*

The image dissolves and I'm left staring at Jack, perfectly fine and unharmed. Pinpricks of nerves climb all over my skin.

"What is going on with you?" Jack shoots me a pissy look, like I'm ruining his big day.

I don't know why it's such a big deal that I'm on that stage with him when he accepts the class presidency. It's not like "first lady" is something I aspire to be. No shade to first ladies.

Jack's voice snaps me from my thoughts. "Why don't you go to the bathroom and splash water on your face? And maybe do something with your hair. They're going to take our picture when I swear in."

His annoying demands jumble into one giant blur as my head clouds and bile rises in my throat.

◈

After spending five minutes puking in a stall, I find my friend Ciel by the sink area, touching up her already-perfect lip gloss.

"You ready for today, Jackie Kennedy?" she says in a singsong voice, then immediately abandons that tone when she clocks my appearance. "Natty, oh my god, are you hungover?"

"No." But it sure feels like I am.

I notice that Ciel seems to have constructed a flower crown from the rose petals on stage. It looks great, just like she always does. I glance at my reflection in the mirror. My skin is pasty and my eyes are rimmed with heavy, dark circles, as if I've been turned into a zombie. I yank out my clip and my hair puffs out in a hopeless cloud of curls.

"Did you see the new guy?" Ciel says, while tousling her beachy waves.

"Huh? What? I don't know." I'm only half-listening as anxiety swirls in my gut, traveling up to my throat.

"The new guy. Scholarship kid. He's hot. Probably poor, but hot. And kinda weird."

Before she can say another word, another image floats into my brain.

It's Ciel, standing on a balcony with some woman I don't recognize.

They're arguing. No, maybe they're about to kiss? The woman leans closer to Ciel… and shoves her off the balcony.

The image vanishes and I'm staring right at Ciel, her eyes dancing over my face. Unease weaves around my limbs, and I'm frozen at the sink, trying to process these weird vignettes that keep haunting my mind.

"Natty? Is everything okay? You want some lip gloss? Lip gloss always makes me feel better." Ciel holds out the tube.

No, things are most definitely not okay. Bizarre images keep scrambling my brain, and the worst part is that they all feel real, like fragmented memories ready to swallow me whole.

❧

My shoes clack down the empty hallway as I head backstage, dread coiling at the base of my spine. I need to find some way to stop these images, daydreams, whatever the hell they are.

My friend Adip's voice rings out behind me. "Natty, wait up!"

Adip is someone I always enjoy talking to, in a very platonic, sibling-like way. But right now, I just want to get through Jack's speech, then spend the rest of the day in bed, sleeping off whatever's glitching inside my brain.

Adip falls into step next to me. "Hey, I had a crazy dream about you last night."

"Oh yeah?" I say, not really paying attention, nor slowing down. Adip keeps up with me as I round the corner, heading backstage to get this whole spectacle over with.

"I was in bed, in my dream, and some dude was sitting on the edge. He woke me up and said he was your dad."

"What?" A laugh bubbles up out of my throat, which feels somewhat relieving after barfing up my guts.

"I'm serious! It was freezing cold, and there was frost on my sheets, like he brought winter inside my room or something."

"Well, my dad is pretty icy, so that tracks."

"It wasn't your dad, like, not the dad I've met. This was some other guy I've never seen. He had these weird blue eyes that didn't look real, if that makes sense."

I pause, turning to face Adip. "None of that makes sense, but it was a dream. It's not supposed to."

"No, I'm telling you Natty, this felt so real. The dude told me I had to watch over you, like some guardian angel. I don't know. I must have been really high."

"Apparently."

"But get this. When I woke up, my window was open. Just flapping in the breeze like someone left and forgot to close it."

As much as I'd like to entertain Adip's weed-induced dreams, I can hear Headmaster Rochester making an announcement inside the auditorium.

"I've gotta get in there. Let's talk later."

As I twist away from Adip, he grabs my hand and gives it a friendly squeeze. "I know you think it sounds crazy, but I swear that wasn't a dream. I feel weird. Do you feel weird?"

Oh boy. Adip must have been smoking some really interesting stuff last night.

"I feel like I have food poisoning, and Jack is going to have my head if I don't get in there with him. We'll talk later, okay?"

Tugging my hand from his, I move down the hall. I don't make it far when another one of those damn images sneaks into my brain.

I'm sitting across from my father at a restaurant on campus. Some guy about my age sits next to me, another person I don't recognize.

"You're not my child. When your mother came to me, she was eight weeks pregnant with you and completely terrified," my father says.

The image vanishes and I'm sick again. Adip just shared some crazy dream, and now I'm having a flash of my father telling me he's not my father? That familiar sense of nausea spikes through my core, followed by a wave of anxious goosebumps.

I manage to get backstage just before Jack goes on stage.

Headmaster Rochester announces, "Let's give a Lockwood chant for our class president, Jack Carter!"

Jack looks back at me and his expression immediately morphs into horror when he sees my appearance. In other circumstances, this might delight me—tossing this act of rebellion in his face. But right now, my mind is vibrating with confusion and pure nausea.

As I step onto the stage behind Jack, I'm immediately blinded by a camera flash. The deafening roars and cheers rippling through the student body make my head want to burst from my neck.

Another flash in my face, and I snap at the photographer. "Stop, I can't see."

The photographer shoots me an annoyed look and backs away. "You look terrible anyway," he says.

When I finally regain my eyesight from the blinding flash, I spot Jack at the podium in all his glory. He raises his hand with a powerful wave and the crowd erupts into even louder tremors of excitement and applause. My body wobbles with dizziness as I take my place behind him, to the right. Attempting to squelch all this mess inside my brain and body, I focus on the crowd—a sea of beautiful faces in designer uniforms.

My eyes latch on to one student, and my stomach tightens as I realize it's the guy I saw in my mind, the one sitting next to me when my father revealed he wasn't, in fact, my father. I'm rendered paralytic as the student grins at me from the audience.

I suck in a deep breath to try and settle down my nerves, averting my gaze from the grinning stranger who somehow managed to claw into my brain.

Then, my eyes land on another strange thing. A line of guards blocks the back of the concert hall, holding rifles. I've never seen them before. As far as I know, we don't have guards at Lockwood.

The guards stare ahead with stone-faced expressions—all except one, whose eyes seem fixed on me. Nerves claw into my bones and spider through the rest of my body as yet another image enters my mind.

I'm outside, wearing that red dress again, but this time, I'm on my knees on the pavement, like I've taken an unfortunate spill. The guard extends his white-gloved hand in what appears to be a kind gesture, and I clasp it. Within seconds, I yank my hand away, scrambling to my feet, racing away from him, terror plastered on my face.

I blink away the image as Jack continues his speech. Fear prickles the back of my neck. Why was I running away from that guard, the one standing across from me right now, staring at me? Are these images some kind of weird premonitions?

I squeeze my eyes closed, trying to steady my breathing, and tune back in to Jack's speech, hoping it will calm me down. I know his speech so well, I can recite it myself. I repeat the words in my mind. Maybe that will halt these horrific slices of a movie I don't want playing in my head.

Suddenly, Jack's words trail off and a loud gasp erupts from the audience, followed closely by several shrieks. I pop open my eyes, noticing the guards pointing their rifles at the commotion.

I crane my neck to try and see what's going on. Shoes screech against the hard floor as students scurry from their seats. Jack whips his gaze around the room, annoyed by the interruption.

As the crowd parts, I'm finally able to get a clear view of what's happening.

It's a student—the other one I saw in my head. The one who was issuing me a warning. He's standing up, clutching his chest, having trouble breathing. He staggers backward, eyes popped wide, a look of sheer terror on his face. No one is helping him. Why is no one helping him?

My heart clenches as another image pops into my brain—

I'm pinned to the ground in the middle of the woods, desperately trying to fight off the guard. I smash my fists into him when suddenly, his body slumps down over mine. The weight of him lifts and I crawl away, noticing the student standing there. The same student having a panic attack right here in this auditorium… saving my life.

The image disappears, and without thinking, I rush to the edge of the stage, heart thundering in my chest. I can hear Jack shouting after me. My shoes smack to the ground and I bolt ahead, shoving my way through Lockwood's elite, and get to the student just as he crashes to the floor.

I lean over him and grab on to his arms. His eyes are squeezed shut, like he never wants to open them again. I give his arms a squeeze and he stirs. His eyes flutter open and clash with mine—deep green with flecks of gold. His eyes, his face, is familiar. Not just from the images in my head, but I have a deep sense that we're somehow connected.

His breathing accelerates, then his fingers snap around my wrists, his nails digging into my flesh as his gaze darkens. His jaw clenches, nostrils flared—the savage pounding of his pulse strumming against my skin.

For what feels like eternity, I can't move. I can't think.

Until finally, a few words escape my throat.

"How do I know you?"

THE END.

The story continues in book three, the final
installment of the heart-pounding Lockwood
Trilogy, UNDONE, releasing February 2024.

A sneak preview of UNDONE - Book Three in the Lockwood Trilogy

UNDONE

CHAPTER ONE

NATALIE

HIS GRIP FEELS familiar.

This stranger lying on the ground in the middle of the Lockwood auditorium, squeezing my hand as if I'm his lifeline.

The orchestra stops playing. The other students are dead silent—watching me on the ground with this student I've never seen before except inside my head. I can even feel my boyfriend's eyes from the stage, burning a hole into my back. Jack must be livid that I ruined his big moment.

"Who are you?" I whisper to the stranger on the ground.

His body trembles, sending an electric bolt pulsing up my arm, making me flinch, but not enough to let go of him.

I search his eyes for any truth, noticing the rise and fall of his chest as his breath quickens, as if he's about to have another panic attack.

As if he can't take it anymore, he shoves me away, sending me crashing against the ground.

"Natty, oh my god." Ciel rushes over, crouching down to help.

But I can't take my eyes off this stranger. He's kneeling now, with a tortured, confused, yet apologetic look in his eyes. He breaks our gaze, scanning the room, seemingly terrified. I follow his eyeline, noticing those strange guards, their rifles pointed at him, like he's some kind of animal. Fortunately, they point their rifles up in unison, now aimed away.

I hear commotion behind me, turning just in time to see Jack flying off the stage, going right for the stranger.

A sharp protectiveness takes over my body as I press to stand, blocking his way. "Stop," I command, which Jack clearly doesn't like, as evidenced by him staring daggers at me. "Just leave it alone."

"This is *my* day," Jack says, fire practically spitting from his mouth.

Out of the corner of my eye, I notice the stranger shoving his way through the guards and fleeing out the exit.

"Are you okay, Natty?" Ciel asks as Adip curls his arm around her.

"She's fine. Let her go," Adip says, as if he knows something I don't.

That same electricity spirals through my body, and I come unglued from the floor, from my pissed-off boyfriend, from all of it—taking off after the stranger. I ignore Jack as he barks orders in the background, demanding that I not leave.

As I move past the guards, the same creepy one casts a glance in my direction. It's quick but noticeable, sending an uneasy shiver down my legs. My hands smack into the heavy metal door, shoving it open into the crisp fall air.

It takes me a moment once I'm outside to find him. He's already several paces ahead, but standing still, like he's frozen in place.

"Hey," I call out, but he doesn't seem to hear me.

I approach him, cautious, noticing his eyes are squeezed shut and he's counting backwards.

"Ten…nine…eight…seven…"

"Are you okay?"

He stops counting and his lashes flutter for a second before he blinks opens his eyes.

Swallowing my anxiety, I try to speak to him again. The sleeve of his uniform jacket is bunched up around his elbow, and on instinct, I reach out my hand to touch him in what's meant to be a comforting gesture. As soon as my finger grazes the bare part of his arm, another shock ricochets through my skin. He yanks away from me and I notice a tattoo on his forearm, some Greek symbol, I think.

"Do I know you?" I ask.

He shakes his head, casting an anxious glance around the campus.

"Because this is going to sound crazy, but I saw you."

"What do you mean you *saw*?" These are the first words he utters, and it's jarring to hear his voice. It sounds so familiar.

"I had these weird flashes in my head, and you were in them."

His eyes narrow and his body is visibly shaking, as if he's trying to control himself. He grabs my arm and yanks me to him as the breath whooshes from my lungs. There's no electric shock this time, just frantic energy.

"What the hell are you doing?"

I attempt to wriggle out of his strong grip as he pushes up my uniform jacket sleeve to reveal the underside of my forearm. He casts a glance of relief before he lets me go.

"What was that about?"

"I was looking for something," he says.

"On my arm?"

But he doesn't answer, and I get the distinct feeling he's about to run.

"Look, I saw you, in my head. You told me I was in danger. You saved my life."

His entire body visibly stiffens as he leans into me. "We shouldn't talk about this here. There are cameras everywhere on this campus."

"They don't work. The school said they turned them off last year."

"And you really believe that?"

My skin pulsates with nerves. I hadn't considered the school was lying and I suppose he makes a good point. Maybe they only said they turned them off so they can catch us doing something illicit. Although, they pretty much let us do whatever we want here, so I'm not sure what they're trying to do.

"I have a place we can talk," he says, motioning for me to follow.

❧

We don't speak a word to each other as he leads me up the steps inside one of the dormitory buildings, onto a maintenance floor. He shoves open a door and leads me inside a private bathroom.

"Is this yours? You have your own bathroom here?"

"Perks of arriving at Lockwood late, I guess."

"I didn't even get your name," I say.

"Henry. Henry Thorne." He leans back against the sink, piercing me with his stare.

"Aren't you going to ask mine?"

"You're Natalie Covington," he says.

How does he know my name? Suddenly, another one of those images enters my mind.

I'm in this bathroom with him, but he has me in the shower, my forearms pinned above my head against the cold tile. Through clenched teeth, he tells me that he saw what was going to happen to me, that he can see the future.

The image dissolves as horror and disbelief sinks in.

"We know each other, don't we? I keep seeing these things, and I feel like they're memories. You told me you can see the future."

Henry doesn't breathe a word, but I can sense his pain—that there's some truth to the images flipping through my mind.

"*Can* you see the future?" I ask.

A shiver seeps into my bones as he stares at me, still not uttering a word. It drives me crazy that I can't tell what he's thinking.

"We were right here in this bathroom, in *that* shower, when you told me. I saw it. I *remembered* it." My words sound crazed, even to me, as they burst from my throat.

The silence stretches on between us as Henry lowers his gaze. My patience loses the battle and I grab at his hands, tugging him into the shower. I spin to face him, pressing my back against the tile, reenacting the image in my mind.

"You were in front of me, you had my hands pinned above my head." I play this out for him, clasping onto his hands and holding them above my head, letting him cage me in.

He squeezes his eyes closed, as if this is all too much to handle.

"You turned on the water. I don't know why. Maybe to drown out any sound? And then you told me you could see the future."

The corners of his mouth twitch as he opens his eyes again. His gaze sears into mine. "Your eyes. They were just brown, but now they're green, like mine," he says.

My heart smashes into my throat. My mom's eyes turned from brown to green, and I always thought that was a strange story— secretly wishing I'd have the same fate. And now it happens, right in this very moment? There's something going on, something I don't understand, but desperately need to.

"Turn on the water," I say.

Henry doesn't make any moves, doesn't even remove his gaze from mine. So I crank the handle, letting freezing cold water pummel down on our clothed bodies.

As the water warms and heats, cascading over us, soaking through our clothes, Henry begins to fray. Time stretches on as our breathing accelerates, locked in the unknown.

Panic seeps through his words as he presses his forehead against mine. "I'm starting to see it now. I remember," he says.

And so do I. Memories flood into my brain like a torrent, our minds melding under the water.

Henry saving my life. Our first kiss. Him leaving. Me searching for him. Killing Oliver. A fight between him and the guy who was smirking at me from the crowd—Wes. Killing Amelia. Waking up on a boat with Henry. Running through the streets with him. Being trapped with him. Standing in a room, Henry, Ciel, and Wes encased in glass—my mom lying dead on the ground. Learning this is all an experiment. Amelia saying that I won't remember, none of us will. Amelia crawling toward a glass object, reaching for the lever. I try to stop her and everything goes blank.

Realization unfurls through Henry and I at the same time. We clutch on to each other, letting the water rain down over us while fear stretches around our bodies like tentacles.

"I remember everything," I say, feeling relieved to be here with Henry, yet terrified of the all the danger that awaits outside of these walls.

Henry releases my hands and cups my face, planting a kiss on my lips. I sink into his embrace, letting the heat from the water and our bodies to consume me.

"Thank god I found my way back to you," he says.

Amelia reset our world and now we're back here at Lockwood, a second round—day one for her twisted experiment.

Except *we remember*. We outsmarted her, out-powered her.

And now we need to stop her for good.

ALSO BY MELISSA CASSERA

Books in THE LOCKWOOD TRILOGY:
CONTROL - Book One
UNRAVEL - Book Two
UNDONE - Book Three (February 2024)

Other books in the LOCKWOOD MULTIVERSE:
BLACK SEA (novella)
OF STARS AND TIDES (June 2024)
SYMPHONY OF ICE & ILLUSION (December 2024)

ENJOYED THIS BOOK?
Please leave a review. I greatly appreciate any support!

ACKNOWLEDGEMENTS

To everyone who took the time to read *Control* and *Unravel*, THANK YOU, THANK YOU, THANK YOU. I am forever grateful that you took time out of your world to read my words. *Sobs in happiness.*

To my Lockwood Elites street team and my ARC readers. Thank you from the bottom of my twisted little heart for all of your support, shares, and sweet reviews.

To my husband, Gary, thank you for always supporting my writing and encouraging me through all my wild ideas and writerly mood swings. None of this would be possible without you.

To Susan Hyatt for getting this series out of a sad desk basket and encouraging me to put it out into the world. Look at us now!

To Dawn Ius, my incredible developmental editor, who always pushes me and cheers me on, no matter what new twist I throw out. I'm so grateful to have you in my corner.

To Jessica McKelden, the most badass line editor/proofreader in the whole world. Your attention to detail is truly mind-blowing.

To my alpha and beta readers, thank you for your invaluable, honest feedback.

To the team at Damonza, my cover designers, who create the most gorgeous designs. I would never have sold this many books without you!

To my friends Alexandra Franzen, Shenee Howard, Lisa Fabrega, Nicole Antoinette, Jessie Rosen, Shelley Cohen, and everyone else who supported and encouraged me along this wild ride. I'm forever grateful.

To my mom for always taking me to the library as a kid, letting me watch soap operas, and for not noticing when I stole your romance novels. Ha!

To Washington state, my beautiful home that partially inspired this story.

To anyone who writes/creates Turkish dizis (quite literally the best TV shows out there.)

To everyone who makes unapologetic, obsession-worthy entertainment. I'm obsessed with you.

CONTACT THE AUTHOR

Thank you so much for giving *Unravel*, book two of The Lockwood Trilogy, a chance! If you enjoyed following the twists and turns of this story, I'd be so grateful if you could rate and review the book.

Join Melissa Cassera's author mailing list for exclusive sneak peeks and giveaways: *https://melissacassera.com/control/*

Instagram: *https://www.instagram.com/melissa.cassera/*
TikTok: *https://www.tiktok.com/@melissacassera*

ABOUT THE AUTHOR

Melissa Cassera is a professional screenwriter and the bestselling author of angsty, twisty romances with a soft spot for the morally grey. She is also the writer of 11 movies for *Lifetime Network*, including "The Obsession Thrillogy," the network's first trilogy of movies.

When Melissa isn't writing twists you won't see coming, she can be found drinking too much coffee, playing at the lake with her dogs, or getting lost in the romance section of a bookstore. You can sign up for her author newsletter *https://melissacassera.com/control/*

www.ingramcontent.com/pod-product-compliance
Lightning Source LLC
Chambersburg PA
CBHW051135130726

47988CB00005B/1843